"Within the harrowing landscape of both the Spanish Civil War and World War II, Escobar shines a light on hope and humanity through Elisabeth Eidenbenz and her work to create the Elna Maternity Hospital and the Mothers of Elne, saving countless mothers and their newborn children. Descriptions and prose, both startling and lyrical, bring you into the scene and into the lives of both Elisabeth and Isabel as they strive to survive, thrive, and care for others in this gripping tale of destruction, war, and the endless potential within the human heart to endure, sacrifice, and rejoice."

—KATHERINE REAY, AUTHOR OF *THE LONDON HOUSE* AND *A SHADOW IN MOSCOW*, ON *THE SWISS NURSE*

"Mario Escobar shares the true story of Janusz Korczak, a respected leader and speaker whose life was dedicated to children . . . Escobar's account draws readers in with compelling, emotional, mind-searing descriptions while delving into human nature, evil, prejudices, and forgiveness."

—HISTORICAL NOVEL SOCIETY ON *THE TEACHER OF WARSAW*

"In *The Teacher of Warsaw*, Mario Escobar tries to recreate Korczak's complexities, which have largely been erased by his martyrdom during the Holocaust . . . *The Teacher of Warsaw* is a nuanced fictionalization, and it may motivate readers to learn more about the real man behind it—whose tragic circumstances left him unable to save the Jewish children in his care."

—JEWISH BOOK COUNCIL

"In *The Teacher of Warsaw*, Escobar's intimate, first-person delivery is flawlessly researched. Its historic timeline unfurls with heightening drama from the vantage point of one selfless man dedicated to the wellbeing of Polish children in harrowing wartime conditions against all odds and costs. It's a sobering, memorable story taking the reader through tragic events in occupied Warsaw, from September 1939 to May of 1943. An important, sensitive look at the triumph of the human spirit over evil, *The Teacher of Warsaw* is based on a true story and epitomizes the very best of poignant historical fiction."

—NEW YORK JOURNAL OF BOOKS

"Through meticulous research and with wisdom and care, Mario Escobar brings to life a heartbreaking story of love and extraordinary courage. I want everyone I know to read this book."

—KELLY RIMMER, *NEW YORK TIMES* BESTSELLING
AUTHOR OF *THE WARSAW ORPHAN*,
ON *THE TEACHER OF WARSAW*

"A beautifully written, deeply emotional story of hope, love, and courage in the face of unspeakable horrors. That such self-sacrifice, dedication, and goodness existed restores faith in humankind. Escobar's heart-rending yet uplifting tale is made all the more poignant by its authenticity. Bravo!"

—TEA COOPER, *USA TODAY* BESTSELLING AND
AWARD-WINNING AUTHOR OF *THE CARTOG-
RAPHER'S SECRET*, ON *THE TEACHER OF WARSAW*

"This is a powerful portrait of a woman fighting to preserve knowledge in a crumbling world."

—PUBLISHERS WEEKLY ON
THE LIBRARIAN OF SAINT-MALO

"In *The Librarian of Saint-Malo*, Escobar brings us another poignant tale of sacrifice, love, and loss amidst the pain of war. The seaside town of Saint-Malo comes to life in rich detail and complexity under German occupation, as do the books—full of great ideas and the best of humanity—the young librarian seeks to save. This sweeping story gives us a glimpse into the past with a firm eye toward hope in our future."

—KATHERINE REAY, BESTSELLING AUTHOR OF
THE LONDON HOUSE AND *A SHADOW IN MOSCOW*

"Escobar's latest (after *Auschwitz Lullaby*, 2018) is a meticulously researched story, recreating actual experiences of the 460 Spanish children who were sent to Morelia, Mexico, in 1937. Devastating, enlightening, and passionately told, Escobar's novel shines a light on the experiences of the victims of war, and makes a case against those who would use violence to gain power. Although painful events in the story make it hard to read at times, the book gives a voice to so many whose stories are often overlooked, while inspiring the reader to never give way to fear or let go of one's humanity."

—*BOOKLIST*, STARRED REVIEW, ON *REMEMBER ME*

"Luminous and beautifully researched, *Remember Me* is a study of displacement, belonging, compassion, and forged family amidst a heart-wrenching escape from the atrocities of the Spanish Civil War. A strong sense of place and the excavation of a little known part of history are reverently handled in a narrative both urgent and romantic. Fans of Arturo Pérez-Reverte, Chanel Cleeton, and Lisa Wingate will be mesmerized."

—RACHEL McMILLAN, AUTHOR OF
THE LONDON RESTORATION

"An exciting and moving novel."

"Escobar highlights the tempestuous, uplifting story of two Jewish brothers who cross Nazi-occupied France in hope of reuniting with their parents in this excellent tale . . . Among the brutality and despair that follows in the wake of the Nazis' rampage through France, Escobar uncovers hope, heart, and faith in humanity."

"A poignant telling of the tragedies of war and the sacrificing kindness of others seen through the innocent eyes of children."

"*Auschwitz Lullaby* grabbed my heart and drew me in. A great choice for readers of historical fiction."

"Based on historical events, *Auschwitz Lullaby* is a deeply moving and harrowing story of love and commitment."

THE FORGOTTEN NAMES

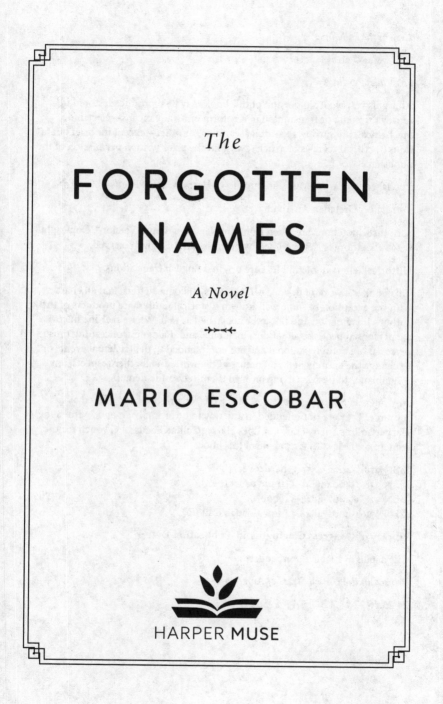

The

FORGOTTEN
NAMES

A Novel

❯❯◄◄

MARIO ESCOBAR

HARPER MUSE

Published by Harper Muse, an imprint of HarperCollins Focus LLC.

Translator: Gretchen Abernathy

ISBN 978-1-4002-4851-3 (hardcover)
ISBN 978-1-4002-4841-4 (trade paper)
ISBN 978-1-4002-4843-8 (ebook)
ISBN 978-1-4002-4848-3 (downloadable audio)

Library of Congress Cataloging-in-Publication Data

CIP data is available upon request.

Printed in the United States of America

24 25 26 27 28 LBC 5 4 3 2 1

To Elisabeth, Andrea, and Alejandra, who traveled to Lyon with me on this journey of memory, history, and passion for freedom.

To the 108 children—and countless others—who managed to escape the clutches of Nazism and who, with their very lives, pulled off the greatest possible act of rebellion against tyranny: being happy.

Sometimes it is only a single light door that keeps children out of the world that we call the real world, and a chance puff of wind may blow it open.

Stefan Zweig, *The Burning Secret*

MOST OF THE CHARACTERS in this novel are real historical people. Some details, including the order of some of the events, have been altered for the sake of the story's development and to protect the privacy of the survivors and their families.

CONTENTS

CONTENTS

PART 2: THE DARKEST HOUR

CONTENTS

PART 3: ANONYMOUS FACES

CONTENTS

A NOTE FROM THE AUTHOR

WRITING A HISTORICAL NOVEL implies describing a part of the world that no longer exists, a part that has disappeared little by little and given way to something else. Someday the impetuous winds of time will buffet us until we, too, are history. The images engraved on our pupils, the sum of emotions and experiences that we all represent, will disappear forever. That futility of life makes us simultaneously giants and pygmies, believing the only way to prolong our existence is to perch atop the shoulders of the next generation and whisper a few phrases into their ears. At its core, that is what literature is: a whisper from people who are no longer. But why is it so crucial that books keep murmuring to us?

In his masterful *Le Livre des Justes*, French Jewish Resistance worker and author Lucien Lazare narrates how the rescue of a baby on the shores of a river changed the course of history. Pharaoh had ordered the extermination of all male Hebrew infants. One poor mother who could not bear to see her son die decided to stick her baby in a basket and float him down the dangerous waters of the Nile. The outcome seemed inevitable, but that very day, the daughter of Pharaoh—the author of one of the most large-scale genocides against children in recorded history—went down to the river to bathe. She saved the baby boy in the basket. That anonymous feat allowed the future legislator and liberator Moses to stay alive.

What is known about the majority of those called "Righteous Among the Nations"—non-Jewish men and women who risked their lives during the Holocaust to save their Jewish neighbors, friends, colleagues, and even strangers—has dissipated with the inevitable passing of time. These were largely anonymous heroes whose only goal was to do good and to act according to their consciences. Today, some four thousand French men and women are recognized by the international community as Righteous Among the Nations. Thanks to these Righteous, three-fourths of the Jews in occupied France did not die. The majority of these were children.

The Forgotten Names is the story of a heroic act without precedent in Nazi-occupied Europe. A network of institutions and people of different ideologies and beliefs came together to carry out one of the largest rescue operations organized during World War II. Cardinal Gerlier, Charles Lederman, Monsignor Saliège, Dr. Joseph Weill, the Protestant pastor Marc Boegner, Father Pierre Chaillet, and the social workers Élisabeth Hirsch, Hélène Lévy, and Maribel Semprún, among others, saved 108 children from the Vénissieux internment camp on the outskirts of Lyon. This novel recounts their experience as well as that of the French historian Valérie Portheret. At the age of twenty-three, Valérie began her riveting research into the rescue of the children of Vénissieux. After discovering a box with the children's files, her research became a twenty-five-year journey to find those lost children and give them back their true identities.

I learned about Valérie Portheret's story in an article in *Le Monde* while researching for my novel *La casa de los niños*. Valérie had been so gripped by the rescue operation that she spent over two decades of her life traveling Europe, Israel, and the Americas to find the children. The story gripped me as well. I was immediately compelled to keep alive the chain of memory. When that chain breaks, we are all left nameless.

In the summer of 2022 I walked the streets of Lyon and visited the Centre d'Histoire de la Résistance et de la Déportation, the Resistance and Deportation History Center. The center is housed in the former military medical school of Lyon-Bron, which was also the former headquarters of the Gestapo and where the infamous SS official Klaus Barbie tortured hundreds of people. The fear and desperation of all those fighting for freedom in those dark hours was palpable.

The Montée des Carmélites is a hill where the former Carmelite convent still stands. In that imposing building the children rescued from Vénissieux were hidden. I paused right where the French gendarmes crouched in waiting to charge the building and seize 108 innocents. That was a time when horror was lord and master of this worn-down city. Then I passed by the plaque that commemorates Vénissieux. The plaque, placed in 2012, is the only remaining vestige of the French internment camp. Time seems to have had its corrosive way with the footprints of all that pain. Yet with rapt concentration, something can still be heard: the stifled cries of the mothers being separated from their children forever, the screams of the children reaching out into the darkest night of the soul for their families. May this book serve as a tribute to them all.

Madrid, September 15, 2022

PROLOGUE

Alba-la-Romaine
APRIL 10, 1942

THE VIOLIN WAS SLUNG over Rachel's back. The case was worn, and the black leather had begun to crack like her grandmother's hands. The cracked hands were all that Rachel could recall of the grandmother she had not seen since she was three. The violin had traveled with Rachel's father, Zelman, from Poland through Germany and to Belgium and later to Paris. By that time he had bequeathed it to his Belgian-born daughter. Their home in Charleroi seemed as far away to Rachel as the morning when the Belgian official rapped softly at the door and whispered to her father that they had best leave everything behind and get moving before the Jews were rounded up and deported to Germany. That very day Zelman; his ex-wife, Chaja; his new wife, Fani; and Rachel fled. They left almost everything behind, but Rachel clung to the violin and her raincoat as they huddled together on the last truck leaving for the French border. After a long and tortuous journey, their new home became Paris, a city whose hostile beauty assured newcomers of their insignificance.

Zelman rented an attic room and the odd family of four survived on his work as a barber until France surrendered to Germany. They joined the hundreds of thousands of Parisians escaping along the crowded streets that led south. Most of those refugees were headed to Bordeaux, but Rachel's family veered toward Valence and from there to the small, provincial Alba-la-Romaine. Bearing evidence of the Roman roots of the village were the stone bridge and the ancient theater, one of the best preserved in France. Rachel loved the solitude of the Roman ruins on the outskirts of the city, especially the theater, which had been witness to so much joy and sadness over the centuries.

That morning the girl was particularly sad. Gendarmes had come at dawn for her father. Things had been taking a turn for the worse in recent months. First, the authorities forbade Zelman from serving non-Jewish clients. Zelman took to going door-to-door, offering his barber services. Then he was forbidden from leaving their neighborhood. The winter was nearly unbearable for the disparate family. With no money for firewood or coal, blankets were their only defense against the cold. Finally, that morning Zelman was taken from them and made to work for the Nazi war machine.

Her father's face had been etched with desolation as he was led away: eyes sunken in fear, face covered with a black beard that, strand by strand, had been softening into gray, and wrinkles that now overextended his forehead and seemed to shrink his dark, expressive eyes. His last words resounded in Rachel's ear. *"Don't lose the violin. Keep playing. Every time you play, you'll know I'm close."*

Yet Rachel felt so alone. Her classmates had stopped talking to her, including Ana, her once soulmate who had shared Rachel's dreams of becoming a famous concert violinist.

Rachel drew out the instrument. It was still a bit big for her, despite her eight years. She nestled it under her chin and took her place on the steps where, hundreds of years before, the sound of peaceful harps and booming drums had marked the pace of comedies and dramas. Rachel closed her eyes and let the music transport her to someplace far away, where no one could hurt her. The wind-tossed notes became a prayer, a plea for her father, for all the fathers who had to leave their families. It was a wish for them to come home soon.

The music stole the magic from the surrounding birdsong, and Rachel's closed eyelids were an insufficient barrier for her tears. Her mother once said that those who sowed the world with tears would someday reap with joy and return with jubilant shouts, and that there was a grief that led to joy, that made people stronger and allowed them to put themselves in the place of those who suffered. But someday was a long way away, and Rachel felt only infinite sadness and fear.

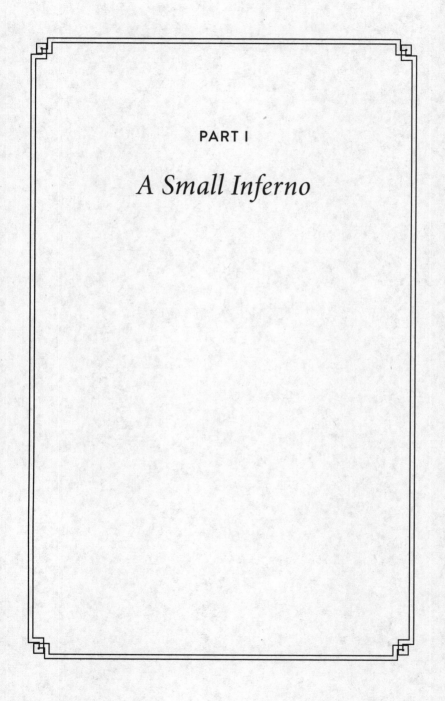

PART I

A Small Inferno

Chapter 1

THESIS

Lyon
SEPTEMBER 20, 1992

FIVE YEARS HAD PASSED since the highly publicized trial of Klaus Barbie, known by many as "the Butcher of Lyon," and France wanted to forget it. The world was changing quickly. The iron curtain had come down three years prior, and the aged prison where the Nazi official had lived out his sentence was now free of its nuisance. With Barbie's death the year before, many former collaborators breathed freely. The past could go back to where it belonged—oblivion.

Valérie headed for Jean Moulin Lyon 3 University. The monumental façade was darkened by soot. Despite bearing the name of a World War II French Resistance hero, everyone knew that the School of Law was a bastion of the extreme Right and anti-Semitism. Valérie planned to direct her research toward the deportation of Jews from Lyon. She vividly recalled the televised sessions of Barbie's trial and itched to do something to recover the history of Jews expelled from Lyon to Germany.

She had an appointment with Jean-Dominique Durand, professor of contemporary history and a dedicated defender of preserving the historical memory of French Jews.

Valérie greeted the professor and took a seat at a table in the school's cafeteria.

"Thank you so much for meeting me, Professor. I'm very interested in studying French Jews, but I can't find anyone to advise me for my thesis."

Jean-Dominique glanced around to see who might be listening. The extreme Right was on the rise, and the law school had become a hive for Fascists. "I'll help you in any way I can," he said.

"So, where should I start?" Valérie asked with a shrug and a smile. She had a beautiful face and dark, energetic eyes. Her slender frame was engulfed in baggy clothes.

"It's a broad subject. You've got to narrow it down a bit."

Valérie's gaze wandered off as she thought. At first she had wanted to study Klaus Barbie and his role in the deportation of Jews from Lyon, but now, after several weeks of reading about the subject, she was more drawn to researching the suffering of Jewish children due to the deportations.

"The children . . ." she mused.

Durand's forehead creased, trying to follow her train of thought. "Which children?"

"The Jewish children. They're what really interests me. I cannot understand how a regime decides to exterminate innocent children."

It was the professor's turn to shrug. "Barbarism is the most primitive state of human beings. Hegel and other philosophers believed that humanity was headed for an era of goodwill and that progress was unstoppable. Marx and Darwin got on board with that positive view of progress, but after two world wars and several pandemics and economic crises, we can no longer say today that humanity is decisively marching toward progress. The narrative that spread through the Enlightenment isn't sustainable, and Nazism and Soviet Communism are the best proof of that."

Valérie nodded and said, "What do you think about studying what happened with the children of Lyon?"

"I'd recommend you start with Le Centre de Documentation sur la Déportation des Enfants juifs de Lyon. It's an archive of documentation all about Jewish children and youth deported from Lyon. It was begun in 1987 during Barbie's trial, to collect all existing data pertaining to child deportees from 1942 through 1944."

Valérie jotted down the details. It was not much to start with, but she would surely find more to go on at the center. She sensed that the road ahead would not be easy. Too many people wanted to forget this most ignominious era of French history, but she was determined to make serious sacrifices to keep the memory of those children from dying out.

Chapter 2

A PERFECT MORNING

Vichy
JULY 2, 1942

LOUIS DARQUIER DE PELLEPOIX slammed his fist down on the table. His broad forehead creased with wrinkles, and his cold eyes flashed. At forty-four, the frenzied anti-Semite had been named director of the Office of Jewish Affairs. He was impatient to get all the Jews out of France. Pierre Laval, who had just regained his title in government, now as prime minister, was less convinced of the wisdom of handing French Jews over to the Germans.

"We need the support of the church. Several bishops have expressed opposition to deporting the Jews, as have some of the Protestant leaders. Marshal Pétain is reticent to go against Cardinal Gerlier. They have long been friends," Laval said.

Darquier swore and let loose a buckshot of saliva droplets over the orders on top of his desk. His colleagues on the cabinet eyed him and his fury fearfully.

"Well then, first expel the Jews that aren't French nationals. Foreign Jewish dross have been basking in refugee status within our borders since 1933. If French Jews, with their libertine men of letters and decadent painters, have destroyed the ancient culture of our beloved nation, the degenerate foreign Jews have done nothing but speed up the process of social decay."

Laval's response was level. "We also need the support of the police. Some of the gendarmes might claim conscientious objection."

Laval, whose complexion was more Algerian or Sicilian than Aryan, fidgeted with his mustache while his cabinet members debated the merits of various ways of dealing with France's Jewish population. He knew he had to tread cautiously. He had already lost Pétain's trust once, and only pressure from the Nazis had allowed him to regain his position. In those two years of erratic, prudish policies, the clergy's critical voice against the government had grown louder. While publicly Catholic, Laval held on to the anticlerical, atheistic notions from his days in l'Internationale ouvrière, the French Section of the Workers' International. Naturally, he kept these opinions to himself. The pious marshal believed that Christianizing the country would solve all of France's problems.

"We've got to get moving on this. We're to send the first shipment of Jews to Germany by the end of the month. For now, let's leave the French nationals alone. We've got to be smart about this. If the Germans suspect that we're not in control of the unoccupied zone, they'll take over the rest of the country in a heartbeat."

Laval's statement indicated that the discussion was over. The ministers left one by one except for Darquier, who clenched his fists as he approached Laval.

"The Nazis are going to be angry. They want to finish the Jewish problem as soon as possible."

"Not to worry, Darquier. All in good time. If we chase the rats into hiding, we make the exterminator's job harder. All in good time . . ."

→>-<←

The prime minister walked among the well-tended gardens of the city of Vichy. The morning heat was already intense, but it was cool and pleasant among the fountains under the ancient trees. Laval mopped his brow with a white handkerchief and loosened his collar. His residence in Châteldon was not far. There his father had horses and a modest coffee plantation and vineyard. There Laval felt something like a feudal lord. At times he wondered if destiny had confused the era in which he was born. At home, his beloved wife, Jeanne, would be waiting for him so they could enjoy their daily coffee. Laval left the machinations of politics and the weight of his position behind in the shadows of the gigantic trees. He drove away from the city and toward one more sweet day of enjoying life and looking forward to what lay ahead. Saving France was, doubtless, a challenge, but he was willing to sacrifice himself for his country.

Chapter 3

THE SHADOW OF DEATH

Alba-la-Romaine
AUGUST 26, 1942

THE DAY BEFORE HAD been happy, which was not a common occurrence. Rachel was able to see and talk with her father for a brief time in the labor camp where he was being held. She missed him terribly. He had been locked up for months and forced to work, though his only crime was being a foreign Jew. Rachel's mother, Chaja, who had managed to avoid being registered as a Jew, had returned to Belgium a few weeks after Zelman was taken. So for months Rachel had lived alone with Fani. Daily survival was increasingly difficult. Fani took every job she could get, but they were only eating one meager meal a day.

Before Fani and Rachel returned home yesterday, Zelman had warned, "Don't go back into town. There's going to be a raid, and this time it won't be just for the men." But Fani found it hard to believe that the French gendarmes would round up women and children. What good would they be to the war effort?

Just after five o'clock in the morning, Fani and Rachel were abruptly woken by loud, insistent knocking at the door. Fani looked toward Rachel and could see the child's eyes shining in the darkness. They had shared a bed since Chaja left.

"Don't worry, it's probably just a mistake," Fani said to calm Rachel. She wrapped herself in her robe and approached the door barefoot.

"Who is it?" she called in a voice still raspy with sleep.

"Police! Open immediately!"

Fani woke fully at the sound of that deep, booming voice.

"Just a moment, please."

"Open up now, or we'll break the door down!"

Fani's heart was racing. She froze for a moment but then opened the door. Two gendarmes stared at her from the landing. One held a nightstick and the other a document that he waved in her face.

"You and all the members of this household must come with us right now."

"But we haven't done anything," Fani protested.

The older of the gendarmes glanced down the dark, empty hallway of the apartment building and, in a moment of compassion, said, "Gather your things; we'll wait for you, then explain what's going on. It's purely a bureaucratic matter."

Those words calmed Fani enough for her to get her body moving again. She turned back to the bedroom where Rachel was sitting up in bed and rubbing her eyes in confusion.

"Rachel, we have to go with the gendarmes."

"Where?"

"I'm not sure, but they'll explain things when we get there."

Rachel was trembling with fright, but Fani wrapped her in a strong embrace that calmed her momentarily. Then they packed a few belongings: some clothes, some food, and Rachel's violin. They got to the door of their apartment looking disheveled, the buttons of their jackets misaligned and dark circles of worry under their eyes.

Down on the empty, dimly lit street, the morning felt cool to them despite it being the end of August. The gendarmes led them to a bus manned by a frowning driver.

"Sit wherever you'd like," the older gendarme said as the policemen settled into a seat at the front.

There were already a few other occupants on the bus. As Fani and Rachel walked down the aisle, the others ducked their heads, ashamed to be part of the macabre convoy. Fani placed their suitcase in one of the last rows.

"I'm scared," Rachel whispered as she took a seat.

"It'll be all right," Fani said automatically but unconvincingly. She feared being locked up in a labor camp like Zelman or being sent to Germany.

Rachel curled up in Fani's lap and tried to rest. It still felt like nighttime. The only light to be seen came from the streetlamps.

The bus drove away from their town. The rumble of the motor managed to relax the occupants into deep sleep, but everyone woke when the bus stopped at the next town and the gendarmes got off.

A boy sitting close to the driver yanked the lever to open the door and shot out running. The gendarmes, only a few yards away from the bus, turned and immediately chased him. In anguish, Rachel watched the boy sprinting toward the forest, but the younger gendarme easily outpaced him. The policeman smacked the boy's face the whole way back to the bus. The driver opened the door, and the gendarme pushed the boy in, growling,

"Keep control of that door or you'll end up in the same camp as the Jews!"

His words had their desired effect. The driver stood and guarded the door with his towering frame.

The boy limped back to his seat and tumbled into it. Rachel caught his eyes fleetingly. His face was reddened, and blood trickled down one eyebrow.

The gendarmes returned with five more people to add to the bus. The operation was repeated from town to town until the bus was full, yet there was still quite a ways to go until it reached Lyon.

Chapter 4

ALEXANDRE GLASBERG

Lyon
AUGUST 26, 1942

TWENTY DAYS BEFORE, GILBERT Lesage had visited Father Alexandre Glasberg to warn him of what the Vichy government was about to agree to. Gilbert was the head of the Vichy's Service Social des Étranger, the social service agency for foreigners. He was also a well-known Protestant. After studying architecture in school, he had switched directions to dedicate his life to the disadvantaged. A committed pacifist, he was horrified about what was occurring throughout Europe and determined not to stand idly by. His anti-Nazi spirit had surfaced several years before the Germans invaded France. In the 1930s he traveled to Germany with a Quaker mission to help Jewish children suffering under the weight of the infamous Nuremberg Laws.

Gilbert had gone to the vicarage to solicit Father Glasberg's help. Glasberg himself was of Jewish background, a Ukrainian emigrant who had suffered persecution at the hands of Soviets in his country.

Glasberg and Gilbert had sounded the alert among a distinguished group of people in Lyon who were opposed to the German occupation, to Vichy collaboration, and especially to the return of Prime Minister Laval to power.

→>-<←

That morning, aware that within hours thousands of Jews would be taken into custody throughout the entire department, Alexandre Glasberg held an urgent meeting with Gilbert and others concerned about the situation. The two men were well aware that the prefect of Lyon, Alexandre Angeli, was eager to oblige René Bousquet, the secretary general of police, regardless of the fact that this meant the illegal detention of thousands of innocent people.

Gilbert knocked at number 17 rue de Marseille, then went up the stairs to Glasberg's office. The priest was waiting with no pretense of calm.

Gilbert spoke before he had crossed the threshold. "The raids have started." He had seen the orders with his own eyes.

"You're the first to arrive, but when everyone's here we'll see what's to be done," Glasberg replied.

"I don't want to be a pessimist, but back in July when thousands of Jews were forced into work crews, no one batted an eye."

Father Glasberg knew all about it. He had begged several bishops to speak out against the policy, but none had done so publicly. The poor devils were foreigners and Jews—people of no real interest to the Catholic Church, which, at that time, was preoccupied above all else with regaining its privileges now that Marshal Pétain was back in power.

"But women, children, and older Jews. They can't look the other way," Glasberg replied, though he was fully aware that human logic did not always follow a logical course, especially when doing so implied opposition to an invader and could lead to detention or death.

The door opened and Pierre Chaillet appeared. The Jesuit was a committed advocate for vulnerable children. He had joined other men of orders like Father Lubac and Father Bockel to oppose the Nazi invaders. His position as a theology professor at the Jesuit school in Fourvière allowed him to maintain contact with a wide network of students and professors. He founded an underground journal of resistance to Nazism and was part of founding Amitié Chrétienne, a rescue organization known as Christian Friendship, in 1941. Amitié Chrétienne was an ecumenical network of Protestants, Catholics, and Jews dedicated to helping the under-served, particularly Jewish refugee children.

"Forgive me for being late, but there are many checkpoints all along the streets. You can smell in the air what the gendarmes are up to."

"Not a problem," Glasberg replied.

"The mayor and Pastor Boegner can't make it, but they're also with us in this."

"Cardinal Gerlier as well, and everyone knows he's quite chummy with Marshal Pétain."

Next to arrive were Marcelle Trillat and Denise Grunewald, workers in the Lyon branch of the Service Social des Étranger. They were soon followed by the final member of the meeting, Georges Garel of the OSE, l'Œuvre de secours aux enfants, the Organization to Save the Children.

"We're all here," Glasberg began. His direct manner contrasted with the bureaucratic approach of some members of the emergency committee. "This is our third meeting, and we can't put it off any longer. We know that today a large number of foreign Jews will arrive at the Vénissieux camp."

Marcelle chimed in, "We've confirmed that there is a list of legally recognized exemptions. They're not authorized to deport Jews who are old, disabled, pregnant, or unaccompanied minors; nor can they deport war heroes who have fought in the French army. We'll have to gather as much documentation as possible in record time. I don't think the Nazis will linger in the task of deporting the Jews."

"First," Father Chaillet offered, "some of us need to go to Vénissieux to get a complete list of the prisoners. Then we'll coordinate and divide up the work of searching through the archives and being in touch with the various embassies. We've got to save as many people as we can."

"That won't be easy. The prefect and chief of police will do as much and more to fulfill the quotas of deported refugees. I get the sense they have no souls," Denise said.

Father Glasberg stood. "Then we'd best get to it. Each to his post. Every minute counts. Godspeed!"

Chapter 5

ARRIVAL

Vénissieux Camp
AUGUST 26, 1942

THE HOURS DRAGGED ON interminably, and thirst ravaged the refugees in the bus, now full to bursting. The asphyxiating heat dehydrated the youngest ones, and several older men and women had fainted. Women tried in vain to revive the weak by fanning them. Children wriggled their heads out of the windows, gasping for breath like fish out of the fishbowl. Rachel's body was drenched with sweat. The melted chocolate that Fani had given her coated her parched throat.

"We'll be there soon," Fani said with false cheer. But Rachel, strangled by heat and exhaustion, could not spare the energy to respond.

The older gendarme, whom they had learned was named Antoine, shuffled down the aisle, trying to calm everyone's nerves. He served water to the weakest of the older refugees. When he passed by Rachel, he stopped and studied her for a moment.

"Don't worry, little one. I've got a daughter your age. They're taking you to a work camp, but you'll be treated well. The French gendarmerie won't allow anything bad to happen to you."

Fani nodded at him, grateful for the gesture. The man was only following orders after all, though Fani wondered how anyone could go along with such inhumane treatment. She had grown up in Belgium, and it was hard for her to accept that the world had gone completely mad. All the hatred she now witnessed—had it been secretly growing for years, just waiting for the moment to strike? She had seen how Jews were treated in Paris. Then, when Fani and the rest of Zelman's family arrived in Alba-la-Romaine, they had been forcibly crammed together with all the other refugees in an abandoned warehouse with no drinking water or heat.

The policeman was continuing his round toward the front of the bus when a woman dressed in a leather coat, despite the suffocating heat, stopped him. Her sons, twin boys, were balanced one on each hip. Ridiculously, they were dressed as little sailors.

"Gendarme, sir, please, if you'll allow me to leave, I can offer you a great deal of money. My husband owned a famous jewelry store in Valence. We have a lot of money hidden away. Please . . ."

The gendarme frowned and shimmied away from her. He did not make it far before another woman stopped him.

"Sir, if you let me and my family go, I'll do whatever you ask," she whispered.

"Good God, woman!" He huffed off and rejoined his companion at the front.

The bus stopped at a railroad crossing. Rachel and Fani's bus was the first in a convoy of half a dozen vehicles. One mother took advantage of the stop. She held her five-year-old son out of the window and let him down as gently as she could. The child was stunned when he hit the pavement but within seconds was up, gripping his pained right arm and running toward a cornfield. The doors of several buses in the convoy opened and two gendarmes raced after the boy. The rest of the police waited to see if anyone else would attempt a similar stunt.

The boy ran like the devil was after him. He scurried into the cornfields and disappeared. Cheers erupted from the crowded buses. From behind Fani, an older man named Jacob said, "We should all do the same. Some of us would make it."

"But where would we flee to?" Fani asked. Since July the authorities had been hunting Jews like rabbits. All they could do was hope for mercy from the French government or hope for the war to end soon.

Jacob sighed and shook his head. "My family tried to get to Australia, but do you know what the Australian ambassador at the Evian Conference said? He said that his country didn't have race problems and he wasn't going to bring half a million Jews in to create one. No one wants us. We escaped from Vienna when it fell to the Nazis. They made me scrub the city streets on my knees and dry the stones with my beard as they kicked me over and over. You know who did it? It was my very own students. I was a high school teacher. I taught philosophy, and the year before my students adored me. But when Hitler took over Austria, the world turned upside down. Vienna had been the most tolerant city for Jews in the entire Austro-Hungarian Empire."

The two policemen returned to the buses without the child. The boy's mother was smiling with relief. She held a baby in her arms and knew that anywhere would be better for her older son than falling into the hands of Nazi collaborators.

A woman across the aisle shook her head and tsked. "Have you lost your mind?" she demanded to the mother. "It's dangerous for your boy to be out in that field alone. He could fall in a ditch or get bitten by a snake or a scorpion."

"That's better than being forced into a slaughterhouse."

"They're taking us to work," Jacob interrupted. "The Nazis need our manual labor in order to win the war."

"That's what the Armenians thought in 1915, too, when the Turks killed millions of them or let them starve to death," the runaway's mother said.

A collective sigh arose as soon as the buses were on the move again, a mixture of relief and renewed fear. At least now there was a bit of airflow from the windows.

Within an hour they had arrived at the gates of the Vénissieux camp. The passengers were greeted with the sight of the French flag snapping above long brick barracks.

Chapter 6

JUSTUS

Grenoble
AUGUST 26, 1942

JUSTUS ROSENBERG STRUGGLED TO accurately recall the faces of his family members in Danzig. He had managed to escape the city just before the Nazis took it over in 1939. His father was a famous watchmaker who served an elite clientele throughout Europe. Before the Nazis arrived, he had prepared an escape route for his wife, Sara, and their daughter, Ruth, but in the end everything unraveled. He got Justus on a ship to Calais the day before the Germans arrived; the rest of the family would sail a week later when all their papers were in order, but by that time it was too late. The Nazis forced all the Jews into ghettoes, and Justus heard no more from them.

Justus had spent his time in Paris studying at the Janson de Sailly School, but when the Nazis occupied Paris, he went to Toulouse, where refugees were being housed in the former Pax cinema. There he met two young women, one of them from the United States. The American took him with her to Marseille where a rescue committee was being organized. The committee was tasked with getting French intellectuals and those of other nationalities out of the country. The US government had sent the journalist Varian Fry to oversee the operation, and Justus soon began working for Fry. When the Vichy government expelled Fry from the country in August 1941, Fry was not able to take Justus with him. The young man then tried to escape over the border to Spain, but he was arrested. The judge over his case was merciful and only fined him a small fee.

After all of that, he settled in Grenoble and rented a room for a modest sum. Yet his money began to run out, and he grew desperate. His father had told him that, if things ever got bad enough in France, he should try to get to Spain, and Justus was ready to try again. He had one uncle in Germany and had seen him before escaping to Paris, but another uncle lived in the Spanish protectorate of Morocco.

But that morning the gendarmes surprised him at the home where he was boarding.

"You can't take the boy! He's done nothing wrong!" Madame Damour, his landlady, protested, though she knew all about Justus's work with the students in the Resistance movement at the University of Grenoble.

"Ma'am, your lodger is a Jew. He's got to be taken to an internment camp."

The gray-haired woman clung to her boarder in defiance. "Since when is it a crime in France to be a Jew?"

"We're just following orders." The gendarme yanked Justus away. Madame Damour lost her balance and fell to the floor.

"Madame Damour!" Justus called.

"Don't worry about me, son. Take care of yourself. You'll be in my prayers."

The gendarmes carried him suspended above the ground between them and shoved him into a truck with other prisoners. Justus picked himself up off the floor of the truck and looked around. Some twenty men were seated in two rows. A teenage boy nearby made room for him.

"You can sit here. Where ten men fit, eleven will too. I'm Lazarus."

The rest of the prisoners on the bench scooted reluctantly.

"Thank you," Justus said.

"We've got to lend each other a hand."

"I'm Justus Rosenberg."

"Are you Polish?" the young man asked.

"Yes; are you?"

The boy shook his head. "Nope, Czech. This truck is a miniature Babel. Juan is Lithuanian, and Abraham is Russian." Lazarus nodded at two boys who raised their eyebrows to return the greeting.

"Do you know where they're taking us?" Justus asked.

"Somewhere near Lyon, and from there to Germany, or to your country, Poland."

Justus shivered.

"What is it?" Lazarus asked.

"I saw my uncle in Berlin just before the war started. He was a professor, but he wasn't allowed to teach anymore. The Jews were treated terribly there, like animals."

Lazarus glanced at his other two companions. "Well, we've been thinking up a way to escape. Don't you think that's our only option?"

Justus did agree. He would rather die shot in the back than fall into the hands of the Nazis. He leaned forward. The canvas cover blocked their view, but from the potholes he could tell they were not on a main road. He wondered for the millionth time what had become of his family. The worst feeling of his life was the sensation of being an orphan and knowing that not one soul cared what happened to him. If he disappeared from the face of the earth, he would be utterly and entirely forgotten. He closed his eyes and tried to remember the prayers he had been taught at the synagogue when he was younger, but his mind was blank. It seemed that his entire life in Poland had been erased. His brain expertly blocked whatever had once been happy to protect him from the melancholy that would otherwise become unbearable.

Chapter 7

THE RESISTANCE AND DEPORTATION HISTORY CENTER

*Centre d'Histoire de la Résistance et de la
Déportation, Lyon*
NOVEMBER 7, 1992

THAT SATURDAY, VALÉRIE WOKE early to go to the Centre d'Histoire de la Résistance et de la Déportation. The Resistance and Deportation History Center had previously been part of the Lyon Natural History Museum. But in the wake of Klaus Barbie's trial, the mayor of Lyon had approved a move a few weeks prior. The center was now housed in the former military medical school, site of the Gestapo's offices during the war. Valérie made her way through the rooms, horrified to see the exhibits about all that had occurred in her city. Innocent people had been tortured in that very building some fifty years ago. She studied the photographs, fragments of handwritten letters, and cleanly typed official reports. What surprised her were the images of children being freed from living in hiding at the Peyrins château, in the department of Drôme.

"They weren't the only ones," an older woman said.

Valérie turned to the woman in surprise. "I'm sorry?"

"I said they weren't the only children who were saved. There was an elaborate rescue plan to save the Jewish children of Lyon."

Valérie's eyes followed the woman, who backed away and sat on a bench.

"Excuse me," Valérie said, "did you say there was a plan to save the children of Lyon?"

The woman smiled and balanced her cane against the bench. "Oh yes. Lyon was one of the best-organized cities in France when it came to saving the children. Many called it the 'Capital of the Resistance.'"

"I had no idea," Valérie said.

"There's a lecture about it tomorrow if you're interested. I'll be going, and you're welcome to join me."

Valérie sensed the direction fate was pushing her toward for her research. She needed to know and understand what had happened, how people from different ideologies and beliefs had come together to rescue the children. She wanted to know how this miracle came to be in that particular dark moment of history.

"Yes, I'd love to. I'll be there." After learning the details of the lecture, Valérie stood and continued taking in the rest of the exhibit. Each panel hypnotized her anew.

An hour later, her body went through the mechanics of leaving the building, going down the stairs, exiting through the yard to the street, and then crossing the bridge heading to her apartment. Yet Valérie's mind and heart were with the children and their families. They captivated her, though she did not yet know the immense sacrifice those parents made to save their children. Their sacrifice would change Valérie's life forever.

Chapter 8

A PLACE BEST FORGOTTEN

Vénissieux Camp
AUGUST 26, 1942

THE ONLY THING THAT could be seen in the distance were the chimneys of old factories and a few trees among the yellowed fields of already harvested grain. Closer at hand, the brick barracks were worn down. The buses drove through the barbed wire fence and dispensed the cargo they had carried for several hours. Hundreds of Jews filed out in rows. Many of the older Jews, famished and dehydrated, did not have the strength to walk. Younger adults supported their weight and took them to the improvised infirmary or simply left them on cots at the front of the building.

Rachel got out of the bus with her stepmother and they stood looking around, unsure of where to go or what to do. Chaos reigned. The day before, men had arrived, but they were separated behind a barbed wire fence, and there was another enclosed section of Indo-Chinese workers.

Rachel pointed. "There are men over there, Fani." They could see a crowd of men pressed against the fence, searching among the new arrivals for their wives and children.

Rachel ran up to the barbed wire to study them. They were all too similar: bearded, torn clothing, and a defeated look in their eyes.

"I'm not sure if your father is . . ." Fani's eyes met Zelman's, and she burst into tears. She had become convinced that she had seen Zelman for the last time the day before. "Darling!" Fani said, thrusting her fingers through the barbed wire. Zelman gripped her tightly, and Rachel wiggled her hand into theirs.

"Oh, daughter. I am so sorry to see you here. I had hoped, had prayed . . . perhaps you had escaped."

Fani shook her head through her tears and said, "At least we're all together again."

The gendarmes pulled the men away from the fence, fearing that it would collapse under the weight of families trying to reunite. Some fathers resisted and received blows for their efforts. Zelman's and Fani's fingers were the last to disentwine.

"I love you, Zelman!" Fani yelled. Her husband said nothing but smiled and held her gaze as long as the shoving of the gendarmes allowed.

A younger man from Zelman's work crew hollered, "Let us see our families!" but Zelman held him back from jumping at the gendarme.

"It's not worth it, Albert. Surely they're sending us all to the same camp, and you'll see them there." Albert bit his lip in helpless frustration.

Fani and Rachel left the fence and walked toward the barracks, Rachel still gripping her violin. They stopped when they came upon the older man they had talked with on the bus. He was lying on a cot.

"Are you holding up?" Fani asked Jacob.

"If I had known this is how things would end, I would've stayed in Vienna. It was pointless to try to escape. I'm tired, and I've lost everyone. My wife died a few months ago. What have we done to deserve this?" he asked in tears.

Fani took his hand. "Nothing, dear Jacob. We've done nothing. But God will get us out of this."

"God?" Jacob scoffed. "He forgot about us centuries ago. They call us the chosen people—chosen for a history of persecution and death. Would that we were the accursed people instead! Perhaps then we'd be less hated."

Fani let Jacob's hand drop as two men lifted the cot and took it inside. "Take care of yourself!" she called after him.

She took Rachel's hand again and they resumed their walk to the first barrack. Finding it overcrowded, they went to the next, but it was just as full. They found a bit of space in the third barrack. People had divided up according to families and nationalities. Fani and Rachel formed a group with two other foreigners, young women who had lived in France for nine years and who spoke French.

→>-<←

The women and children were exhausted. A loud noise startled them, and many of the babies began crying.

"What was that?" a woman asked in German.

"Perhaps it's the dinner bell?" another offered in French.

The women left their belongings beside the bunk beds and hurried to the dining hall. Some of the more improvising women had packed a bit of bread, butter, sausages, and canned food when the gendarmes came to get them that morning, but most had had nothing to eat all day.

Rachel and Fani joined the end of the long line. They salivated at the smell of the vegetable stew. The line advanced slowly. They spoke with the family in front of them, a mother with her daughters, Sonja and Lucy, and her eighteen-year-old niece, Ruth.

"Are you hungry, Sonja?" Fani asked.

The girl, no more than five, smiled, but her older sister answered for her. "Food is the only thing Sonja thinks about."

When their turn arrived, the cooks were scraping the bottom of the pans. Fani and Rachel were served on metal plates and took their seats at the long tables in the former army mess hall.

"I thought we'd never get here," Sonja and Lucy's mother said.

"How long were we on the bus?" Fani asked.

"It was nine hours for us. So many people passed out. The old men and women and the children couldn't help but wet themselves. How it reeked! They're treating us like cattle," she huffed.

Lucy glanced at Rachel and cocked her eyes at the violin case. "Why didn't you leave that piece of junk in the barracks?"

"It's the violin my father gave me, and it isn't junk," Rachel snapped.

"Don't be rude, Lucy," Ruth said, frowning at her cousin. "It's completely normal to hold tight to the few things we've got left. The Nazis want to erase us from the face of the earth. Sometimes when I get up in the morning, I wonder if I've disappeared completely."

Some of the women went out to smoke after dinner while others put the younger children to bed. Despite their exhaustion, it was very difficult for the little ones to fall asleep with so much going on. Some women were sick and feverish, and they moaned in delirium.

"We might be better off sleeping outside," Fani said to her new friend.

"I don't know which is worse. This heat is insufferable, there's no water to wash up with, the latrines are disgusting, and the stench in the barracks . . ."

The two women shared a last cigarette and breathed out all the smoke before entering the barrack. It was a desolate site. A pigsty would have been preferable lodging.

Chapter 9

FALSIFICATIONS

Lyon
AUGUST 26, 1942

DENISE AND MARCELLE HAD made a list of all the legal exemptions, but the hardest work lay ahead: acquiring proof of residency and, if necessary, altering the date of entry. French laws only protected refugees who had arrived prior to 1936 from being deported.

"So, the exemptions are for people over sixty years of age, those who have served in the French army, those who have French children or French spouses, pregnant women, parents of children under five years of age, those whose jobs fulfill a vital service for France, and unaccompanied minors," Denise rattled off to her boss, Marcelle.

"That's over a thousand people. There's no way we can prepare reports for so many in one night."

Denise made a quick count of the papers stacked in front of her. "We've got fifty so far."

"We'd better call the whole crew of social workers. It'll be a sleepless night if we're going to try to save as many people as possible."

Denise felt the weight of the responsibility but was less optimistic. "Why can't we ask the prefect for a few more days?"

"Because the prefect and the chief of police want to be done with this whole business as soon as possible. As soon as the transportation is ready, they want to get these people to Drancy and then to Germany."

"But why do they want to take them away?" Denise asked.

"All we have are rumors. The ghettoes of Poland, Austria, and the Czech Republic are full to bursting. So they're sending the people to live in miserable conditions in concentration camps. The weakest ones die off quickly." Marcelle spoke softly, preferring to work instead of talk.

"Worse than here in Vénissieux?" Denise continued.

Marcelle looked up. "The Nazis are nervous because of what's going on with the front in Russia. They've been fighting there for a year, and the Soviets are holding out. They need more weapons. And the Jews are cheap labor."

"So then why do they want children, old people, and pregnant women?" Denise insisted.

A chill ran up Marcelle's back. "I don't know," she said. "But it can't be good. Go ahead and call the rest of the team. We've got to get everything ready for tomorrow morning."

→>-<←

Denise called everyone who worked for the Lyon branch of the Service Social des Étranger. Within minutes, twelve women showed up to the office and got to work. The French government was highly bureaucratic, and the Vichy regime was no less; these women were experts at preparing reports and filing requests.

The afternoon light slowly dwindled, and the street outside was calm. The human drama unfolding a few miles down the road at Vénissieux seemed hardly real. The citizens of Lyon went about their evening routines and dinnertime peacefully enough. Food was in shorter and shorter supply, and the ration cards barely provided what was necessary for survival, but they were alive. The war was still too far off to be truly terrifying. Most citizens hardly noticed that hundreds of their neighbors had been taken from their homes that morning. If they did notice, few were concerned—it meant fewer mouths to feed and less racket from the foreign Jews who seemed incapable of adequately adapting to French customs and values. Yet it was a frenzied, sleepless night for others: the men and women trying to fight the hell that Lyon's Jews were experiencing. Their resistance was a feisty wave on a vast ocean of placid indifference.

Chapter 10

THE INFIRMARY

Vénissieux Camp
AUGUST 26, 1942

NO ONE EXPECTED THE camp doctor to quit that afternoon. Up to then he had tended to the Indo-Chinese workers, but when he saw the avalanche of sick Jews that arrived, he hung up his coat and walked away. Élisabeth Hirsch took the reins. There were cases of dehydration, panic attacks, suicide attempts, low blood pressure, high blood pressure, badly bruised children, and a woman going into labor early. Élisabeth had served in difficult conditions at the camp at Gurs, but at least there they had been prepared for the massive arrival of refugees. At Vénissieux, the authorities of Lyon had improvised a detention center in a space unfit for that many people. All the authorities wanted was to get rid of the region's foreign Jews as quickly as possible.

Élisabeth approached an older man who had nodded off. "What is your name, sir?" she asked, gently shaking his shoulder.

Jacob looked up and wiped the drool from his mouth. His throat was dry, his head ached, his whole body hurt, and he was shivering with chills.

"Jacob, but I'm bad off. Don't waste your time with me; I don't have much left. All these others need you more than I do. I'm just an old man whose time has come. The first fifty years of my life were happy. Then things got twisted up, and the last five years have been constant grief. María's gone. I'm just waiting to die so I can rest. Most people don't understand this, especially not young folks, but when you get to a certain age, you see how your whole world starts slipping away little by little. First it's your parents. They go, along with the aunts and uncles you spent your childhood with, and then your friends, and then your soulmate. There's nothing left of the world I grew up in, of my little village outside of Vienna, of that Jewish community that was like one big family."

"Oh, sir, but there's still hope," Élisabeth answered.

"Not for someone like me, but maybe for those children." Jacob nodded to the youngest patients. "Though I don't envy them. The world I grew up in was kinder than this one. We fought in the Great War and faced crises and plagues, but human beings still had souls. I've seen so much, madame. I wish I could drive it all out of my mind and heart. These people don't know the hell they're about to be taken to. The Nazis are devils with no souls."

Élisabeth dabbed at the sweat on the man's fevered brow.

"Let me give you something to bring your fever down."

"Don't waste your meager supplies on this old man. All I want is to go to sleep and never wake up. Every night I lie down hoping this will be the night. And I wake up desperate. Life refuses to leave me. But there's nothing left for me here."

Élisabeth thought of her own grandfather. At twenty-one, she had seen more in her time than most and was still not jaded by tragedy. She had been in France for twelve years but had grown up in Romania. Her brother taught her the basics of medicine. Armed with those skills, she worked in the Gurs internment camp starting in 1940. She had poured herself into the work of freeing hundreds of children and getting them to safety and was in Paris helping Jewish children during the raids in July. Now she was seeing what she could do to help in Lyon. But the years of difficult work were beginning to take their toll. Sometimes Élisabeth wondered how much more she could take.

Jacob looked at her with eyes that were tired of living. Élisabeth handed him water and a pill to help him sleep and eased him up to swallow it.

"Thank you," the old man said, reclining again and closing his eyes.

Walking away, Élisabeth could not keep herself from crying.

"Are you all right?" her colleague Madeleine Dreyfus asked. She was a psychologist.

"No, no, I'm not." Élisabeth could not say why the story of that man in particular touched her more than the children lying on cots all around him or the terror in the face of the mother who was about to give birth.

"Take a break," Madeleine said. "Most everyone in here will be asleep soon; they're worn out."

"You do understand that a lot of these people won't wake up tomorrow?" Élisabeth asked.

Madeleine gave a sad sigh. "That might be for the best."

Élisabeth headed for the room at the back of the infirmary, a small office with a bed. She allowed herself to lie down, and sleep came quickly.

→>←←

Élisabeth started awake a few hours later. She could not remember where she was and did not know what time it was. Everything was quiet. She studied the light coming through the opaque window. In her groggy haze, she did not notice the man sitting in the room's only chair and working under a dim lamp on the desk.

He cleared his throat, and Élisabeth jumped again.

"I'm sorry to have frightened you. I'm Dr. Weill, Joseph Weill."

"Oh, Dr. Weill, we met one time at Gurs."

"Indeed we did. You're Élisabeth, correct?"

She nodded.

"Gilbert Lesage asked me to come by. Apparently the camp medic resigned? I can't say that I blame him. It's complete chaos around here. I left my family at home and came as quickly as I could. Madeleine has briefed me on most of the cases here at the infirmary."

Élisabeth sat up and held out her hand to shake the doctor's. "We've got a very difficult couple of days ahead of us."

"My father, who was a rabbi in Strasbourg, once told me that the great rabbi Simcha Bunim always carried two pieces of paper with him, one in each pocket. On one was written, 'The world was created for me.' And on the other, 'I am but dirt and ashes.' When he felt weak and powerless, he would take the first piece of paper out and read it. When he was tempted to forget that he was a mere mortal, he read the second."

Élisabeth smiled. She understood perfectly what the doctor was trying to say: they were there to fulfill their duty and do all that they could. The rest was not up to them.

Chapter 11

SICKNESS UNTO LIFE

Vénissieux Camp
AUGUST 26, 1942

A S MOST OF THE men had arrived the day before, there was no room for Justus in the barrack when the police dropped off his group. Most of the prisoners were already asleep on their bunk beds. The young man stretched his blanket on the floor and was about to lie down when he heard a voice from one of the upper bunks.

"Come on up here. It's hot as hades, but you'll be better off than on the floor. The place is crawling with rats and cockroaches."

The voice came from a dark corner of the room, but the tone was friendly, that of a young man, perhaps even a boy.

Justus climbed up to the bunk where the young man had already made room for him.

"I'm Samuel."

Justus introduced himself and then settled in to sleep. He had been in the truck all day and had not eaten anything, but at that moment exhaustion was greater than hunger.

Yet his bedmate was chatty. "I shouldn't be here, but the stupid police don't listen to anything. I'm French; I was born here. My parents emigrated to Paris seventeen years ago, but our papers were lost when my parents were taken in the big raid. I managed to escape to Lyon, but that's done me no good. If I'd known this would happen, I would've gladly gone with them to their bus instead," Samuel explained.

Justus turned toward him. "So you were in Paris too?"

"Yes," Samuel answered, "in the Marais neighborhood. My parents came from Russia. First the czarists were after them, and then the Communists. They ran a café in Marais. It was small but classy, really close to Victor Hugo's house."

"I know that area," Justus said, now awake again.

"I want to get out of here," Samuel groaned.

Those words surprised Justus. "Escape? But how? I checked out the fence. It's high and well guarded."

"You think they'd shoot us if we tried it?"

"When I was in Marseille, I saw gendarmes kill more than one Jew. They know that no one will say anything if they kill off a few of us. We're trash to them."

Samuel was quiet for a few moments, weighing the words of his new friend.

"So are you just going to wait around here twiddling your thumbs?"

"No, Samuel. I'm going to fake an illness. I hope it'll be enough to get me transferred to a hospital, and hopefully from there it'll be easier to get away. I'm aiming to cross the Pyrenees."

"An illness? Like what?"

"Appendicitis. It's serious, and they have to operate on you right away. Once I'm at the hospital, I'll find a way to get out."

Someone from a nearby bunk growled at them to be quiet. The two boys looked at each other, barely able to see the other's face in the dark. Justus marveled at how easy it was to speak frankly with people sharing the same dire situation. There was no time for formalities or social games or wondering who could be trusted. The danger was constant, death was around every corner, and it was enough to know that the primary interest of the other was survival. Yet no one could pull it off without other people's help. The individualism from before the war—that sense that a person's life mattered to only the one who lived it—was a daydream from the past. The only way to survive in the world they now lived in was, simply, to trust others.

Chapter 12

SURVIVOR

Lyon
NOVEMBER 8, 1992

VALÉRIE PORTHERET WALKED INTO the head-quarters of Amitié Chrétienne. Twenty or so people were milling about the chairs lined up in rows in the conference room. Valérie got the sense that most of them knew one another well. The older woman from the Resistance and Deportation History Center the day before was not there. Valérie felt like an intruder. She fidgeted with her long blond ponytail and sighed with relief when a man announced that they were about to begin. Then the woman who had agreed to meet her there slipped in through the door, puffing with haste. She eased into the seat next to Valérie, placed her hand on Valérie's knee, and whispered, "I'm so sorry; forgive me for being late. I missed my bus, and at my age, I can no longer run."

"Don't worry about it," Valérie whispered back, relieved to no longer be completely out of place.

The older gentleman at the front of the room wore a frayed gray suit with a shirt that had not been ironed in decades. But as soon as he began speaking, Valérie forgot all about his disheveled appearance and focused on his words.

"The conference room is almost full today. What a change from five years ago when we started these lectures! Back then there was only a handful of us."

The man's enthusiasm in a room full of octogenarians took Valérie by surprise.

"For years we've been studying what happened in the summer of 1942 in Lyon and the surrounding areas. We've gathered quite a bit of information, but there are still important gaps. We know that an ecumenical Christian fellowship organization, Amitié Chrétienne, coordinated the aid to the foreign Jews held at Vénissieux. With the help of a few government employees, the workers of Amitié Chrétienne gathered the reports and legal documentation necessary for obtaining deportation exemptions for the greatest number of people possible. They focused on children and saved 108 from sure death."

Valérie's eyes were wide. This was the subject that interested her most.

The man continued, "Those children managed to escape and go into hiding, but we know almost nothing about them. We have a handful of names, though most of them adopted new names to avoid being tracked by the Nazis." The audience listened with rapt attention to each word. The speaker pulled out a yellowed piece of paper and shook it gently in the air.

"Records like this give us valuable information about what happened at the camp on those sad August nights. The more we find, the more we'll be able to unravel the mystery of those children, what became of them, and how they survived the war."

->-<-

When the lecture was over, Valérie's older companion greeted several people and introduced Valérie to them. Then she motioned toward the speaker and asked, "Would you like to meet Joseph?"

Valérie nodded shyly. Her typical assertiveness had dried up.

"Joseph, this is Valérie Portheret, a doctoral student. Valérie, this is Dr. Joseph Weill."

"I'm so pleased to meet you," Valérie said, shaking his strong hand.

"Where are you studying?" Joseph asked.

"At Jean Moulin Lyon 3."

Joseph pursed his lips. "That place is a brood of Fascists. I've had to lecture there a few times, and they've all but kicked me to the curb. I don't know why the government allows it."

The old woman tried to defuse the tension. "Lyon used to be considered the capital of the Resistance. Now it's a bastion of the extreme Right. That's one of the consequences of forgetting the past. Joseph, Valérie wants to write her thesis on what happened to the Jewish children of Lyon."

The man's face relaxed and he smiled. "What aspect in particular?"

"That's what I'm trying to figure out. At first I thought about focusing on Klaus Barbie's trial, but I'm more drawn to the subject of the children."

Joseph nodded. "Klaus Barbie arrived in Lyon in July 1942. Before that he'd been in Holland and on the Russian front. That spring he'd been named chief of security in Gex, near the Swiss border. We know that he was sent to Dijon in June, but then by July he and other Nazis were staying in the Charbonnères-les-Bains casino outside of Lyon. He was going after spies who transmitted their messages by radio frequencies."

Valérie was pensive. "So he wasn't involved in the deportation of Jews from Lyon?"

Joseph put his hands to his waist and leaned back. He was enjoying the conversation now. "Well, no, not directly. The French gendarmes did all the dirty work, but the members of the SS and the Gestapo supervised the work of the prefect and the local government. Not long ago I discovered a very interesting photo."

"Of what?" Valérie was keen to hear.

"It's of Klaus Barbie in the Vénissieux camp. Some people believe he could sniff out what was happening with the Jewish children and that he tried to stop it, but at that moment in time, the Gestapo could not take open action in the unoccupied zone. Not until November 1942 did they have full authority to pursue Jews in the free zone."

Valérie shook her head in fascination. "That's incredible."

"Well, the children aren't my specialty, but there's a lot of information in LICRA, the International League Against Racism and Antisemitism."

The older woman rested a hand on Valérie's shoulder. "If you'd like, I can go with you to meet those folks. I was thinking to pass by the offices next week. Joseph would agree with me that they're extremely jealous of their time and resources, but there's a very nice man, René Nodot, who would be happy to tell you more about what happened with the Jewish children from the camp."

The two women bid farewell to Joseph. They went down the stairs and back out onto the street where daylight was giving way to a chilly darkness. The streetlights snapped on suddenly, allowing the older woman to study Valérie's face.

"Are you all right after all of that?" she asked.

Valérie nodded resolutely. "As Dr. Weill was talking, I felt more and more sure that I need to research more about the children from Vénissieux and their rescue. It takes me farther away from my original subject of study, Klaus Barbie, which was going to be extremely interesting, but the lives of those young ones mean so much more than the life of that murderous butcher. Have you noticed how the executioners often end up as celebrities? There are books and books about them. But so few write about their victims. The victims are mere numbers, faceless statistics, figures on the yellowed pages of history."

The old woman held Valérie's gaze and said, "I was one of those faceless statistics."

Valérie stepped back in surprise.

"Yes, I come from a family of French Jews. We didn't flee the country in 1942. When the Nazis took over the free zone, they arrested us."

Valérie could barely breathe enough to eke out, "Dear God, I'm so sorry." Her legs refused to move from where the women had paused.

"It was a long, long time ago, but it's still painful. They arrested us in 1944, when the end of the war was in sight. In August of that year, in fact, just a few weeks later, the Allies arrived in the city. Ironic, isn't it? A neighbor denounced us. We had spent two years locked up inside the house, surviving thanks to the kindness of some of my father's friends, who brought us food. I was a young woman of twenty-two, dreaming of becoming a schoolteacher. I lost two years of my life locked up in that house, buried alive within four walls. The Gestapo detained me along with my parents and sent us on a transport to Auschwitz. My parents were gassed immediately when we arrived, but I worked in the laboratories of Auschwitz III. I was forced to go on the famous death march. We made it to Bergen-Belsen, where the British freed us on April 15, 1945. I was so skinny I thought I'd never recover."

"When did you come back to Lyon?" Valérie asked in awe.

"A few weeks later. Our house was still standing, despite the bombing. I waited for my parents, who were never officially declared dead, though I saw them being walked to the gas chambers, and we all know what happened there."

At that, the woman started to cry.

Valérie hugged her and said soothingly, "I'm so sorry; I had no idea."

"I've been a teacher for over forty years, but I never married. I didn't want to bring children into a world like this. I've seen too many things, things that still come back at night to haunt me."

Valérie hugged the woman again and tucked the woman's frail arm under her own as they resumed their walk toward the river again. The thesis research was already opening Valérie's mind to a new world. It was a cruel, pitiless world that refused to be erased. Valérie needed to know and, above all, needed everyone else to know the truth.

Chapter 13

GOOD OLD KLAUS

Lyon
AUGUST 26, 1942

KLAUS BARBIE WALKED BY the church and caught the chords of a hymn that floated out from the half-open front door. The Catholic church was in the center of the city, and its towers stood out from the rest of the buildings in the tightly packed plaza. The building reminded him of the Catholic chapel in Godesberg, his hometown, near the Rhine. His ancestors had been French. Until age ten, he went to the school where his father taught and then to a Catholic boarding school in Trier. There he learned to love God and got involved with Catholic youth events, but once the Nazis came to power, Klaus switched to the Hitler Youth. A few months later, Klaus's father, Nikolaus, passed away. Their relationship had been strained. When Nikolaus returned from the Great War, he had taken to drinking. He was constantly furious and often beat Klaus's mother.

A few years later, Klaus entered the SS. He had worked as a mole within Catholic youth organizations, betraying and denouncing his own peers and friends. By 1938 he was already part of the Reich's intelligence services. Little by little he had climbed the ladder in his SS career. He had gotten married at the beginning of the war, but constant transfers kept him estranged from his wife and children. Now he spent most of the day moderately intoxicated.

The German official marched into the church building, well aware of the reaction his SS uniform would cause. For many, he was just shy of the angel of death. The priest, in the act of raising the Host to bless it, suddenly stopped, petrified with fear. The congregation turned, and many were visibly angered at the sight of the officer.

Klaus sat at the back and bowed his head. The priest resumed the Mass. Klaus enjoyed the fear that he caused. He had been an easily frightened weakling as a boy, an open target for teasing. And now he was one of the most powerful men in Europe. As his boss Himmler always said, they were the masters, the race that would govern the world and rule humanity for at least a thousand years.

Klaus's mind flashed with image after image. He had been chasing Jews, Communists, and Masons for years. He had thrown hundreds of them into prison in the Netherlands and had been obliged to break a few heads to procure necessary information. The work had gotten back to normal for Klaus once he was in France, but the spiral of personal degradation that had begun was unstoppable. Orgies, prostitution, alcohol, drugs, and all sorts of excess had all but destroyed him. Now that his chief pursuit was clandestine radios, he had too much free time.

→>—<←

At the end of Mass, everyone stood and filed out in silence, intimidated by the presence of the Nazi.

In an act of true valor, the priest approached and asked, "Can I help you with anything?"

Klaus studied him, intrigued. The man had guts to come up to a German SS official.

"No, thank you, I'll be going now."

The Nazi stood, and his eyes met the priest's.

"It's never too late to return to the ways of the Lord," the priest whispered.

Klaus shrugged and walked off. He knew that his soul was completely lost. All he could do was survive. He no longer believed that the Third Reich would last one thousand years— perhaps not even five more. Everything he had built his life on and that had gotten him up in the morning was slipping away.

Chapter 14

FALSE HOPE

Vénissieux Camp
AUGUST 27, 1942

T HE BAD PART ABOUT waking up was discovering that it had not been a nightmare. Fani looked at the child beside her. Rachel was not her daughter, but she loved her as if she were. She and Zelman never had children, and now Fani was glad. Bringing an innocent life into a world like theirs would have been madness.

They were allowed to go to the bathrooms for a few minutes, though it was hardly enough time to empty their bladders, wash their faces, and freshen up. Fani would have liked a shower, but the showerheads did not work. Fani made do with splashing water on her armpits, washing Rachel's face, and taking their place once again in the interminable line, this time waiting for breakfast.

From the start of the war, they had been constantly waiting for something, stuck in one unending, dignity-eroding line after another.

One of the women in front of Fani was pregnant. She looked exhausted but had to keep standing.

"Why don't we let the pregnant women go ahead of us?" Fani said to the women farther up the line.

A thick redheaded woman retorted, "I've got three little ones to feed."

"I'm barely standing upright," an older woman said as she leaned heavily on a cane.

Complaints of problems, aches, and pains came from all sides.

Fani crossed her arms and resigned herself to waiting.

The pregnant woman leaned toward her and said, "Thanks for trying. I'm Esther Abeles. My sister, Martha, is here too."

"Oh, I'm sorry. This is my daughter, Rachel. How far along are you?"

"Eight and a half months, though with the malnutrition and all this upheaval, I'm likely to go into labor at any moment," she said, stroking her belly.

"And the father?"

Esther shrugged. "The fact is that we shouldn't be here. We arrived in France in 1933, but since we fled to the free zone, they said that was suspicious criminal activity. It's suspicious, you see, to get as far away from the Nazis as possible."

Finally they arrived inside the mess hall. Breakfast was a very hard piece of black bread, a sliver of rancid butter, and a piece of fruit. Rachel scarfed her portion down so quickly that Fani, knowing she could wait till the noon meal, gave her half of her own.

→>—<←

After the meager breakfast, they were not allowed back into the barracks, so they all went out to the yard. There was nothing to do. The heat grew more intense by the minute. Most people idled in the shade of the barracks and spoke of their woes to any who would listen.

Fani went to the infirmary, hoping to be able to offer a hand and keep busy with something. Élisabeth and the other nurses were exhausted after a long night.

"Can I help in any way?" Fani asked. "I know how to give injections, bandage wounds, and that sort of thing."

"Thank you," Élisabeth said, smiling brightly. "For now, if you could bring water around to all the patients, we would be so grateful."

With the heat, the men, women, and children were eager for the water that Fani brought to their cots. On one cot she saw Jacob, the older gentleman who had been on their bus to Vénissieux. He seemed to be asleep.

"Jacob, would you like any water?" Fani asked.

The man did not respond. Fani touched his shoulder gingerly and confirmed that he was cold. Her eyes filled with tears.

"Did you know him?" Madeleine Dreyfus asked as she tended to a patient in the next cot.

"Not much. We just met in the bus on the way here. The poor man was all alone in the world."

"We all are, in a way," Madeleine said, giving Fani a hug, "which is why we need to keep each other company on our short journey."

⊁⊰⊱

As Fani helped at the infirmary, Rachel found a spot outside the barracks. She pulled her violin out of the case and started playing. A crowd gathered around her, eager for a break in the monotony and drawn by the beauty and peace of Rachel's playing. As the notes stretched out across the camp, tears descended from many eyes. The sun continued to rise and to bear down unflinchingly. But they were alive. They were breathing and at least had this day, an opportunity to show the world that they were much more than poor vagabonds with no country; more than outcasts who had been longing for some two thousand years to return to their lost Jerusalem where they could once more be a people, a nation, no longer persecuted the world over. At least that was the dream of many of those in Vénissieux, those who were forever treated as strangers and newcomers wherever they tried to put down roots.

Chapter 15

OPPORTUNE CONFUSION

Vénissieux Camp
AUGUST 27, 1942

J EAN-MARIE SOUTOU ARRIVED VERY early at the
camp in a black Citroën that had been loaned to him by a
friend who worked in business. Alexandre Glasberg was
beside him in the passenger seat. They feared that the guards
would not allow them through even though they had all their
papers in order. The truth was that they were not welcome; their
demands exasperated the regional intendant, Lucien Marchais,
and the regional intendant of police and director of the Vénissieux camp, René Cussonac. Everyone knew that Cussonac was a
declared anti-Semite.

Jean-Marie did not slow down as they approached the checkpoint
at the camp's entry. Glasberg glanced over with concern, wondering
if Jean-Marie was going to roll through the barrier. He knew that the
peaceful Catholic could be fearsome, despite his intellectual look.

The black Citroën stopped just in time. The police stood at
attention and let the car through without even asking to see

identification. At first Jean-Marie hesitated, unsure whether to drive on or clarify the situation, but he decided to go with it.

"What just happened?" Glasberg asked.

"I think they thought we were the prefect. He drives the same make and model car as this."

The two men chuckled over the mistake that saved them time and paperwork.

Alexandre Glasberg looked around the former arsenal of the French army. Vénissieux was by no means an adequate holding space for over a thousand people, and even less so in the heat of summer. But it was a strategic location: outside of Lyon, so the citizens could not see what their government was doing; near the train lines; and kept up by a team of Indo-Chinese workers.

Jean-Marie took in the parched grass, the dull bricks, and the dusty streets. The multitudes were crowded into the shade of buildings or under the few living trees. Everyone seemed to be busy, though no one was doing anything or going anywhere. It was clear that these people did not want to sit around waiting for their inescapable fate of being deported to the country they had all been fleeing.

"What are the Indo-Chinese doing here?" Jean-Marie asked when he saw a group of the camp's workers sitting by the mess hall. Most of them were smoking and watching the recently arrived multitude with rapt attention. The influx of Jews had been an unexpected diversion for the Indo-Chinese, a break from two years of the same rote work, day in and day out.

"They're part of MOI," Glasberg explained. "Main-d'oeuvre Indigéne, Nord-Africaine et Coloniale—the Indigenous, North African and Colonial Labor Service. They were recruited from

French colonies to work in the factories that make planes for the army, but now there's not much for them to do."

One of the workers studied the Citroën with open curiosity until the approach of a woman broke his gaze. She was very pretty, and she held out a shoe. Glasberg and Jean-Marie parked next to the infirmary close to where the scene unfolded.

"Could you fix this heel for me? It broke, and it's the only pair of shoes I've got here," the woman explained slowly.

The worker took the shoe and examined it closely. Then he nodded his head. He patted his chest and said, "Pham Van-Nahn fixes this for you." Then he took the shoe with him to a building farther away.

Jean-Marie and Glasberg got out of the car carrying briefcases stuffed with documentation about the detainees and hundreds of exemption requests based on numerous factors. The social workers had been up all night gathering the information and preparing reports. Now the countless files had to be compared to the list of prisoners themselves before being presented to the Rhône Office of Foreigners, headed by Claude Cornier. Gilbert Lesage, leveraging his position within the Vichy administration, was the head of the commission determining the exemption cases. But before that could happen, Gilbert Lesage, Jean-Marie, Glasberg, and Father Chaillet, who was waiting for them at the door, had to meet with Lucien Marchais and René Cussonac, the director of the camp.

Dr. Jean Adam was already there in the infirmary with Joseph Weill. He was in charge of the medical reports to be included with the exemption requests.

Glasberg had been at Vénissieux the day before to receive the buses as they arrived. He did not want the first face that the detained Jews saw to be that of René Cussonac. He had met with people seated on the ground and with the injured and ill lying outside the infirmary due to lack of space. He had smelled the stench of the unbathed multitude, many still in the clothes they had been wearing when the gendarmes awakened them. Glasberg understood that the sense of urgency was not just to stop the refugees from being transferred; it was also a question of public health.

>—<—

The group gathered in a room near the infirmary that had been hastily outfitted for the commission. The furniture consisted only of one long table with six chairs on one side and two on the other.

They sat and took out their paperwork. Jean-Marie was the first to speak.

"We've cobbled together 936 reports. The majority of the people here have the right, for one reason or another, to be exempted by law."

Father Chaillet buried his face in his hands. "This is lunacy. The authorities will never agree to it. This would only allow them to deport fewer than one hundred people. The government has promised a certain number of prisoners, don't you see? Prime Minister Laval, the chief of police, the prefect, and the intendant have to meet that quota."

"So what do you suggest? That we hand over half the refugees without protest? Most of them are women, children, and older people," Jean-Marie said.

"Well, let's start by giving them the men. If they're needed for work, at least they won't be harmed," Father Chaillet said.

"But they're the husbands and fathers of these families. How will the women and children survive without their help?"

"We'll take care of the families. Amitié Chrétienne has the resources for them."

Jean Adam had remained silent up to that point. Two of the other doctors sent to tend to the refugees had quit. If it had not been for the cooperation of Dr. Weill and the support of the Red Cross nurses, there would have been more deaths in the camp already than the six registered thus far.

"Our duty is to present the exemptions. Let them do the work of rejecting them. Seeing so many, maybe they'll just usher them through," he suggested.

"We'll know soon enough," Gilbert Lesage said. "The camp director and the intendant should be here at any moment." His words seemed to have clairvoyant power. Within seconds, René Cussonac and Lucien Marchais entered. They sat in the two chairs at the front. Intendant Marchais broke the uncomfortable silence.

"Gentlemen." He gave a quick nod that took in the men across from him. "I hope you're well. Our mission is very simple: to determine which individuals are exempt from deportation to Germany. The people out there aren't French. They're foreigners who have been leeches upon French hospitality for too long. The war is getting worse on the eastern front, and it's harder and harder to keep our own population alive. The presence of foreigners is no longer convenient."

His words were a bucket of cold water for the commission. Marchais had clarified the Vichy's position: they would attempt through any and every means to send as many refugees as possible to Germany.

"Sir, the law allows—" Jean-Marie began.

"We're living in a state of emergency," Marchais interrupted. "We've had to double our agricultural exports to Germany this year. Do you recognize what that means?"

No one answered.

"Well, it means that thousands, perhaps tens of thousands, of French are going to die this winter, and the future doesn't look any brighter. The fewer mouths to feed, the better off we all are."

Father Chaillet asked, "So then which exemptions are allowed?"

"Only unaccompanied minors." With that, the intendant stood to leave. The room filled with voices of incredulous complaints against the draconian measures.

"This is unjust; it goes against all humanitarian laws. We cannot call ourselves civilized if we allow innocent people to fall into the hands of those—"

The wagging finger of René Cussonac cut Jean-Marie off. Cussonac roared, "What are you implying? Most of those people out there are German or from territories controlled by our German allies. Their government demands their return so that they can support the German war effort. You people on this commission are making a mountain out of a molehill. Why are you so taken with the Jews anyhow? They killed our Lord and Savior. They're leeches wherever they go. We've treated them like human beings, which is much more than they would do for us, I can assure you. We've got enough French Semites without having to keep the rest of Europe's leftover Jews as well."

The intendant nodded and added, "The Germans have assured us that they will create a Jewish state in Poland or Madagascar. They're solving a problem that's been two thousand years in the making."

"Getting to the root of the problem," Cussonac added.

"But what about all those who are old, disabled, or pregnant? They won't survive a long journey on cattle cars. Not to speak of the children. You're sending them to their deaths," Gilbert said. He was typically one of the more diplomatic members of the group, but he had never imagined that the authorities would dismiss all of the commission's hard work so flippantly. There were perhaps a dozen orphaned children at most.

"As the chief doctor of this camp, I cannot go along with this. My moral code requires that—" Joseph Weill began, but the loud smack of Marchais's fist on the table cut him off.

"We can include veterans who've served in the French army, but that's it. We aren't negotiating with this commission. We're informing you. The orders are coming from very high up. And now, please excuse us."

Marchais and Cussonac got to their feet. Fittingly, their black suits gave them an aura of gravediggers.

When the group of Amitié Chrétienne workers was alone, they all started speaking at once.

Gilbert gestured with his hand and asked for quiet. "Please, we've got to act, not react."

"Well said." Father Chaillet nodded.

Jean-Marie laid out a plan. "First off is to talk with Cardinal Gerlier and ask him to intercede with Pétain, and then to talk with the archbishop of Toulouse, Monsignor Saliège. And to write a letter to the prefect. We need to buy ourselves some time and ask them to increase the exemptions."

"Let's do all of that, but we also need a plan B because all of that might come to naught," Father Glasberg said.

Everyone looked at him, waiting for his suggestion.

"We need to ask parents to make the greatest sacrifice to save the lives of their children . . ."

His unfinished phrase hung in the air. Glasberg was unwilling to spell out what he meant, knowing the crushing weight of those words.

Chapter 16

COMPASSION

Vénissieux Camp
AUGUST 27, 1942

DESPITE HIS EXHAUSTION, JUSTUS had not been able to sleep at all. One thought consumed him: getting out of the camp. He did not know why he kept fighting. The animal instinct surpassed reason. He was young with abundant energy and simultaneously alone and lonely. The only way to deal with his situation was to hold fast to the fight and resist. He was not born to give in.

Samuel, who had arrived at the camp before Justus, showed him where the bathroom was and then the mess hall. There, Justus introduced his bunkmate to Lazarus and the young men he had befriended on the truck the day before.

"Are you still thinking about how to get out of here?" Lazarus asked.

"What other option do we have? Let ourselves be led like lambs to the slaughter? I'd rather die fighting."

Lazarus and his two friends looked at Justus with a mixture of admiration and fear. They were drawn to his confidence and clarity of thought.

Inside the mess hall, they were served watered-down coffee and black bread. It was far from filling to four growing young men.

"You see the hogwash the French give us? So just imagine what the Germans will do to us," Justus said, trying his best to gnaw off chunks of the hard, tasteless bread.

Abraham asked, "How will you get out of here?"

"Well, I'm going to fake peritonitis. It's hard to detect and very dangerous. They'll have to take me to the hospital, and the security won't be as tight there."

Lazarus and his friends were unimpressed. They had begun to think of Justus as a kind of savior who could help them all get out of their circumstances.

"So then how can we get out?" Lazarus finally said.

At first, Justus had no answer. He did not feel qualified to give advice, but he came up with something. "Ambulances are pretty big, and underneath they have crossbars for the suspension or something. If you grab on to them from underneath, you could maybe get out without being seen."

"That's a crazy plan," Juan said, breaking his silence.

Justus shrugged. It was the best he could come up with, and he felt like he had done his duty by them. His plan could cost them all their lives. If the gendarmes discovered them and stopped the ambulance, they would all get sent back to camp.

"Well, we'll try it anyhow," Lazarus said.

Samuel was unconvinced. "Not me, friends. You three go ahead, but I'll figure out something else."

→>—<←

There were fewer people at the infirmary than the day before. Several patients had died, but many others had recovered enough from the long bus journey to go to the barracks.

Justus put his hand on his stomach. He went inside the infirmary and explained to one of the nurses that he felt really bad and was in a lot of pain.

"You can lie down here," she said and went to get the doctor.

Jean Adam came directly from the commission meeting as most of the other Amitié Chrétienne workers dispersed for their various tasks.

"What's going on, young man?" he asked Justus kindly.

"It hurts really bad here on my side. I don't know what it is."

"Does it hurt here?" The doctor applied pressure to the skin.

"Yes, a lot."

Jean Adam frowned. "It could be peritonitis. I'll have to send you to the hospital right away for an operation."

Justus nodded but, to his surprise, the doctor leaned over and whispered, "When you get to the hospital, fake it on the other side. The appendix is on the right."

Justus was momentarily speechless.

"Nurse!" Dr. Adam called. "Call for the ambulance! This young man has to get to the hospital right away!"

Within minutes, two men with a stretcher were carrying Justus to the ambulance. As soon as they went to the front, two of Justus's new friends hid below the ambulance, and Juan crept into the back.

"What are you doing?" Justus asked, startled.

"It's a terrible idea to hide underneath, but there's room for me here." Juan crouched down under the stretcher and covered up with a blanket.

At the camp gate, the gendarmes stopped the ambulance and checked the drivers' paperwork. They opened the back doors and gave a cursory glance before waving the vehicle through.

A few miles down the road, when the ambulance stopped at an intersection, Lazarus and Abraham let themselves fall to the ground. Juan slipped out and shut the door gently behind him, ducking so that the driver would not see him in the mirror. The boys were already hidden in a clump of trees when the ambulance started up again. They had agreed to try to find Justus in Valence and escape south together, crossing into Spain.

Fifteen minutes later, Justus arrived at the hospital. The medics took him right away to the operating room. Justus tried to talk with the doctor, but a nurse placed a mask over his face, and he was soon in deep sleep. Two hours later he woke to searing pain in his right side. He looked down in horror to find an angry incision still red with blood. His plan had worked too well. They had indeed removed his appendix.

Chapter 17

TO SAVE JUST ONE

Vénissieux Camp
AUGUST 27, 1942

GILBERT WANTED TO LEAVE with Father Glasberg and Jean-Marie, but first he needed to talk with the staff of l'Œuvre de secours aux enfants, the Organization to Save the Children. They needed to share ideas about the days ahead and how to drag out the exemption process to buy all the time they could.

There were several OSE staff workers at the camp. While some continued the ceaseless labor of tending to the refugees, Élisabeth, Madeleine, Joseph, Georges, and Charles Lederman came to the ad hoc meeting.

Gilbert began, "You are aware that the intendant has informed us that there will be hardly any exemptions allowed. But we're not going to sit around with our arms crossed. We'll try to negotiate with the higher-ups and put pressure on the authorities. We've got to free these people one way or another."

His colleagues nodded collectively as he continued. "It won't be easy, and I won't hide the fact that it could be extremely dangerous. Yet I believe this is worth all the effort and sacrifice. There are over a thousand people here who have committed no crime and have done nothing wrong to anyone. They're being persecuted for the simple fact that they are Jews, and this is unacceptable. Our ancestors were the first to formulate the fundamental rights of human beings and of citizens. I'll go even further, though I know not all of us are believers. The rights of human beings are inalienable because they are granted by our Creator. So, my friends, let us work with strength and resolve."

When Gilbert finished his speech, Madeleine approached him. There was another young woman with her whom Gilbert had not met before.

"Forgive me for bothering you, Gilbert, but I wanted you to meet someone who's been working with the OSE locally here in Lyon for over a year. This is Lili Tager. Last night she came and offered her services for our work in the camp. We need all the hands we can get, but I wanted you to meet her first."

"It's a pleasure to meet you, Miss Tager."

"The pleasure is mine."

"Yesterday Lili worked alongside Dr. Weill and is with Dr. Adam today," Madeleine explained.

"Last night we had about fifteen attempted suicides. They all tried to hang themselves. We saved almost all of them, but a young woman named Clarise and an older gentleman were too far gone."

"How tragic; I'm so sorry," Gilbert said, looking at Lili kindly. It pained him to see people so young dealing with such difficult situations.

"Thank you, sir," Lili answered.

"Well, welcome to the club of desperados," Gilbert said, patting her shoulder before making his way to the next room, where Father Glasberg and Jean-Marie were waiting for him.

"I'm sorry for keeping you," Gilbert said.

"Don't worry about it. Training your staff to tend to the prisoners is of upmost importance. We're all in such a state that, without the help of the social workers, it'll be impossible to get all the forms filled out," Father Glasberg answered.

Jean-Marie sighed. "If it's even worth trying. You heard what the intendant said."

"Don't be pessimistic, my friend. There's plenty of game left to play," Glasberg answered.

A movement at the back of the room caught Gilbert's attention, and he noticed a boy in the corner for the first time. He looked at his colleagues with eyebrows raised in question.

"He has no family. He was in the infirmary last night and was supposed to go back to the barracks today but has been crying all morning," Jean-Marie explained.

"Did anyone see him come into this room?" Gilbert asked.

The two men shook their heads.

"And your car is parked at the door, right? We could put him in the trunk and cross our fingers."

Glasberg nodded, but Jean-Marie was less convinced. "To save just one we could jeopardize the entire plan."

Gilbert understood his friend. It was undoubtedly reckless and risky.

"But what value can we place on one human life? We don't know what's going to happen. The hopes we have right now of saving as many as possible could disappear in an instant, yet we might be able to save just one."

Jean-Marie studied the boy and then turned back to his colleagues. "Oh, all right. May God spare us."

The three men left by the back door. While one kept watch, the other two helped the boy into the trunk, covered him with a blanket, and then got in. At the checkpoint, the punctilious gendarme Philip Moreau was on guard.

"Papers, please," he said as the car slowed.

A gendarme holding a machine gun scrutinized the back of the car.

"Everything is in order, officer," Gilbert said. Among the three, he had the coldest blood.

Moreau studied Gilbert's face but saw nothing behind the broad smile. Meanwhile, the three men in the car collectively held their breath as the other gendarme approached the trunk.

"Leave off," Moreau called. "What do you think they've got, a Jew hidden back there?" The two gendarmes guffawed in laughter, and the three occupants of the black Citroën followed suit. Jean-Marie accelerated cleanly through the raised barrier and did not stop until they were well outside of Lyon.

"So what do we do with the boy?" he asked.

Gilbert shrugged. Father Glasberg answered, "There's a convent not far from here, and I'm sure they'll take him in. They'll pass him off as a novice."

They drove into the yard of the Carmelite convent and helped the young man out of the trunk. The abbot, a burly man with dark hair and glasses, immediately hugged the boy and assured the three men that he would be welcome in their community.

→>-<←

As the men drove away from the convent, they were relieved to have helped rescue at least one refugee. The task ahead of them was enormous, but they would move heaven and earth to complete it.

As soon as they were back at the Amitié Chrétienne office, Father Glasberg called the office of Cardinal Jules-Géraud Saliège while Jean-Marie contacted the prefect and Gilbert sought the assistance of the French Protestant Federation. Their request of all of these parties was to pressure for the official release of the refugees held at Vénissieux.

The Amitié Chrétienne office was a hive of frenetic activity. It was a race against time to save as many as possible. Meanwhile the bureaucratic machine of the Vichy regime was at full tilt, placing every barrier possible before the benevolent workers' task. The fate of foreign Jews mattered to very few in that dark moment of history.

Chapter 18

AN UNCOMFORTABLE MEETING

Lyon
AUGUST 27, 1942

THAT MORNING KLAUS AWOKE with an annoying hangover, which was not helped by the constant ringing of the telephone in his room at the casino. He grabbed the receiver and straightened his shoulders. It was the Reichsführer-SS, Heinrich Himmler.

"Sir!" Barbie said, swallowing down his nerves.

"Our office in Paris has informed me that the quotas of Jews promised to France are not being met. You'd better get in the car right now and head to Vichy. Make Pierre Laval keep his word, and remind him that we want Europe to be cleansed of the Jews before the war ends. Is this understood?"

"Yes, Reichsführer-SS."

"I'm expecting a report from you tonight."

Klaus wiped the sweat from his brow after hanging up. He had only spoken with his boss one other time, and in that instance the conversation had consisted of one phrase. If the SS chief had called him, it meant that the matter took precedence over everything else. The capital of the free zone was over two hours from Lyon. If he left right then, he could be there before noon.

Klaus dressed in haste and called for his chauffeur. He told the man to get to Vichy as fast as possible. Each minute counted. About two-and-a-half hours later, they were at the Vichy government's headquarters at the Hôtel du Parc. Marshal Pétain resided next door with his wife at the Hôtel Majestic.

Two French soldiers saluted Klaus at the entrance. At the front desk his demand to see Prime Minister Laval was accommodated immediately. Within minutes Klaus had the second most powerful man in unoccupied France sitting before him.

"Mr. Barbie, to what do I owe the honor of this unexpected visit?"

"This morning Heinrich Himmler, Reichsführer-SS, called me himself. He is worried. The promised shipments of Jews aren't arriving."

Pierre Laval cleared his throat nervously. He knew that the Nazis did not play around. "Things are proving more difficult than anticipated."

"Our information services in Lyon and other cities have alerted me to the fact that certain associations are attempting to rescue foreign Jews from deportation. They are claiming what I believe are called exemptions." Klaus leaned in closer and spoke very softly. "There will be no exemptions. Is that clear?"

Laval swallowed before answering. "We'll inform the prefects and intendants, never worry."

"I *do* worry. The damned clergy and Communists are behind all of this. If your people can't get control of the unoccupied zone, the Germans will."

Klaus Barbie stood, and Laval followed suit.

"We want at least sixty thousand Jews before the end of the summer, and we don't care how you get them."

The SS officer stormed out. As he descended the stairs two by two, he mused on what Himmler's call meant. Klaus was reaching the heights of the SS ladder. His hard work had not been in vain. Before returning to Lyon, he had the chauffeur stop at a bar. It was to calm his nerves, he explained. Klaus felt the strong call to a new mission: to oversee the shipments of Jews from Lyon and keep his superiors informed of all the happenings of that region in France.

Chapter 19

THE CARDINAL

Lyon
AUGUST 27, 1942

CARDINAL PIERRE-MARIE GERLIER WAS a church leader of the old guard. Born in Versailles sixty-two years prior, he had studied to be a lawyer before committing himself to an ecclesial path. He had been wounded and captured while serving as an officer in the Great War. His career had been slow and challenging, but he had now been archbishop of Lyon for five years. As a cardinal of the Roman Catholic Church, he held one of the most revered positions possible for a man of orders. An intimate friend of Marshal Pétain, Gerlier had put all his energy into leading the city to obediently comply with the new Vichy regime. The cardinal's anti-Semitism was a well-known fact. Initially he had not opposed the racial laws or raised a finger to defend the Jews.

Cardinal Gerlier believed that Marshal Pétain was God's gift to France to save the country from the decadent times it was forced to endure. But things had changed. Gerlier had access to privileged information that allowed him to read between the lines and understand what was happening to Jews in Poland and other occupied territories. It was one thing to want all Jews to leave Europe; it was something else altogether to approve of their complete annihilation. Therefore, when the raids against the Hebrew people increased earlier that year, the cardinal started thinking that the Catholics should do something.

That afternoon his secretary informed him that Alexandre Glasberg had requested a meeting. The day before, the cardinal had received Rabbi Kaplan, who came to intercede on behalf of the foreign Jews in Gerlier's diocese. Everyone presumed that Gerlier's ecclesial position gave him some sort of power, but his only authority was in the moral and spiritual realms. He wanted to think that this still mattered in France, but he had his doubts.

The secretary announced the abbot's arrival, and the cardinal donned his robes before Glasberg entered the lavish office of the episcopal palace. Glasberg bowed his head and kissed the ring on the cardinal's outstretched hand.

"Most excellent and reverend sir, thank you for receiving me on such short notice."

"Abbot, forgo the formalities. What brings you here?"

The priest sat on a nearby chair. The cardinal listened in attentive silence as Glasberg explained the Vénissieux problem. When the priest was finished, Gerlier summarized, "From what you've told me, the government is denying exemptions. This is inhumane and contrary to a government with Christian morals."

"I'm sure that Vichy fears retaliation from the Nazis."

"Without a doubt," the cardinal said pensively, "but we are still in France, a civilized, Christian nation."

"On behalf of Amitié Chrétienne, I would like to ask you to intercede directly with Marshal Pétain."

The cardinal rested his chin on his hand, let out a long-held breath, and allowed his eyes to drift to the window. It looked like a storm was brewing.

"What has happened in France over the past few years has been a true disgrace. The Third Republic spun out into one of the darkest eras for our beloved country, and everything that is of any worth has disappeared. Human beings have become depraved. No God, no fatherland, no family. The Great War sped up the process, and the mad years of the 1920s turned the world into a great garbage heap. The crisis of 1929 impoverished hundreds of thousands of French, and just when it seemed like things could not get any worse, Communism and Fascism threatened what was left of the ashes of our civilization. The Nazis took over the country, and the government and the politicians did not turn down the invitation. They were already rotten to the core. In fact, they contributed decisively to France's great weakness. The Germans, our eternal enemies, humiliated us, just like what happened last century with Napoleon III. Then, by some miracle, Marshal Pétain committed himself to saving France, not from the Germans but from herself. In his first speech he announced that he wanted to build a nation free from the teachings of Socialism and Communism and that France would once again be strong and great. He put the foundational values of Western society back on the table: work, family, and fatherland. What good are freedom, equality, and fraternity if there's no bread, family, or nation?"

"But all of that has turned out to be a show," the abbot dared to venture.

"Indeed, indeed. And so we can no longer keep silent. I'll write to the marshal and beg him to save the Jews. If that's not enough, I'll write a letter to all the parishes of France and raise the people up against this form of tyranny."

The cardinal's passion shocked Alexandre Glasberg. He knew of Gerlier's earlier anti-Semitism and was well aware that most of the high-ranking church officials had not spoken against the injustices committed by French society against the Jews. But something seemed to be changing at last in France. "Thank you, Your Excellency."

"May God grant us the help we need."

The cardinal raised his hand, and the abbot kissed it again before quitting the room.

→>-<←

A few miles away, at the Vénissieux camp, Rachel was staring hard to see if she could spot her father again. Worrisome rumors were circulating that the men would be taken away the next day.

Zelman had not slept the night before. Everything seemed pointless—their journey of crossing border after border and leaving behind all they had known. The evidence was all too clear: he was a weak failure incapable of keeping his family safe. He had spent his time at the camp so far giving haircuts to dozens of prisoners tired of the pesky lice. He wanted to get the money he had earned to his daughter, but he could not find her in the crowd across the barbed wire fence.

Standing on tiptoes, Rachel thought she saw her father. She waved and called out. Then a Chinese-looking man came up to her.

"What is it, little girl? Why are you shouting?"

Rachel studied the man without answering.

He smiled at her and said, "It's all right. My name is Tuan."

This seemed to satisfy the girl, and she explained. "My dad can't see me with all these people around. His name is Zelman."

The Indo-Chinese worker smiled again at her and knelt, patting his shoulders. Rachel understood and climbed up.

Zelman spotted his daughter above the heads of the rest of the crowd and ran to the fence. He wiped his tears to keep her from worrying.

"Rachel! Where's Fani?"

"She's been helping in the infirmary all day."

"Are you all right?" Zelman asked, suspiciously eyeing the Indo-Chinese man who had Rachel on his shoulders.

"This is Tuan. He helped me find you."

"Hello, Mr. Zelman." Tuan was still smiling widely.

"You can set her down now. Thank you," Zelman said dryly.

Rachel got as close to her father as the fence allowed, and Zelman stroked her cheek.

"Look, I have a bit of money for you. I want you to keep it safe. You may need it. If you and Fani get the chance to escape, head for Italy. They aren't arresting Jews there. Then find a boat going to Brazil or Argentina. Do you understand?"

Rachel nodded. "But we don't want to leave without you."

"They're transferring the men tomorrow. So I'll meet up with you later on," he lied.

Rachel started crying. "I'm scared, Dad."

Each tear broke his heart anew. "No, honey, don't be afraid. I'll always be with you. Every time you look up and see the clouds, think of me. Wherever I am, I'll be looking at the same sky and thinking of you."

Rachel's grip on her father's hand was tight. He handed her the money just as a gendarme approached and waved them apart.

Rachel stayed crying at the fence as her father was led away. She did not know if she would ever see him again or if misfortune would separate them forever. She thought of something her mother had said at bedtime once: the stars were God's diamonds, but people were even more valuable to him; Rachel was the apple of his eye and God wouldn't let anything bad happen to her.

Night was falling as the exhausted refugees waited in the supper line at the mess hall. The heat had been suffocating, but distant clouds bespoke a coming rain. Perhaps it would bring hope as well. A few weeks prior, they had all been going about their daily lives, albeit under the threatening shadow of Nazism. A few months prior, they had still hoped to sidestep the terrible tide of war. A few years prior, they had lived happily without even knowing it. Back then they had wasted their days worrying about ridiculous little things and watching the clock anxiously. But now time had run out on them. The dark red evening sky was suddenly of utmost importance. It now seemed entirely possible that they would not live to see a new dawn.

Chapter 20

THE UNTHINKABLE

Lyon
NOVEMBER 20, 1992

T HERE ARE MOMENTS IN life that can change a person's existence forever. Valérie Portheret did not know that that chilly autumn afternoon would be one of those. Despite her youth, she was a determined woman, capable of ordering her entire being around a just cause. She felt more comfortable in the presence of the dead than the living; she was at her happiest in the archives, surrounded by old files and documents. The voices of those who were no longer whispered into her ear and begged her to tell the world their stories, but she did not yet know how to interpret the language of the dead, their desires and hopes and dreams. The lost names of those rescued at Vénissieux were still unknown to her, though she was aware that there were more ghosts than living inhabitants circling the streets of Lyon.

The LICRA meeting was even more stripped down than the gathering the week before at the Amitié Chrétienne headquarters. The walls of the dilapidated LICRA office were lined with shelves that barely supported the weight of countless yellowed notebooks. It had the bored look of a municipal archives office. Six or seven people were chatting and milling about, occasionally casting a curious eye at the young blond woman across the room. Valérie smiled at everyone but secretly wanted to run out of the dirty, dust-caked building. Then the man who was going to lead the meeting came up to her and held out his hand.

"Hello, and thank you for coming. There are so few young people interested in the past. Sometimes I think about how, when those of us here are all gone, everything that happened will die with us."

"Thank you for having me. I'm researching the children who were housed at the Peyrins château."

"It's a fascinating subject. Allow me to introduce you to one of our LICRA members."

The man led Valérie to a man with short, curly gray hair who was deep in conversation with an older woman.

"This is René Nodot. He was a member of the Resistance and has put together a pamphlet on some of the children in Peyrins."

René turned and stared in surprise at Valérie.

"You're Valérie Portheret, yes? I believe we're neighbors, though it hasn't been long."

Valérie's jaw dropped. "Goodness, you're right. You live on the top floor."

"Indeed I do. I had no idea you were interested in these matters."

Valérie's mind was blown that one of her neighbors had been part of the French Resistance.

The man who had introduced them nodded and said, "Well, we're going to start now."

The lecture lasted about an hour. The speaker talked some about the Resistance in 1942 but focused more on the dangers of the extreme Right and the recent rise in anti-Semitism in France.

René walked Valérie to the door and was bidding her farewell when she asked if he would like to go out for coffee.

"You see, I'm very interested in what happened at the Peyrins château."

René nodded and said goodbye to the rest of the LICRA members.

→>-<←

They walked along the bank of the Saône River as the evening sun seemed to set the façades of the houses behind them on fire. The city had once been wealthy due to the silk trade but was now in slow decline.

They entered a nearby café. The light from the lamps on the table struggled to filter through the thick cigarette smoke. They sat at the back, though the place was not crowded. As the season turned colder, more and more people stayed home instead of venturing out.

"I had no idea you were part of the Resistance," Valérie said when the dark coffee arrived.

"Well, it's not something I go around trumpeting. To be frank, a lot of people now claiming to have been part of the Resistance never really were."

"Ah, I see."

"Think about it: until 1942 there was hardly any true Resistance since most French saw the occupation as a lesser evil, with the exception of a few left-wing militants, of course."

Valérie held her cup between both hands to let its warmth chase away the cold. "People always prefer tranquility over freedom," she mused.

"Absolutely. I couldn't have said it better myself. For most French, the occupation seemed to chase away the phantom of the war. That reminds me of Winston Churchill's famous phrase after the Munich Agreement, when he wrote to a friend. Churchill said that Prime Minister Neville Chamberlain had been given a choice between dishonor and war, and he chose dishonor, but Churchill said that he would have both."

Valérie took a long sip from her steaming mug while René lit a cigarette.

"Will you tell me what happened with the children at the château?" she asked.

"It's a sad and beautiful story."

"Like all war stories," she added.

"Well, in war there are a lot of stories that are only sad."

Valérie nodded. She had heard a few like that. "War is the paradigm of sadness."

René took a sip. The coffee cleared his head, and he began. "What happened at Peyrins was all thanks to an incredible woman named Germaine Chesneau. During the Great War she served as a nurse and had always felt a keen vocation to spend her life serving others. In 1926 she married Marcel Chesneau, and they moved to Peyrins. About a decade later the count of Sallmard rented them part of his castle. After the death of her husband in 1939, and with three young children, Germaine decided to turn the château into a refuge for children, like a summer camp during those first summers of the war. At one point the Nazis used part of the castle for their own purposes, but after France surrendered, Germaine got her space back. She was forty-six years old when France started deporting Jews to Germany. Starting in 1942, when the persecution against Jews spread all over the country, Germaine started receiving them in her residence, including some of those who had escaped from the Vénissieux camp."

Valérie was riveted. "How many children from Lyon were at the château?" she asked.

"Around fourteen."

"And what happened after that?"

"Well, when the front got too close, Germaine was advised to evacuate. How prudent that she did, because the Nazis got to the castle on August 29, 1944, with the intention of using the children as human shields."

"What an incredible story."

"You don't know the half of it."

"How did the 108 children manage to escape from Vénissieux? From what I've read, the Vichy government authorities rejected most of the exemption requests."

René smiled, stubbed out his cigarette, and said, "The parents rescinded their rights."

Valérie's throat caught. "What rights?" she asked, fearing the answer.

"Their rights as parents, Miss Portheret. They gave up their own children."

Anguish pierced Valérie's heart. She began to imagine the pain those mothers and fathers would have suffered in giving up their children, losing them in order to save them.

PART II

The Darkest Hour

Chapter 21

LILI

Lyon
AUGUST 27, 1942

IN HER TWENTY-ONE YEARS of life, Lili had seen many things she was not prepared for. The war had stolen the innocence and joy of life from more than one generation. But Lili was not one to lie down in defeat. Lili had joined the OSE, the same organization where Georges Garel worked, and given her youthful energies to helping the children of France. She was on a project spearheaded by Charles Lederman. Since the Nazis came to power in 1933, the trickle of refugees, particularly Jews, had grown into a flood. Having come from a family of Russian Jews, Lili knew what exile and persecution were. She and her family had fled Paris and hoped that the unoccupied zone would be safer as things turned uglier in France.

She was a fearless young woman. In November 1940, not long after the Nazis had set up shop in the country, Lili had brazenly participated in a protest in front of the Tomb of the Unknown Soldier. When her father was forbidden from practicing his profession, the family had an inkling of how bad things might get. That is when Lili decided to support the teams working to help children in French internment camps. In the camps she met Joseph Weill, who had suggested she join the operation to rescue the children of Lyon.

Like the rest of the volunteers, Lili was deeply concerned. A few days before, on August 11, a train destined for Drancy stopped in the city, and the abject conditions faced by the passengers came to light. Rabbi Kaplan had recounted with vivid detail to Lili and the team what he had seen. The train was stopped for several hours. The people crammed inside begged for water, food, and for a bathroom. The rabbi went up to one of the cars to pray for the passengers. He heard a woman begging for help, begging for someone to do something about what was going on. This was not an isolated event. The mistreatment and harassment of the Jews was spreading throughout the country, but most people turned a blind eye and hoped that the angel of death would pass them by.

Rabbi Kaplan had written to Cardinal Gerlier and then had paid him a visit. Up to then, the Catholic Church had not taken a formal position. Its silence owed to several factors. On the one hand, the Catholic hierarchy feared that squarely opposing the Vichy regime would block their efforts to assist the refugees and would bring an end to any privileges the church enjoyed. On the other hand, bringing the problems into the light might intensify negative repercussions against political and religious dissidents.

As a volunteer at Vénissieux, Lili attended the meeting that morning at the OSE office. There were several organizations represented, and Gilbert Lesage presided.

"The authorities have made it very clear that they intend to send over a thousand refugees to Germany and will tolerate almost no exemptions. The only one currently allowed is for unaccompanied minors, which allows us to save two or three, perhaps four, children total."

"That's unacceptable!" Rabbi Kaplan exclaimed.

Similarly disgruntled cries arose from those the various volunteers and organizations represented.

Madeleine looked at her colleagues and spoke gravely. "The only solution that I see is to increase the number of unaccompanied minors."

Eyebrows raised all around the room, and heads cocked with hesitant curiosity in Madeleine's direction.

"And how do we go about doing that?" Jacques Helbronner, president of the Consistoire Central des Israelites de France, the Central Consistory of French Jews, asked.

"We ask parents to relinquish custody of their children."

A long, uncomfortable silence ensued. Everyone mulled over exactly what that meant.

"You're suggesting we separate the children from their parents?" Rabbi Kaplan asked.

Madeleine shot straight. "It's the only option I see. Between today and tomorrow the men will be shipped off. The rest will be gone by the twenty-ninth at the latest and sooner if the transports materialize. We're working against the clock, and everyone we ask for help gives us the same answer. No one in the government is going to lift a finger to help the Jews or risk their neck in front of the Nazis."

Lili spoke for the first time. "But it's criminal to ask parents to do that. We'd be taking their children from them."

"We all know what's happening with the Jews in the ghettoes of Poland and other countries, and we know the deplorable conditions of the German concentration camps. Children under thirteen or fourteen years of age will never survive if they're deported to Germany or Poland," Glasberg added.

Everyone looked at one another, knowing that the priest was right but not knowing what to say about it.

"Well," Gilbert said reluctantly, "this presents three challenges. First, acquiring all the abdications of parental responsibility today and tomorrow. We've got to explain how serious the situation is to the parents, though this may cause them even more trauma. Second, transporting all those children. We have no idea how many there will be. And third, figuring out where to place them. This could be up to one hundred minors." The rest of the workers started taking notes.

Jacques said, "Here in this room we've got representatives from the Red Cross, Amitié Chrétienne, the OSE, the Boy Scouts, and other organizations. Working all together, we can pull this off. But we've got to get started ASAP."

"We'll work up a document template for relinquishing paternal rights for parents to sign," Madeleine volunteered.

"We'll work on arranging transportation," Glasberg offered.

"We'll help with finding families to take the children," Rabbi Kaplan said.

The meeting wrapped up a few minutes later. The attendees were exhausted by the daunting task of asking parents to give up their sons and daughters, but they knew that the alternative was much worse.

Chapter 22

THE FIXLERS

Vénissieux Camp
AUGUST 27, 1942

EVA FIXLER WAS THE mother of four girls. She had not rested one moment since arriving at the camp. When one or two of the girls were asleep, the others would wake up and start crying. Though she was only forty, she was depressed and spent. She had never imagined anything like this could happen to her or her family. She was Romanian but was registered as a Czech, and the gendarmes had detained her illegally. No one had listened to her protests until she met Lili that morning. The young woman was handing out water among the refugees when she saw Eva struggling to settle her four daughters. When Lili served them some water, Eva burst into tears.

"Forgive me," she said, sniffling. "It's just that this is the first time since we were herded onto that terrible bus that anyone has shown me kindness. My name is Eva Fixler."

"Eva, it's good to meet you. I'm Lili."

"I shouldn't be here. I was born in Romania, but I'm a Hungarian citizen, and my country has not demanded our repatriation. But neither the police nor the government officials pay any attention to me."

"I'm so sorry about that."

"It's not your fault. These are my daughters: Hélène, who's nine; Sarah, who's eight; Esther, who's six; and Isabelle, who's four."

"And your husband?" Lili asked gently.

"He jumped out of the window of our house in Savoy and escaped. He never believed any harm would come to us. They always left the women and children alone in the raids before this."

Lili set the metal bucket of water down on the ground and pulled out her notebook to write down the woman's information.

"We'll get in touch with the Hungarian consul and will try to get you and your daughters out of here."

Eva, still holding Isabelle, leaned over and hugged Lili. Lili was initially stiff with professionalism. She always tried to keep a certain emotional distance from the people she worked with, knowing that getting too involved would make it impossible for her to do her work. That was the risk of dealing with human beings. But she relaxed and gave Eva a reassuring squeeze.

She left the Fixler family and went to the infirmary to discuss their case with her colleagues. Everyone agreed that something must be done. They called Father Glasberg and asked him to get in touch with the Hungarian embassy. They knew full well that embassies were not always willing to help. Most were indifferent to the plight of their Jewish citizens or were reluctant to risk going against the Nazis.

While the social workers prepared the forms for parents to sign, Father Glasberg and Jean-Marie Soutou continued their attempts to negotiate with the French authorities regarding increasing the exemptions. They were aware that some officials had received requests from religious authorities and people of clout. But after two hours of attempted negotiations, the intendant had not ceded an inch. Jean-Marie was exhausted and at the edge of his patience. The hundreds of exemption requests on the table were much more than paper forms for him. They were people's lives, families who would disappear forever if they crossed the Rhine and reached Germany. The land of Mozart, Goethe, and Immanuel Kant had become a nation of barbarians, of heartless warriors whose driving desire was to control the human race and conquer the world.

After the arduous meeting, Jean-Marie and Father Glasberg were alone. Jean-Marie's head was buried in his hands as if to keep it from exploding.

"Do you see? For them, human life has no value. People are just numbers, animals, rats that must be driven away from the ruling class's little bourgeoise paradise. Don't they see that they'll be next? When they wrap up their war in the East, the new rulers of the world will turn their gazes to France. They'll divide it up like a pagan land, and the French will become mere manual labor."

Glasberg studied his companion. Though Jean-Marie was correct, for Glasberg the time had not yet come to give up. He was the type of man who grew taller and stronger when facing adversity.

"My dear friend," he said, "for centuries the West has blindly believed in the progress of humankind—secular progress, that is, of a material nature, but nonetheless one that would have repercussions throughout all levels of society and would do away with social injustices. All philosophers and intellectuals believed that, if citizens were educated like Socrates talked about, they would become good people. The intellectual elites believed evil was simply ignorance. But they were incorrect. Others put their faith in technology and science. Yet these are mere instruments that, in the hands of humanity, can be used for good or for evil."

"It's true; they diagnosed the illness incorrectly," Jean-Marie agreed. He himself had spent many years numb with dreams of reason.

Glasberg continued to muse. "Human beings aren't naturally good, but neither are we irrationally evil. It's just that our hearts house evil and selfishness. I've heard some say that the Nazis are cruel because they aren't human. But turning them into wild animals or beasts doesn't help undo the horror they cause. That's what the Nazis have done against the Jews: attributed to one nation the ills of the entire world. The truth is that all of us are prisoners of egocentrism and all of us are capable of horrible wickedness."

The priest's words restored Jean-Marie's strength. He stood and said, "If we're made only of matter, if there's nothing for us beyond the stars, if the moral laws are not based on a just God, then we're just a cluster of atoms that will one day disappear. All of humanity will be extinct once the sun burns out. We'll be little more than a minuscule, passing flash compared with the immensity of the universe, and there will be no intelligence there to remember or value what we were. Nazism is the fruit of such an idea: since we'll all be annihilated, let's act like animals. Let's eat, drink, and devour the weak, for tomorrow we'll die."

Jean-Marie's words were drenched in sadness. The futility of life rendered everything useless, but the two men knew that the one thing they could hold on to was love—that mysterious choice to give oneself to others without expecting anything in return.

Chapter 23

THE HUMAN SPIRIT

Lyon
NOVEMBER 27, 1992

AFTER COFFEE, RENÉ NODOT had given Valérie a pamphlet he wrote about what had occurred at the Peyrins château. Since then Valérie's mind had been spinning with those facts and trying to work out how the handful of children from Lyon had ended up there. How many were there? What had become of them? These and many more questions cropped up every time her research unearthed an actual name.

A few days later, the young woman met with her professor Jean-Dominique Durand to update him on her discoveries and share her questions.

Durand was waiting for her in his office. Carrying a blue notebook with René's pamphlet and her handwritten notes, Valérie sidled into a chair on the other side of the worn mahogany desk.

"I've been talking with people and asking a lot of questions over the past few weeks," Valérie began, "and I'm more and more drawn to researching what happened with Jewish children in Lyon."

Durand's face registered surprise. "I'm not sure why, but I figured you would end up settling on Klaus Barbie. Despite all that's been written about him in the past few years, to date there's no serious analysis of his life and actions."

Her professor's words gave Valérie pause. She was not entirely sure of anything when it came to her research path.

"Well, I've thought a lot about that, too, but I just know that I've got to learn more about those children."

"A research project should not attempt to address a personal or emotional need. It's got to fill a knowledge gap. We're here to discover the truth, the pure historical fact."

After an uncomfortable silence during which she studied the swirls of the wood grain before her, Valérie raised her head.

"Yes, but I think that the research and the researcher have to be in sync. If I commit to something I'm not passionate about, it'll end up as just one more thesis on a shelf that no one ever reads. I have no pretension of convincing the academic world of anything. I want to make a difference, to rescue from oblivion the lost names of those children."

"I understand that, and I respect it, but you're at great risk of veering off course. As scientists, we've got to maintain our distance from the object of study."

"We're not scientists, Professor. Historians are humanitarians. We're trying to measure something much deeper than mere archaeological remains. We're after the reasoning of the human soul, the spirit that moves the world."

Durand smiled. Valérie was an exceptional woman; no one could argue the contrary. Advising her thesis would not be easy, but the challenge was a bright prospect that counteracted years of erudition. Those crusty years had made Durand forget that history could not and should not be in competition with other sciences. The materialism of the past two hundred years had distanced humanity from truth and had circumscribed human beings to merely intelligent animals. But human misery and greatness indicated otherwise.

"Very well, but allow me to give you one piece of advice."

"I'm all ears, Professor." Valérie beamed with a flash of her big dark eyes.

"Let the facts speak for themselves. Don't be tempted to prematurely conclude who the heroes and the villains are. Human beings are much more complex than that."

"I'll do that, sir. I'll remember that facts are just the echo of the fears and longings inside of us all."

Chapter 24

POISON

Vénissieux Camp
AUGUST 27, 1942

I RMA GOLDBERG HAD BEEN in the infirmary at the same time as Justus, but they had not spoken. She was eighteen years old and in all sorts of pain, none of it physical. Her face reflected the distraught state of her heart. When Dr. Adam saw her, he suspected that the girl had lost all interest in living.

The young doctor took a seat beside her. Irma was beautiful, angelic even, if not for the constant grimace.

"Doctor, I don't want to be deported. I don't have anyone left. It's pointless to face the terrible journey ahead all alone."

"Life is generous and opens up a way out."

"You know that's not true. You deal with death every day. You've seen it in the faces of newborns, in the eyes of a young woman on her wedding day, on the purple lips of an old man who just wants to rest. You of all people know that life is a fickle traitor. I want to be done with mine. It may be an offense to God, and I know that you've been trained to save people, not to help them die, but that's all I want."

Dr. Adam's eyes pricked with tears at the desolate words, and he swallowed hard.

"You're asking me to do something I can't do. My conscience..."

Irma turned away and let her tears fall silently, soaking the coarse, stained pillowcase where before her hundreds of heads had suffered alone and hundreds more would after her.

"Please," she whispered. "I'm begging you."

Dr. Adam stood. He wanted to get out of there and plug his ears to the sound of that young woman's voice, like the cry of a drowning soul in a stormy sea. A few moments later he returned with a pill.

"I can't put you to death, I'm sorry. But if you take this pill, you'll be so sick that they won't be able to put you on the transport. After that, we'll find a way to get you out of here. There's always a way."

"I don't want to die, Doctor; I promise. But I don't want to live in a work camp. I'm just not capable of it."

"I can promise you they won't deport you with this," he said, handing it to her.

The young woman observed the pill in the palm of her hand for a few moments. It was long, thin, and pink, with a tiny inscription. Irma wondered how something so small could save her life. She also wondered if the doctor was tricking her. Since losing her family and being on her own, Irma had known very few people of goodwill, so few who were kind and trustworthy. Finally, as a small act of faith, Irma cocked her head back, dropped the pill into her mouth, and swallowed it with a gulp of water. It scraped her throat, and she thought she could feel it going down her esophagus.

Dr. Adam had waited patiently during the process. He said, "Now lie back and rest before it starts hurting. But don't worry; it isn't going to kill you."

Irma thought that closing her eyes and not waking up would actually be a gift. Sometimes life was so difficult that disappearing into sleep was the only option for something akin to happiness.

The doctor walked away, and Irma's mind slowly started to detach from her body. She felt a peace that had eluded her for months—years—and was convinced that she really was dying, or perhaps being reborn. It was never entirely clear if death was the end of something or just the beginning of something else.

Chapter 25

EIGHT HUNDRED LIVES

Lyon
AUGUST 27, 1942

L UCIEN MARCHAIS REVIEWED THE list of exemptions before going to Vénissieux. The do-gooder associations would put up a stink, but it would be a passing row. Within a few months no one would remember the poor devils from the camp. The intendant himself had nothing against the Jews. He was just doing his duty. He did not give the orders; he followed them. If the Germans wanted the foreign Jews, he would hand them over since, after all, those people belonged in their country of origin. After that he would head back home to spend time with his family.

The intendant arrived at the camp in his black Citroën. Jean-Marie and the rest of the commission were waiting for him. It was their second meeting of the day, and exhaustion was etched on their faces. The city government had received all sorts of missives begging for the liberation of the prisoners. But they all knew that the masters of France were not the prefect or the regional intendant, not even Prime Minister Laval or Marshal Pétain. The Germans held all the cards.

"Ladies and gentlemen, forgive me for being late. Discussions about what measures to adopt are ongoing, and I still cannot tell you which people will be exempt."

A murmur passed through the room.

"Do you mean to say that other groups besides unaccompanied minors will be considered for exemption?" Jean-Marie asked.

"I did not say that," Marchais snapped.

René Cussonac, the camp director, spoke up. "Don't get your hopes up; it'll only be worse later."

His words were met with disgusted stares. Everyone saw through Cussonac's bravado to the heartless, cruel man that he was.

Jean-Marie noticed the briefcase at the intendant's feet. He had a feeling that it contained the names of exempted people. If he could get a look at that list and see the arguments against the rejected requests, perhaps they could do something to counteract what was happening.

"What do you say to a coffee break?" he suggested to Father Glasberg. Everyone got to their feet and headed for the adjacent room.

Jean-Marie seized the moment of Marchais's and Cussonac's absence. He grabbed the briefcase, ducked into a side room, and began rifling through the papers. There were so few names accepted for exemption. Surely it was incomplete. He jotted the names down, put all the documents back, and hastily returned to the meeting room. People were already returning to their seats. The intendant was looking all around the floor.

"Where's my briefcase?" he demanded.

Everyone looked up at him in surprise.

"I left it right here! One of you Communist collaborators stole it!"

"Mr. Marchais, my colleagues are not Communists, and we haven't seen anything," Father Glasberg answered calmly.

Cussonac went to the door to call for his men. Jean-Marie hid the briefcase behind his back, turned without taking his eyes off the two authorities, and set it down off to the side. He calmly stepped as far away as he could.

"Isn't that it?" he asked, pointing to the corner where the case now sat.

Everyone turned and Marchais grabbed it.

"I didn't leave it that far away; I know I didn't."

Jean-Marie shrugged. "Someone probably moved it accidentally when we all went to get coffee."

Marchais had the briefcase open on his lap and was thumbing through the papers.

"Is anything missing?" Jean-Marie asked.

"No, everything's here," Marchais said warily.

"Very good. Then can you proceed to tell us about the exemptions?"

The intendant was fed up. He glared crossly at Jean-Marie and said, "Tomorrow we'll get to that." He stood and headed for the door.

"But we need to know the names today so we can file the appeals," Madeleine objected.

"All in due time," Marchais snapped.

"Please, Mr. Marchais," Father Glasberg called, "this is all most irregular. There are norms and processes to follow."

Cussonac got in Glasberg's face. "Are you accusing us of doing something illegal?"

"I'm just pointing out the fact that these proceedings are highly irregular, sirs. The lives of over one thousand people are at stake, most of them helpless women, children, and older adults."

"They aren't soldiers or criminals," Jean-Marie added. He could barely contain his fury.

"Everything will be carried out according to regulation." Marchais's parcity of words indicated that the meeting was over, and he opened the door.

But Madeleine called out, "When is the deportation and transfer scheduled for?"

"Tomorrow, the men. The night of the twenty-eighth to the morning of the twenty-ninth, the rest," Cussonac announced, proud that his work there was coming to a suitable close.

The authorities quit the room, and the members of the commission stared at one another dejectedly.

Again, Madeleine spoke. "What are we going to do?"

"Let's all have a seat again. On the one hand, the release forms for parents to sign are being printed, and those cases can't be rejected. On the other, there are those who've served the country of France."

"Those groups combined hardly amount to two hundred people," Jean-Marie said.

"So they're going to report upward of eight hundred?" Madeleine's tone held the shocked grief they all felt.

"There's still time, and we'll fight to the end," Father Glasberg said. He turned to Jean-Marie. "What did you see in the briefcase?"

"There was a list with a lot of names granted exemptions, but then later a pen had scratched off hundreds of them—the majority, in fact."

"So at first they accepted our requests, and then someone gave a counterorder," Glasberg concluded.

"We've got to make our reports watertight," Madeleine said with tears in her eyes. "If we can save even one more person, it will be worth it."

The commission members knew that most of the camp's inmates were already condemned to die. For many, the sentence would not be carried out immediately, but eventually the Nazis would erase the souls crammed into Vénissieux.

Chapter 26

ORDERS

Lyon
AUGUST 27, 1942

MARCHAIS WENT BY HIS office before returning home. He picked up the phone and called the Ministry of the Interior. A few moments later, the minister angrily asked what he wanted.

"I'm calling about the foreigners being held at Vénissieux. Several networks are pressuring us, and more and more people are speaking out against deportation."

"What the hell is going on in Lyon? I thought you were the spiritual reserve of France. Are you all just a bunch of Communists now?"

"Cardinal Gerlier has threatened to write an open letter to all French Catholics."

"Oh, the damned crows think they're something else. They've swallowed the hogwash about God, family, and country. The orders are clear: you've got to hand over at least eight hundred prisoners. We've got quotas to fulfill at the request of our allies, the Nazis.

Those prisoners have nothing to do with France. They're just disgusting Jews. Tell your goddamned priests that the Jews were the ones who murdered their precious Jesus. Don't bother me again with this unless you want to end up on that train to Germany, you understand?"

"Yes, sir," Marchais said, squaring his shoulders.

He was sweating profusely when he hung up the receiver. He was not going to risk his career, his life, and his family for a few foreigners. All he was doing was allowing them to leave France. Whatever befell them after that was not his business. Marchais smacked his hat down over his brow and headed for home. He did not know how he was going to look his children in the eye, but it was for their sakes that he was doing all of this.

Chapter 27

THE LONGEST NIGHT

Vénissieux Camp
AUGUST 28, 1942

THE SOUL'S BITTEREST HOUR is when it comes face-to-face with its deepest fears. Many of the men were already gone from Vénissieux, primarily the young, single men. Mothers clung to their children, sensing the impending danger. Eva Fixler was still hoping for an answer from the Hungarian consul that would get her released. Her daughters meant everything to her. Her life would be completely devoid of meaning if one day they were no longer with her. She had always wanted to be a mother. When that joy came her way, she poured herself into the task fully, making up for what her own distant mother never offered. But the hours of not seeing the Hungarian consul passed slowly. The rumors about deportation grew more intense. Eva Fixler could not stop staring at her daughters and trying not to cry.

"You all right, Mom?" the oldest asked her.

Eva nodded unconvincingly. "One day, if I'm no longer here, do you promise to take care of your sisters?"

Hélène's eyes opened wide as she tried to process her mother's request. She bit her lips, cracked from lack of proper hydration, and nodded resolutely.

"Your sisters are quite little, but you'll be able to take good care of them."

Just then several of the camp's social workers approached the barrack where the Fixlers had found a spot. Some children were playing on the floor while older ones were reading silently. Some mothers were doing their best to wash clothes without the necessary tools while others sat in groups chatting. Everyone noticed the arrival of the social workers. It could mean only one thing: bad news.

Maribel Semprún was one of the workers. This Spanish woman, who had fled Spain after the defeat of the Republic, had been in Lyon for a few months since marrying Jean-Marie Soutou in March. Her father was an ambassador in The Hague. Though she and her brother, Jorge, had studied in France, they had never forgotten Spain. Beside her was Father Glasberg, who could speak the languages of most of the refugees and always showed deep empathy for them. Hélène Lévy, a psychologist with OSE, joined the social workers in case any of the mothers had a breakdown or suffered some other crisis.

Maribel caught Hélène's eye and nodded to the Hungarian mother. They approached slowly and, with soft, gentle tones, began.

"Mrs. Fixler, we need to speak with you for a moment."

Eva's big gray eyes were trimmed with wrinkles that bore testimony to the suffering of the past few years. Yet she retained her beauty.

"How can I help you?" she asked.

Hélène held Eva's gaze and said quietly, "At dawn you'll all be deported to Germany."

Eva's face broke. The news did not surprise her, but reality was harder to face than suspicion.

"But I can't be deported. The other workers talked with the authorities, and they understand that everything has been a terrible mistake. Hungarians can't be deported; it's illegal."

Hélène and Maribel exchanged a glance. They were aware of Eva's situation. "The consul or the ambassador might come to set you free, but there are very few hours left, and we have to ask you something . . ." Hélène searched for the right words, but there were none.

"We have to ask you to sign away your parental rights," Maribel finished.

Eva was petrified. She presumed she had not understood, but then her knees sagged, and she grabbed onto the bunk bed for support. Her chest was tight and her face very pale.

"My daughters—why do you want my daughters? I won't be separated from them, not if I can help it."

Maribel placed her right hand on Eva's shoulder. Her left hand held the abdication forms, which she placed on the bed. She willed strength and comfort to flow from her hand into Eva.

"What we know is that children aren't allowed into the work camps. As soon as you get to Germany, you'll be separated, and we fear for what the Nazis will do to the little ones. Do you see?"

Eva was still in shock, breathing in short, rapid bursts.

"The Nazis are eliminating the children and older people. That is what we've heard from eyewitnesses." Hélène's words got through to Eva.

"They kill the children? That's impossible; it's absurd," she said.

"We have every reason to believe that it is exactly what they do," Maribel insisted, picking up the paperwork again.

Eva shook her head. "I can't. It's impossible. The Nazis are cruel and evil, but not even they could do something that vile."

"I can assure you that they are and that they do. The war in the East is going very badly for them. They don't want any more mouths to feed." Hélène swallowed hard to chase her tears and bear up under the tension.

"Sign the papers to hand your children over to us. Later, if it becomes unnecessary, we will destroy the releases; we promise."

Eva glanced at the paper through a squint, not wanting to fully read it. It felt like looking at her own death sentence. Without her daughters, she did not want to remain alive. Nothing would make any sense. But she did not want to put them in further danger either.

"Are you sure?" she whispered. She still could not accept the fact that the Nazis would murder her daughters.

"I'm afraid we are. We're going to be asking the rest of the mothers to do the same."

The other women had kept a prudent distance. Though they could not hear the words being spoken, the horror they saw on Eva Fixler's face assured them that bad news was coming for the rest of them.

Eva wiped her tears. She had to be stronger now than ever before. Just a few minutes ago she had asked her oldest daughter to look after the younger ones. Though Eva herself would be gone, at least the children would have a chance at life; her memory would not disappear as long as one of the four was alive.

Maribel handed her the paperwork and a pen. Eva held the Spaniard's gaze, pleading for a way out of this terrible dilemma. Then she took the pen with a trembling hand and filled out the information. She signed it and watched the wretched papers go back into the social workers' folder.

"Don't worry—we'll take good care of them," Maribel said.

"If I do get released, where do I go to find my daughters?"

The workers looked at one another gravely. That was a hard question to answer. The plan was to disperse the children among families in the area and then get them out of the country.

"If you return . . ." Hélène's voice faltered. As far as they knew, no one who had been deported came back alive. "Then we will get you to your daughters."

Eva nodded, understanding. "Thank you," she said, crying again.

Hélène and Maribel turned to the next mother, leaving Eva desolate. Her entire soul had been ripped out from her. Her daughters were playing near the bed, seemingly content, unaware of what was going on around them. Eva envied their innocence and their ability to just let things happen. She could hardly recall her own childhood but had a vague recollection of what it meant to live in absolute and blissful ignorance of the evil that ruled the world.

Chapter 28

SIGNING

Vénissieux Camp
AUGUST 28, 1942

FAJGLA BAUMEL WAS ABOUT to take a walk outside around the barracks with her son, Jean, when Raquel, one of the social workers, approached. Fajgla had heard what was going on. The social workers were taking children to the mess hall after the mothers signed paperwork rescinding their parental rights. Fajgla had arrived with a group of families from Saint-Sauveur-de-Montagut, and all the mothers from that group had stuck together to help one another.

"You already know what I'm coming to ask you?" Raquel asked.

Fajgla took a deep breath and dropped her head. She closed her eyes and wished the presence of the social worker away, as if the woman were a bad dream.

But Raquel was still there, and she went on. "We have to take the children for their own safety. We don't know what the Nazis are capable of doing to them."

"So then if you don't know, why do you want to separate us from our children? They're all we have left. First the government took our livelihood, since we're just animals to them. Then we had to leave everything and flee to a foreign country, where we've been treated like a plague. When we thought things might get better, the Nazis came to France and took our husbands away. Now they've taken our freedom, and all that's left are our children. If you take them, we'll have nothing—my soul goes with my son."

"We're not taking them from you. You'll have to sign Jean over voluntarily. It will just be for a time, until you can return for him. Then we'll reunite all the parents who return with their children."

Fajgla snorted. "Return? I don't see that happening for any of us. I've got family in Poland. They've told me what's going on with Jews up there. They're worked to death and those that can't work are just . . ." Fajgla swallowed.

Raquel looked at the child playing nearby. There was hardly any light in the barracks. Even though it was still daytime, the sky was dark with threatening clouds. It was fitting that the sun refused to shine on a grim day like that.

"So that's even more reason for you to allow your son a chance to survive, don't you think?"

"Survive? What for? Is a world like this worth living in?"

Raquel did not know how to respond. She had been trained on how to speak with the mothers, but she herself wondered the same thing every night when she returned home. The Nazis had stolen much more than people's freedom—they had taken all their hope.

"Sometimes we must hold on to whatever life offers us, no matter how small. Every day that your son lives, he's one day closer to surviving the war and this monstrous regime."

Raquel's words did little to comfort Fajgla, but the mother knew that the social worker was right. Taking Jean with her on the train would be condemning him to death. She could not do that.

Fajgla took the paperwork, filled it out, and signed without even reading carefully.

Raquel put it in her folder and asked, "Do you want to say goodbye to Jean?"

Tears were pouring out of Fajgla's dark eyes and spilling down her face, but she shook her head.

"I can't. I don't want him to see me like this. I don't want this to be the way he remembers me."

"I understand," Raquel said.

She took Jean by the hand, and he followed her willingly. When the boy turned back to look at his mother, Fajgla had stepped back into the shadows.

Once she left Jean in the mess hall, Raquel broke down in tears. Jean was the fourth child she had led away from their mother. Her sense of guilt grew by the moment. She knew that she was saving lives, but she was destroying others in the process.

→>-<←

Georges Garel tried to get the mother to see things rationally, but she clung to her daughter as if Georges were trying to kidnap the girl.

"Give her a chance, please," he repeated patiently. "Léah deserves to live."

Léah's mother studied the man in front of her with confused eyes, incapable of understanding, while the girl, sitting on the floor, clung to her mother's skirt and cried in terror.

"Do you know what you're asking of me?"

"Yes, I'm asking you to make the most difficult choice in the world. But if she goes with you, she'll have zero chance of survival. Do you understand?"

The woman started moaning and beating her chest.

"This is infamy! By God, how can you ask me to do this? You're stealing our children! God can't be allowing something this terrible!"

"God is giving you a chance. Léah has to survive. If she does not, then the Nazis have won. Don't you see that?"

"They've already won if we have to give up our children."

Georges did not know what to say. The woman was pulling her hair out and crying bitterly.

"Look, right here, Léah's father already filled out the paperwork and signed. We only need your signature." Georges held the paper out for her. Those words got through to the mother.

"Her father signed?" she asked in disbelief.

"Yes, right here," he said and pointed.

That was her husband's signature all right. Everything changed in an instant. She dried her tears and signed.

Léah was thirteen but did not want to leave her mother. They were very close and did everything together. They talked for hours on end, laughing and crying, dreaming about the future, creating a world in which Léah would study and become a nurse.

"My daughter, go now," her mother begged.

"No, Mom, don't make me leave!"

"For God's sake, go now before my heart breaks in two."

The mother kissed her daughter's cheeks and tasted her salty tears. She held Léah's face in her hands for a brief second, that beautiful face she loved so dearly. She looked at Léah's big brown eyes and long brown hair one last time—her precious doll, whom she would never see again.

"Mom, please," Léah pleaded, but Georges took her by the hand and pulled her back.

As soon as they were out the door, the mother let out a long, desperate wail. Léah heard her as they crossed the yard to the mess hall. It had begun to rain. The sky was weeping all the tears of those ravaged souls while time crept on toward the terrible sentence looming over the camp's refugees.

The number of children in the mess hall was growing. Most were crying. The older ones tried to console and distract the younger ones, but their efforts were in vain. Fear and suffering were contagious. Thunder began to rumble, muffling the wailing of the mothers who cried like the mothers centuries before in Bethlehem. They, too, had lost their children to a cruel tyrant. That one had sought to snuff out the life of the Messiah promised to humanity and announced by a star in the sky. History's sad song repeated itself: mothers paying the cost of the evil actions of angry men.

Chapter 29

BLUE PAPERS

Peyrins Château
DECEMBER 18, 1992

VALÉRIE TOOK THE CAR and headed for the château despite the snow. It was not too far, and the roads were passable. She was listening to an old tape of France Gall, and the song "Ella, elle l'a" was on full blast as the barren, frozen fields gave way to leafless wintry forests. Since deciding to write her thesis on the children of Vénissieux, she felt a positive sense of energy flowing through every aspect of her life. Almost every door she knocked on opened willingly. She had managed to get in touch with the people who currently managed the château, and the manager had told her that they still had unopened boxes from the time when the building housed a number of Jewish children.

René Nodot had told her about one of the children hidden there from the Nazis, Eva Stein. The Spielman family had also found refuge in the château when Germaine Chesneau was in charge. She saw what was going on in France and in 1942 decided to turn their home into a refuge for persecuted Jews. Her previous experience as a nurse served her well during that time.

Valérie drove through the gate and into the château grounds. The spacious yard was unkempt. There was a long pond in the middle and several walkways flanked by enormous plane trees. The main house was divided into two wings. It was a dingy cream color with wooden shutters that gave it a country look. Ivy grew up the façade all the way to the rounded roof.

When her car stopped on the gravel near the front door, a well-dressed man came out to greet her. He smiled, led Valérie inside, and said, "Welcome to the castle. The château is not in its finest moment, but it still retains something of its former glory."

"The most beautiful thing about this place is that it was a safe haven for some of those who suffered most during the war."

"That it was." He nodded, indicating for Valérie to enter a spacious room that was brightly illuminated despite the dim winter light coming through the windows.

"Is this where the families were housed?" Valérie asked.

"They were spread throughout the various buildings. Germaine had installed a bell and a telephone to sound the alarm whenever the Gestapo showed up."

The man gave Valérie a tour of the first, second, and third floors. They ended in the attic where one dingy bulb provided the only light. He took down a box and handed it to the young woman.

"No one has touched these things since 1944 when the Allies liberated the region."

Valérie went back down to the well-lit room, holding the box like a delicate china vase. She placed it on a table and looked at the man, silently asking for permission before opening it.

"Please, go right ahead. I'll leave you alone with history."

"Thank you so much," she said as he left the room. But he turned on the threshold to ask, "Coffee? It's terribly cold out."

"Oh yes, thank you."

He nodded and left.

Valérie breathed in the solitude for a moment before opening the box. It was soft from decades of dampness and dust. She pulled out several books, a few notebooks, a pen, some photographs, and, finally, a small box. She studied it before trying to open it. It took her a while to find the golden clasp under the lid.

"There we go," she said, raising the wooden top.

Inside were a number of purplish papers, though perhaps they had once been blue.

Her hands trembled as she pulled out the first. The heading told her what they were. Two large tears rolled from her blue eyes down her neck to her white shirt. She read the documents in silent reverence. The weight of history bowed her forward, and her head dropped. They were the releases, the papers signed by parents on that fateful night in August 1942. The box contained at least sixty of them. Valérie studied them one by one as the names of the children reverberated throughout her core.

Chapter 30

MISSION

Lyon
AUGUST 28, 1942

KLAUS BARBIE LOOKED AT his files and then took another drag of his cigar. Things at Vénissieux seemed to be going swimmingly well. His superiors would be pleased that the deportation quotas were being met. His job officially consisted of tracking down members of the Resistance, but a friend in Berlin had asked him to personally oversee the deportations. The French authorities could not be trusted to do the job well. To the Germans, the French were like all Latins—too sensitive, not trustworthy, susceptible to whatever their bishops thought and said. That was especially true of their patron saint Marshal Pétain.

The SS-Hauptsturmführer sipped on his cognac and felt the alcohol burn his throat. Then he called his secretary and asked for his car to be brought around. Klaus was ready to visit the camp. It was under French jurisdiction and in the free zone, but the SS and the Gestapo could do pretty much whatever they wanted. In fact, several high-ranking French officials had asked the German services to help them fight the growing Resistance movement. France had always been a complex territory. The Germans could not afford to send hundreds of thousands of soldiers, and their soft-line policy had been met with rebellion. The Resistance had even infiltrated the Vichy government.

When the car was ready, Klaus polished off his cognac, settled his hat on his head, and descended the stairs two by two. He was humming a little melody until he reached the door and saw the rain. His good mood soured. He dashed into the car and took a seat on the warm leather. Through the window, the city seemed to be drugged to sleep under the summer storm. Many of Lyon's inhabitants had relocated to their country homes or to the Mediterranean beaches. The war did not seem to have curbed French decadence, Klaus mused as they left the city behind.

The Vénissieux camp was on the outskirts of Lyon, near an industrial area, in the abandoned military barracks of the French army. When Klaus's car came to a stop at the checkpoint on the muddy street, the SS official regretted having left his rooms that afternoon. Two sorrowful excuses for policemen raised the barrier as soon as they saw Klaus's uniform, and the vehicle parked in front of the administration building. Klaus loved showing up unannounced and taking the French government workers by surprise. Their shocked faces displayed the cowardice of a people who had submitted to the superior race with hardly a fight.

Klaus waited while his assistant opened the door, spread a cloak over the muddy ground to keep the official's boots from touching the dirt, and covered him with a black umbrella. Under the porch roof, the SS officer stomped his boots on the wooden floorboards and entered without knocking.

René Cussonac was already on his feet when Klaus crossed the office with his powerful stride.

"Captain, a pleasure to see you here," the camp director said.

The man's lie pleased Klaus, who knew that his presence was far from welcome, though he also knew that Cussonac was a committed anti-Semite.

"At ease. I'm only here to check up on how the deportations are coming along."

"Everything is proceeding according to plan," Cussonac said. He wiped his brow with a handkerchief, finding himself suddenly covered in sweat.

"How many tomorrow?" Klaus asked.

"Would you like a drink, Captain? I have a magnificent Calvados, the best spirits Normandy has to offer."

Klaus never refused a drink, no matter how strong it was.

Cussonac poured the tinkling liquor into a small glass and then poured another for himself. Both men downed it in one gulp. Then the Frenchman began to explain the plan.

"Many of the men have already been shipped off, and tonight the rest of the refugees will head out in buses. Altogether it's thirteen hundred people, though we've had to allow a few exemptions required by our laws."

Klaus frowned, and Cussonac filled his glass again. "How many of these rats will get away?"

Cussonac began to stammer. "Oh, j-just a few old and sickly folks, and a few dozen unaccompanied minors."

"I want exact numbers, Officer!" Klaus roared.

"Two hundred and eighty."

The eyes bulged out of the SS officer's face. "What the hell? If you don't meet your quotas, you'll all pay for it."

"We've rounded up more. We'll make the quotas, don't worry," the gendarme promised.

"I *am* worried. Unlike you, I am fulfilling a sacred mission. The Führer wants all Jews in Europe to disappear. He warned everyone that if Germany had to go to war because of the Jews and the Communists, all the Jews on the continent would be exterminated."

"You're aware of my feelings toward the Jews. The damned race has corroded the eternal values of France and reduced us to a mixed-race, immoral, decadent country. We share the same objective, Captain; I assure you."

Klaus slammed his fist down on the table, and Cussonac watched him fearfully. "I want each and every one of the Jews here in Vénissieux on a train to Germany by dawn. If everyone's out by dawn, no one will halt the operation."

"But my superiors . . ."

"I'll take full responsibility. Understood?"

"Yes, sir."

"I don't want to have to come back to this pigsty that reeks of swine and cow shit. If Berlin's orders are not carried out, you and your family will be next in line for deportation. Meet the quotas, whatever it takes."

Klaus drank down the last of the liquor, put on his hat, and slammed the door on his way out. A smile crossed his face as he went down the wooden steps and ducked into the car.

The chauffeur closed the door after him and then got behind the wheel. "Back to headquarters?" he asked.

"No. I feel like having a good time. Work gets me riled up. Head for Madame Boyer's brothel."

Klaus Barbie's unrestrained appetite for luxury prostitutes had already resulted in syphilis, but he could not deny himself. The only time his mind was off work and relaxed was when he was mounting a good-looking whore in a conquered country. Then he knew himself to be one of the lords of war like Adolf Hitler promised to those who served him faithfully.

Heading back to Lyon and crossing the wide river, Klaus leaned back in the seat and determined to return to the camp that night to see if his orders had been carried out. A good German never trusted the French to follow through.

Chapter 31

THE GENERAL

Lyon
AUGUST 28, 1942

GENTLEMAN, I REFUSE. MY men are not jailers, especially not of innocent women, children, and old men and women," General Pierre Robert de Saint-Vincent answered. For emphasis, he shook his head at the intendant and the chief police of the division of Rhône.

The general had faithfully served France throughout a long military career. His division had not receded an inch in the Alps, and after the armistice he had been named the military governor of Lyon charged with one branch of the army.

"We need your men to supervise the transfer of the Jews to the northern zone. They've got to be at the border by tomorrow."

"My troops will never be part of any such operation." The general's thin face, sunken eyes, and small military mustache were set in opposition.

"These are the president's orders," Lucien Marchais, the intendant, insisted.

"My conscience answers to an office higher than the president of the Republic. How can you even consider sending civilians for the Nazis to exploit and kill? Those aren't the values of France."

"You might have noticed that things have changed a bit," Cussonac retorted.

"Not for me. I'm bound by the honor of my position and France, but also to God. I cannot act against my conscience. What would be left of the French if we acted with such vileness?"

The intendant rose to his feet indignantly. "You're calling us murderers? Those Jews are foreigners, and most of them are here illegally. If the Nazis want them, they must have done something."

The general remained seated, calm, implacable. He raised his head and met Marchais's eyes squarely. "Most of those children were born in France. Even if the rest are foreign-born, they are human beings. Our country was the first to codify human rights. Those values still hold meaning for some of us."

Cussonac waved his finger in the general's face and, enraged, Marchais said, "This won't be the end of it. You'll be removed from your position and stripped of your honors. You're a traitor to France."

"I'm the traitor? I'm serving my country to the best of my abilities."

"Don't you realize that if we don't comply with the Nazis' demands, they'll take over the unoccupied zone, and then we'll be powerless to help the rest of our citizens?"

General de Saint-Vincent got to his feet, still a gallant figure despite his age. "Then perhaps the country will rise up against those tyrants and their accomplices. Now, please see yourselves out of my office."

As they descended the stairs, Marchais told Cussonac, "This won't be the end of it. We're in a very delicate position. The Germans are weighing the merits of continuing to allow the free zone. What does a handful of Jews matter? Bah! Has the whole world gone mad? The marshal will eat that traitor alive."

The angry words did little to calm Marchais's fury. As soon as he got to his office, he contacted Vichy. The entire deportation affair was rotten, and lower-ranking officials tended to be the scapegoats for such debacles. "I'm not going down with this ship, no sir," he vowed.

Chapter 32

MARY

Vénissieux Camp
AUGUST 28, 1942

THE STORM RAGED AS the social workers tried to convince more parents to voluntarily give up their children.

Father Glasberg was with Déborah, an older woman in charge of her granddaughter, Dawia. She was so rattled that she had stood in silence with her hands resting on the release papers for several minutes.

"I'm not the child's mother. Making this choice is too big a responsibility for me."

"But surely your daughter asked you to take care of the child?"

"Yes, but she also told me not to let anything in the world separate us."

The priest's gaze held endless compassion.

"I want you to understand, sir," the woman went on, "I don't have much time left. The war found me already old and weak. I've been living on borrowed time for years now. But this girl, she's got her whole life ahead of her. She deserves to live; she deserves a chance." Déborah's eyes were glassy with tears.

"That's exactly what we're trying to give her, a chance to live. If she goes to Germany, you'll both die."

Glasberg felt the harshness of his words acutely, but speaking with so many mothers and fathers had showed him that the only way to get them to take action on this horrible decision was to lay out the facts.

Déborah signed the paper and handed it to Glasberg, then drew Dawia close and kissed her cheeks. "Behave yourself. Make me proud. We can't keep walking the same path together. God is calling us to different roads from here on out. But I know for sure that his angels will protect you."

"But, Grandmother, I don't want to go without you. Who will take care of you if I'm not around?"

The old woman smiled. Dawia had always been a sharp, happy child, the light of Déborah's life.

"God will see to that, little one, never you mind. You'll be with other children, and that's good for you. Be strong and courageous. Don't be afraid or discouraged. Be just like Joshua when he had to face all those armies in the promised land."

One of the social workers led Dawia to the mess hall. Unlike most of the children, she walked with calm confidence, seeming to understand what was necessary.

The priest went up to another group of mothers. They knew what was going on, and it was growing harder to convince the parents to agree. Time was running out, and Glasberg expected the gendarmes to enter any minute and make his team leave the barracks.

He held out the paperwork to one woman and said, "You're Mary, yes? Your husband has already signed. We just need your signature."

The mother did not take her eyes off her children. She was used to making difficult choices, but this was the most wrenching yet.

"I . . . I . . ." the woman stuttered.

"Mary, please, sign the papers."

"I've seen so much. In Brussels I tended to soldiers wounded in the fighting. I know how heartless war is. But I never imagined any of this—" She waved to indicate Vénissieux and everything it represented. "Do you understand what you're asking of us?"

Glasberg's voice cracked with pain. "Once there was a mother who had to give up her son to die for humanity. Two thousand years have passed, but we still remember her. Thanks to the sacrifice of that mother, I myself am here, and so are the other workers with me. Her name was also Mary."

The Mary of Vénissieux signed the document and then hugged her children tightly.

"Don't forget to dress warmly and to wash your hands before eating. Don't bicker. Go to bed on time and don't ever talk back to adults. Understood?"

The little ones nodded gravely. Mary hugged them again and her tears drenched their blond hair.

Father Glasberg left that barrack for the next. It was past ten o'clock in the evening, and the rain was falling hard. Not far off he saw Hélène Lévy and Charles Lederman escorting a child who seemed calm enough. They were singing a lullaby. That broke the priest. He stepped aside to weep in the shadows. Across the dark of night, their song broke the silence:

One kilometer on foot, wears out, wears out,
One kilometer on foot, wears out your shoes.

Two kilometers on foot, wears out, wears out,
Two kilometers on foot, wears out your shoes.

Three kilometers on foot, wears out, wears out,
Three kilometers on foot, wears out your shoes.

Four kilometers on foot, wears out, wears out,
Four kilometers on foot, wears out your shoes.

Five kilometers on foot, wears out, wears out,
Five kilometers on foot, wears out your shoes.

Six kilometers on foot, wears out, wears out,
Six kilometers on foot, wears out your shoes.

Chapter 33

LOTTE

Vénissieux Camp
AUGUST 28, 1942

WHILE DRAMATIC SCENES UNFOLDED across the camp, the social workers carefully filed each signed release into a wooden box. There were still so many children unaccounted for, though, and it was almost eleven o'clock at night. Time flew by. They did not want any little one to be sent off to their death. The Weichselbaum twins had joined in with the rest of the children singing in the mess hall. Singing was their attempt to fight their sadness and fear of the dark. The two girls nervously rocked back and forth. If they had to go to the bathroom, they were too embarrassed to admit it. Beside them were Élisabeth Hirsch, Lotte Levy, and Madeleine Dreyfus.

Though she was only fifteen, Lotte Levy concentrated on taking care of the younger children, trying to convince them that they were going on a field trip.

Around sixty children were packed into the small mess hall. They were sweaty, thirsty, and hungry. The room stank of urine and feet. By that time, though, the children were all used to being in uncomfortable, dirty, and dark spaces.

Father Glasberg went up to Lotte and placed his hand on her shoulder. "Thank you for your help. Your singing has calmed their nerves, I believe."

"I've always liked children. When I'm older I want to be a teacher."

"You'll make a fantastic teacher someday."

"Will there be many more children coming?" Lotte asked.

"Hopefully at least forty more. The social workers are making the rounds as we speak."

Lotte sighed. The war had caused too many children to grow up too fast, stealing their fleeting innocence.

"You're a priest, right?" she asked, eyeing his collar. "So why does God let things like this happen?"

Father Glasberg was quiet for a few moments. He had often wondered the same thing, and he was sure that millions of others across Europe and the rest of the world did as well.

"Can I tell you a story?" he finally answered.

When the children around them heard the word *story*, they gathered around eagerly.

"There was an old man who'd had a very hard time having a son. The man's name was Abraham, and he had left his hometown in search of a promised land. God had promised that Abraham would have as many children and grandchildren and great-grandchildren as there were stars in the sky and grains of sand by the sea. But he had only had one son with his wife, Sarah. The child was born when they were very old—older than I am!" At that, several children giggled. "One day Abraham received a message from God. The message was terrible: Abraham was supposed to take his son, Isaac, up on a mountain and sacrifice him. Isaac was no longer a boy. He was a young man, so his dad didn't tell him what the plan was. They walked all day. Isaac was carrying the firewood. At one point along the way, he stopped and asked his father what they were going to sacrifice. Abraham answered that God would provide it for them.

"When they got to the top of the mountain, Abraham prepared the altar. That's when Isaac realized that he himself was going to be the sacrifice. It ended up that Abraham found a ram caught in some bushes, and he sacrificed the animal instead of Isaac. That was how God showed that he forbade humans to be sacrificed to the gods that lots of people worshipped back in Abraham's day. It was a really hard way to learn that lesson. But now everybody—at least in the West—knows that it's wrong to sacrifice humans. Maybe war will teach us a lesson we can't learn any other way: the lesson that killing one another for our ideas, beliefs, or flags is absurd, because we all belong to the only human race there is, and we're all brothers and sisters of one another."

Chapter 34

GEORGES

Vénissieux Camp
AUGUST 28, 1942

AS MORE CHILDREN ARRIVED at the mess hall, the heat and the crowdedness reached intolerable levels. Maribel Semprún and the social workers tried to keep the children calm while another group of workers tried to convince the remaining parents to sign over their children. Then Georges Garel entered with two girls clinging to an older boy. They were sisters who refused to be separated from their brother. The girls were both sixteen, but being short and slender, it was easy to pass them off as younger.

"Don't let them take our brother!" the girls begged while Georges tried to untangle the mass of arms and hair.

Maribel came up to offer a gentle presence. "Girls, it's a miracle that you two are able to come with us. But your brother is too old and looks it, and we can't claim that he's younger. The gendarmes could get mad and question us and then put the rest of the children here in jeopardy as well. Does that make sense?"

The girls nodded but still begged through their tears. "He's all that's left of our family. We've lost everyone else. Please, save our brother. He's only seventeen."

At that the young man spoke up. "It's all right. I'll always be in your memories. Mom and Dad would want any of us who could to be saved, and right now that's you two. You two are the best sisters any boy could have. Help each other. Don't forget, we're always Jews, no matter what they do to us."

He backed away, maintaining their gaze until he shut the door. The girls tried to run after him, but Maribel embraced them and wept with them.

"I'm here for you. Who knows, your brother might come back some day. Don't lose hope."

Maribel's words still circled the heads of everyone listening when two boys brought in Eva Fixler's daughters. The Hungarian consul had not been able to get the family out of Vénissieux, and their separation would be permanent.

➤═◄

Amid the chaos, a policeman entered the barracks and found Glasberg.

"Keep the mothers from screaming, please. If they keep this up, we'll put them all on the buses right now."

The priest looked at the man in surprise. "Wouldn't you scream if your children were taken from you?"

The gendarme frowned. He had not put himself in those people's shoes until right then. For him, this was just a job; these were not human beings going through the worst moment of their lives.

Glasberg waited. The policeman imagined his own two young ones. He eventually nodded.

"I would scream too. But please, try to keep them calm. If the camp director hears of what's going on, all the work you people have put in will have been in vain."

"Thank you," the priest answered.

The blind eye turned by a handful of gendarmes was a crucial ally for the children's escape that night.

→>◄◄

Midnight was coming. The workers knew that they could do nothing more after that. Lili tried to obtain more signatures, but the last groups of mothers was fiercely hesitant to turn their children over to strangers without having absolute certainty that the children would be better off with them than with their own parents.

Lili found Maribel and started crying.

"What is it in particular, Lili? I mean, besides the whole situation?" Maribel asked.

"I just saw a mother give her son a necklace and tell him to wear it always so he would always remember her. Oh God, this is terrible. I haven't been trained for something like this."

Maribel hugged her friend. It was a night of very intense emotions, and it was far from over. They had to keep going. There were more children to save.

Lili went out to the barracks again with Maribel. The storm was still raging, and the air stank of wet dirt. They were soaked within seconds, but the women paid no heed to the pounding drops. There were signatures to get, and the clock was ticking. Just as they entered a barrack, the camp lost electricity. The thick cover of darkness was broken only by flashes of lightning. The roaring thunder made the glass windows rattle.

Lili and Maribel went farther inside the pitch-black barrack. The phantasmal faces of the mothers studied them from the dim light of a candle someone lit. Most women were clinging to their children, fearful that the social workers would take them by force.

"We're almost out of time, so we're begging you all to listen to us. What I'm going to tell you is very difficult. If you take your children with you, you're taking them to certain death. If you sign the release papers, you'll save their lives."

Lili's desperate plea had the desired effect. Several women came up to them.

One mother held her son's hand out to Lili and said, "Please, save him. May he at least survive. I've heard what happens in those camps in Germany and Poland."

The child looked at his mother with a serious, aged expression, but he did not cry. Lili handed the woman the release form, and she filled it out quickly and signed.

Another mother refused to let her son go. Georges Garel went up to her, knelt, and gently urged, "Please, give him a chance to live."

The woman opened her arms and allowed her son to walk away. But she wept and writhed in uncontrollable grief as he left the barrack with a worker.

Anna, an older girl, put her hand in front of her younger brother's eyes so he would not see the suffering. She herself filled out the paperwork, since her mother was too indecisive, and pointed for exactly where her mother should sign. Maribel felt sick watching the daughter's caring efficiency.

The mother looked to Father Glasberg and said in Yiddish, "They're what I love most in this world."

"We'll take care of them," he replied, lifting the lightweight suitcases of the children.

Jules and Anna waved goodbye to their mother, who fought back her tears. Anna was seventeen, but she looked much younger. It was a bitter day for Jules especially. It was his birthday.

Lili approached another mother who had decided to sign. Her daughter, Mela, was closing her small traveling case. Before her mother hugged her for the last time, she knelt and put her own earrings on Mela's ears.

"Don't forget me. I'll always be with you, like these earrings."

The child had a confused look on her face but dutifully nodded.

When the last of the children who had been entrusted to Glasberg's workers left the barrack, the cries of desperation and pain from the mothers soared to heaven. The sound grew to a roar louder than the thunder. Several women fainted as they watched their children walk away into the night—their little ones, the ones for whom they had given everything. Outside, the storm continued. The dark August night was the stark opposite of the bright morning that the next day would bring. For the moment, the moon hid behind the skies, weeping for all the broken families and abandoned children.

Chapter 35

MUSIC AND LOVE

Vénissieux Camp
AUGUST 28, 1942

ZELMAN BERKOWICZ HAD SIGNED away his parental rights over Rachel a few hours before. It was the hardest decision of his life. He had always tried to do what was right, though he was all too aware of his countless failures. Father Glasberg had explained the situation clearly, and Zelman immediately understood. Zelman had learned long before that being a parent meant suffering and worry, though Rachel's smile more than compensated for all the sleepless nights. The inability to protect her made him feel so weak and insignificant that he was tempted to follow the trend of many men around him and do away with his own life. But some ridiculous spark deep inside compelled him to keep fighting to survive, though Zelman was under no illusions about the futility of that fight. Beside him, Jankiel Raychmann's downcast head was shaking.

"I would never have dreamed we'd have to do something like this. My daughter, my precious Hélène . . . The world has gone mad," Jankiel said, his gaze boring a hole through the dirt below his feet.

Zelman shook his head as well but for a different reason. Genocidal tyrants like Adolf Hitler had always existed, but they only triumphed when an entire people became willing accomplices to their crimes.

"Don't forget what happened in Egypt, when Pharaoh decreed the murder of all male Israelite infants. God sent that genocidal dictator's daughter—his very daughter!—to take care of Moses, who went on to save our people from the darkness of Egypt and get them out of there."

"God? Curses upon him! He calls us his chosen people?! What kind of God would allow something like this to happen?"

Zelman did not argue with his friend. Jankiel, and every other Jew in Vénissieux, had every right to be infuriated. After a brief silence, Jankiel looked up at Zelman.

"So you think there's still hope?"

"If your children live, yes, there is."

The men bore their sadness by continuing to debate their misfortunes. Across the camp, Rachel stared sadly at Fani. Lili had come for her. While the girl packed her violin and suitcase, Fani took deep breaths to keep from wailing.

"Don't ever forget me," she said as she held Rachel in a tight embrace.

"No, never ever," the child answered. Her sweetness made Fani's task all the more bitter.

"Someday we'll see each other again. This isn't the end." Tears puddled in Fani's beautiful eyes, the eyes that had made Rachel's father fall in love but were only a pittance of beauty compared to her soul. "Play the violin and get all the sadness of your heart out by sharing your music with others."

The girl walked away hand in hand with Lili to the room that held nearly all the children from the camp. Lili was depleted. The clock was about to strike midnight. Like in a fairy tale, the magic that had helped them overcome all the barriers to saving the children would run out. Bitter hours awaited them, including the moment of the children's parents being driven away for good.

Rachel looked around at the children who were scared by the storm and the darkness. She settled down on top of her suitcase, pulled out her violin, and started playing. The cries and whining of the younger children succumbed to silence before the music. The notes filled the steaming mess hall, a lullaby for the little ones and a message of inexplicable peace to the older ones. For those moments, their hearts could rest within a refuge of ordered calm. They could almost touch the beauty hidden within the melody. It did not erase the pain but did make it bearable. Rachel's playing lit up a piece of heaven within the hell that a few greedy men had turned the world into.

Chapter 36

TEMPER

Lyon
AUGUST 29, 1942

KLAUS BARBIE STUMBLED OUT of the brothel and his assistant helped him into the car. It was three o'clock in the morning, and the storm had not let up. The electricity was out in part of the city, and the deserted streets were eerie. No other cars were out, and the water gushed like improvised rivers over the elegant sidewalks of Lyon. The city had its less-desirable section of working-class neighborhoods. It was home to the thousands of people whose lives were consumed by the country's luxury fashion industry. But in the Saint-Jean neighborhood, the historic city center that had once served as the capital of Gaul in the Roman era, the lavish streets and mansions put other European cities to shame.

In Lyon the SS captain enjoyed a level of luxury undreamed of in his hometown of Godesberg, or in Trier, where he had studied. His parents' income had never allowed the family to live large, and, like most everyone else in Germany, the crisis of 1929 had brought them to ruin. Joining the Hitler Youth was how he had survived. He knew he was smarter than most of his militia mates and comrades at arms. Mediocrity was the leading tendency within the ranks of the SS. But that was of little import. What made a man superior was his race. In France he was no lower-middle-class fop. He was a god, feared and respected by all.

"Where to, sir?" the chauffeur asked.

Klaus debated a moment. The thought of sleep was tempting, but duty called.

"To the camp. I've got to make sure the damned French are doing their job."

"It's pouring out, sir."

The captain leaned forward, suddenly completely awake. "Since when have I asked for your opinion?"

The chauffeur nodded and turned the key. The rest of the journey passed in silence. Fifteen minutes later, they were at the camp gates. The guards recognized the vehicle and waved it through immediately. Parked in front of the administrative offices, Klaus could see buses on the other side of the street. Several policemen, sleepy and irritated at having to work the night shift, stood watch over the transports that would take the camp's internees away.

The German official paused in quiet for a few seconds in the back of his car. His head was spinning, and he needed coffee, but his mission was clear: get all those Jews sent off to Germany. He knew exactly what awaited them there. The orders of the now deceased SS chief, Reinhard Heydrich, remained. The Germans would solve the Jewish problem as quickly as possible. To the hordes of Polish Jews there were daily added thousands more from Russia and other eastern countries. Keeping them in ghettoes was not a viable option. Jews were like rats. They could outlast almost anything. So they had to be treated like the infectious animals that they were. There could be no mercy or compassion. Though the Nazis' victims at times could look like innocent women, children, and older people, in actuality they were a dangerous plague that corrupted entire nations.

Klaus stepped out into the raucous wind of the storm. Everything was dark except for the headlights of the buses and of his own car, lighting up the barrack in front of it. Klaus sloshed through the mud and up to the office of the camp director. According to custom, he entered without knocking.

Near the barrack, one of the social workers glimpsed the figure of the SS officer and ran to the mess hall to alert Father Glasberg. Just as they were so close to saving the children, everything could go wrong.

Chapter 37

FAREWELL

Vénissieux Camp
AUGUST 29, 1942

I T WAS AFTER FOUR o'clock in the morning, but no
one at Vénissieux had slept that night. The prisoners' nerves
were shot as they waited in the dark barracks for what they
knew was coming. Father Glasberg was beyond exhausted. He
had worked until the last possible moment to save as many
children as possible. The last count his coworkers provided
was 106 children. But he thought of all the others who were
not in the mess hall, especially the children under five years of
age. The babies and youngest children had to stay with their
mothers. He knew what that meant.

The buses were parked and waiting, the police weaving in and
around them restlessly like caged lions waiting to devour their
prey. And to top it all off, now there was a Nazi loose in the
camp. They had to think up a distraction and keep their plan
from being detected, at least until the children were away from
the camp.

The transports for the children were parked outside the camp in a discreet spot, but if the gendarmes or the Nazis spotted them, everything would come to naught. No one would be saved.

Glasberg returned to the mess hall and observed the scared, sweaty children packed in like sardines. The adults were doing their best to comfort and calm them. He wondered how in the world they would get them out quietly. It was nigh impossible for over one hundred children to remain calm and quiet at the same time even in the best of circumstances, much less in their current situation.

Lili, Maribel, and Élisabeth stood together in the doorway, sharing a cigarette to calm their nerves. They trembled when they noticed shadows moving just a bit away. It was the men and women being led by the gendarmes to the buses. The group progressed slowly and in order, with no fuss despite the rain. Perhaps they feared that any show of desperation would put their children at risk.

They were to be taken by bus not far away to the stop at Saint-Priest, where a train would then take them to Drancy and from there to Germany.

The three young women were speechless before the macabre spectacle.

Father Glasberg left the mess hall with papers in hand. He approached the buses intent on saving more, even one more person.

"Where are you going?" a gendarme corporal asked, extending his arm to stop Glasberg.

"Some of these people qualify for exemptions," the priest explained.

The policeman frowned. He did not want problems or a last-minute riot. The job should be simple enough: get these last five hundred people to the train and hand them off to French police and German custody.

"Please, go back. Don't make things harder than they already are."

The priest took a few steps back. The rain pouring down his face mixed with his tears. Some of those filing out of the barracks nodded in his direction, gratefully acknowledging his attempts to help.

The eerie calm of the scene was interrupted just then by shouts in front of one of the buses.

"No, I'm not going in there! I'm a war hero and should be exempted!"

The gendarmes wrangled with Erich Altmann and he managed to stun one of them with a punch. The police then beat him into submission and forced him onto the bus. Bleeding and bewildered, Erich dragged himself along the floor until Julius Stein helped him to his feet.

"Give it up now, friend. Sit here."

The first bus slowly filled with men and then headed for the camp gate. A few yards away another bus was waiting for the line of deportees to enter. Mothers crowded together in a stupor until the gendarmes ordered them to get on the bus. The first to enter were the women from Saint-Sauveur-de-Montagut. As soon as every seat was taken, the bus revved up. To turn around more easily, the driver steered toward the mess hall. The social workers tried to usher the children away from the windows, but at the sound of the motor, they jostled and jockeyed for positions against the glass. The eyes of mothers and children met, and loud lamentation erupted. The yards of dark rain that separated them were an entire abyss of pain and desperation. The mothers knew that this was their last glimpse of their children. They held one another and wailed uncontrollably on the bus.

Lili and the rest of the workers tried to back the children away from the windows, but the situation was uncontainable. The boys and girls were beating the glass and screaming for their parents. Only the older ones looked toward the buses with calm resignation. They were regretting all the stupid arguments over things that were now pointless, all the harshly quipped words, all the time they had not spent with their mothers. Fate was stealing their mothers' company away, and their anguish came out as stony silence.

When the bus had completed its turn and driven away, Georges entered the mess hall with two more children. One was balanced on his hip; the other held his hand. Oscar and Manfred Furst were the last two children to join the group. They were calm until they saw all the other children crying and calling for their mothers. They joined the chorus.

Looking around as the buses of adults continued to file out of the camp, Georges wondered if they had done the right thing. Those young ones would be marked for life. They would never forget that sad, stormy August night.

Chapter 38

DANGER

Vénissieux Camp
AUGUST 29, 1942

K LAUS BARBIE STARED THE camp director down.
They had both watched the buses drive away, but the
German was perplexed.

"Five hundred people? That's all? Where are the rest?"

"Well, some were already sent, and like I said, we had to free
some of them because of exemptions."

"I'm commanding you to go get them back and deport them
once and for all!" Klaus roared into Cussonac's cowering face.

"It's not up to me. My superiors have to remove their immunity.
I'd lock them all up if I could—you know what I think of the Jews."

Despite the coffee he had just drunk, Klaus felt dizzy. A pounding
headache distracted him from his typical clarity of thought.

"Well then, you'd better get them on the phone. Wake up whoever
you have to. If not, those Jews will slip away and scatter, and it'll be
much harder to track them down."

Cussonac picked up the phone and held the receiver in his hand a moment while he took a deep breath. Then he started dialing the intendant's number, knowing how Marchais hated to be disturbed off-hours.

Klaus stood and looked out the window. Then he turned and glared again at Cussonac, who was wiping his sweating forehead.

"Why aren't there children on those buses?"

Cussonac put the receiver down without placing his call. He loosened his tie. "Children? What do you mean?"

"I saw a few babies, but where are the rest of the children?"

"As I reported earlier, there have been a series of exemptions."

Klaus settled his hat on his head without breaking his cold stare into Cussonac's eyes. "Where are the children? I won't ask you again."

Cussonac shrugged. He was paralyzed by fear and nerves.

Klaus pulled out his pistol and pointed it at Cussonac. "You'll take me to where they are right now, understood?"

Cussonac raised his hands and nodded. He gingerly scooted out from behind his desk and cautiously walked to the door. He knew that if he did not give Klaus what he wanted, he was a dead man. No one would hold the captain accountable for Cussonac's life, so it was better to obey than to die in that human garbage dump. Cussonac was willing to do what he had to in order to get out alive.

For his part, in his fury Klaus was capable of doing whatever he had to in order to satisfy his superiors. With his gun trained on the camp director, he wondered when he could go home. At his core, the whole war effort left him with a gaping emptiness inside. The more efficiently he did his job and hardened his heart, the harder it was to continue to feel nothing. Alcohol and sex partially took away the sting of deep loneliness, but he missed his wife and children. War was harsh, as he knew from his time on the Russian front, but at least his position was secure, not to mention privileged. The longer he stayed away from actual fighting, the greater his chance of survival and reaching his dreams in the Third Reich. Klaus hoped the Führer's thousand-year promise held.

Chapter 39

ESCAPE

Vénissieux Camp
AUGUST 29, 1942

T HE SKY WAS STILL dark. The light attempting to peak over the horizon was halted by the dense clouds that refused to disperse. Most of the gendarmes had gone with the buses of prisoners, but a few were still stationed at the gate and in the offices. The plan was to take the children to a large hall that the Jewish Scouts had outfitted for them in the Carmelite convent of Lyon. From there, they would be dispersed to safer places. Since the hall was frequently used by the scouts, the adult workers hoped that a large gathering of children would not raise any suspicions.

Father Glasberg and Gilbert Lesage called all the volunteers together to lay out the plan. Though they had already explained some of the details, the tension of the moment had them all on edge, and Glasberg wanted to make sure everyone knew exactly what to do. The faces of Lili, Madeleine, Hélène, Élisabeth, Maribel, and Jean-Marie were gaunt with anxiety and sleepless nights. Outside the camp gates

Claude Gutmann would be waiting for them. He was the head of the Jewish Scouts in Lyon. Glasberg emphasized that for things to go well, the children had to file out in order and in complete silence. Any whine or cry could ruin the entire plan.

David Donoff was behind the wheel of one of the other buses. The two huge vehicles were waiting with their motors running.

Father Glasberg and Gilbert Lesage hoped that the gendarmes would not find the sight of two more buses odd but would interpret them as merely the continuation of the transfer of the prisoners. They placed all their bets on this one card and trusted for fortune to smile on them.

The group of workers had acquired releases and permissions from the parents, but they did not actually have permission to remove the children from the camp. Their only chance was to act in front of the guards as if they did.

Father Glasberg saw that it was time. He started giving orders.

"It's time to head out. The few guards that are still here are nodding off now at the end of their unexpected night shift."

The social workers could not manage all the children on their own, so they had equipped some of the older children as leaders for the younger ones. Hélène Fixler and Anna Szrajbe were among the adolescent leaders.

"You two take care of this group. Follow closely when my group leaves, and keep the children from making any noise, even a peep," Élisabeth told the girls. Her coworkers gave the same instructions to the other teenage helpers.

The women got the children lined up in order. Older children carried the youngest ones. There was collective calm after the exhausting night of intense emotions.

Father Glasberg opened the door and the first workers filed out at the head of their lines of children, nervous but determined. At the gate, they all stopped. Father Glasberg and Jean-Marie Soutou went up to the solitary guard who came out to meet them at the checkpoint.

"The children are being transferred now. They're the last of the prisoners."

The policeman looked at the well-ordered lines. There was nothing suspicious. The camp was to be evacuated that night. Though no one had told the guards that the children would be the last to go, there was nothing necessarily odd about it.

"And the transports?"

"They're out front. Turning around inside the grounds is difficult," Jean-Marie explained.

"All in order. Go along."

→>-<←

In the Citroën, Jean-Marie, Georges, and Father Glasberg drove out of the camp slowly, eschewing any indication of hurry. They followed the perfect lines of the small army of children. When they reached the buses, the women divided the children up as Father Glasberg prayed for everything to go smoothly.

Lili and Élisabeth sat in the first bus with Esther Fixler and Rachel Berkowicz. Hélène and Maribel were settling children into the second bus, and Lotte and Joseph oversaw the third.

The first bus started moving, much too slowly for the nerves of Georges and his companions in the black car. They wanted the children away from camp as soon as possible. Daylight was coming ever so slowly as the convoy headed into Lyon with the hope of hiding the children and saving them from a terrible end.

As the Citroën drove away, absolute silence reigned in the Vénissieux camp. The abandoned barracks now held only the few items and cases left behind by the prisoners who had taken their own lives.

Though the long, difficult night was coming to a close, the children were far from safe. The dangerous plan was about to enter its most dangerous phase: in the middle of a large city, over one hundred children would be sent into hiding within different families.

As the citizens of Lyon awoke from the stormy night and the heat descended once more upon the flooded streets, three buses and a black car parked inside the grounds of a Carmelite convent. The various stages of the complex plan were unfolding one by one. But there was someone not far behind who intended to put it all to a stop.

Chapter 40

HIDING PLACE

Vénissieux Camp
AUGUST 29, 1942

K LAUS BARBIE LEFT THE camp director's office with his pistol in hand. Cussonac had said that he thought the children were being kept in the mess hall, though he was not entirely sure. Klaus's assistant followed with his pistol raised as well. They opened the doors of the mess hall and were greeted by a gust of foul heat. There were toys and drawings on the floor but not a child in sight.

"Where the hell are they?" Klaus growled in anger. "One hundred children can't disappear all at once!"

Klaus then checked all the barracks, but the camp was deserted.

The two Nazis walked through the sticky mud to the front gate. A gendarme snapped out of his stupor and saluted when he heard their footsteps.

"Where are the children?"

The policeman tried to make out the Gestapo officer's French.

"Where are the children?" Klaus barked again, this time picking the man up by his jacket flaps.

"W-well, the children have gone like the rest of them," the gendarme stammered.

"Why did you let them leave?"

"It's evacuation day. All the prisoners had to leave."

Klaus threw the man against the guardhouse and screamed in his face as he hit the ground, "You damned, inept traitors!"

Then the German stormed back to his car with great strides. The imprecations did not cease until they had driven away from the camp. Now he had a new mission. One hundred children could not be easily hidden. They must have been taken somewhere in Lyon to then be dispersed around the area. He would find them and send them all to Germany, and then he would take care of everyone who had made their escape possible. He would not rest until the last collaborator was behind bars and then swinging from the gallows as a nice example for their compatriots.

Chapter 41

A MISSION

Lyon
MARCH 13, 1994

S INCE MAKING THE DECISION to write her thesis on what had happened to the 108 children rescued from the Vénissieux camp, Valérie Portheret had developed a new habit: sharing her research progress every month with René Nodot over coffee.

"Two years ago when you found that box of files, how many families were you able to identify?" René asked as Valérie watched the wind whipping the rain against the café window.

"At first I thought it was more, but it turned out to be only thirty-three. So there are still a lot more to find."

"Wouldn't the diocese of Lyon have files in their archives? The Catholic Church is known for holding on to things."

"You're right about that. Pierre Gerlier was a very orderly man, but they haven't granted me access to their files. I think that some members of the church hierarchy feel the same way as most of society; they'd like to turn the page and move on.

Klaus Barbie's trial a few years back coughed up all sorts of controversy."

René sipped his coffee, which was still too hot. He recalled the taste of chicory root from his younger years when coffee ran scarce and then ran out. Real black coffee still tasted like glory to him.

"Klaus Barbie," René mused. "Did you know that I met him in 1942? He'd been sent to Lyon to hunt out clandestine radios, but what he liked most was hunting people. He was obsessed with finding the children. For days it was all he did. He couldn't believe that a hundred children had been rescued right under his nose."

Valérie smiled. That must have been a memorable defeat for the man, she mused while biting into the pastry the waitress had brought with her coffee. Then she winced and said, "It's not for nothing that they called him the Butcher of Lyon."

René nodded. "He'd been sent to Dijon but then was named head of the Gestapo in Lyon. Not far from here, just a few blocks, is where their headquarters were. It still gives me chills to think about."

Valérie studied René. It was still hard for her to grasp that people like him had lived through the events she was writing about. World War II was so near and so far away at the same time.

"He more than deserved to end his days in jail," she said.

"Well, human justice is always debatable. After all that he did in the Netherlands and in France, torturing his victims with his own hands, he was in a comfortable cell in Lyon, practically a hotel. This was a man who was responsible for the death of some four thousand people. He even imprisoned the legendary Resistance fighter Jean Pierre Moulin. Perhaps his most heinous crime was capturing the forty-four children of the Izieu children's home and seeing to their death."

Valérie set her mug aside. She had something important to tell René.

"You know that I've been trying to trace the children."

René nodded.

"Well"—she cleared her throat—"I've decided to try to find each one of them." René cocked his head at her, unsure of exactly what she meant. "I mean to actually search for them wherever they are in the world and, when I find them, give them back their real names, their lost identities."

René took her hand. Her statement had shaken his customarily passive expression. "Tracking down those children will be a titanic mission," he warned.

"I know. But I believe that we're all here on earth for a reason, for a purpose, and mine is to find those children. They come to me in nightmares about August 28, 1942. It's like their little faces are begging me to find them. Their parents sacrificed everything for them, and they don't even know who they used to be."

"God help you; it's a magnificent project. You know you can count on me for all the help you need."

"Thank you," Valérie said, resting her hand on her belly.

"Ah." René cocked his head again. "And I see that you no longer smoke."

Valérie smiled.

"So you're expecting?"

Valérie's smile widened and her eyes shone. "I imagine what that night must have been like for the mothers and fathers of Vénissieux and . . . Mercy, this child hasn't even been born and I'd already give my life for them."

Her words floated in the air, the same air breathed fifty-two years before by the families of the Vénissieux camp.

Chapter 42

MONTÉE DES CARMÉLITES

Lyon
AUGUST 29, 1942

THEY ARRIVED AT THE convent at six in the morning, when the soaked streets of Lyon were still empty and the sun impatiently tried to reinsert itself over the previous day's storm. It would be another scorching day. The clouds had dissipated and the wind blew up from the south again, making the buses uncomfortably hot. Before the children in the first bus were allowed to get off, Lili stood and spoke to the rest of the adult workers and teenage helpers.

"We've got to get out in complete silence again. The less attention we draw to ourselves, the better. This neighborhood is used to seeing children coming in and out of these grounds, but not usually at this hour of the day."

Most of the young children were asleep. The older ones were nearly catatonic after the night of strong emotions and no rest. They stared blankly with resignation about whatever lay ahead.

The first volunteers got down from the bus with the youngest children and quickly crossed the short distance to the side door. There the shade of plane trees hid them from the curiosity of any onlookers. As the children began entering the convent, Lili glanced around for the car where Georges still sat, and her eyes met his. She could not deny that over the past few days, as they planned out that harebrained rescue operation, she had begun to feel something for the man. She did not know if it was love or just the capricious result of the extreme adventure they were living. Working for the Resistance and facing constant life-and-death danger was certainly stressful. At the same time, it kept Lili in a state of perpetually heightened emotions.

The motor of the Citroën revved up. Father Glasberg wanted to alert his superior, Cardinal Gerlier, right away of their progress. Lili watched the car drive away and felt the pang of separation. Every time Georges went away from her, she wondered if she would ever see him again.

The children walked through the convent yard in silence as the Carmelite brothers lit the way with lanterns and led them to a large, unused room. The number of monks was greatly reduced from the convent's early days, and several sections of the grounds and buildings were permanently closed off. The hall to which the monks led the children was spacious enough to hold them all. It would not be needed long. The plan was, within twenty-four hours, to place the children in safe homes. The workers knew that it would not take the Nazis and the gendarmes long to track them to the convent. They were also sure that, if that occurred, the children would be captured again and sent by train to Germany right away, even if such action meant sidestepping the laws of the Third Republic and of morality.

The Jewish Scouts had spread hay on the ground to soften the surface so the children could rest. As the boys and girls settled into the straw, Joseph Weill went to an adjacent room and studied his notebook with the list of the children's names and the families that would come to retrieve them. Placing the children was tedious work. First, it was not easy to locate enough families willing to risk their lives for the sake of strangers. Second, in some cases the families would have to take in several children together so as not to separate brothers and sisters from one another. The rest of the children would be dispersed to the various camps and homes run by Jews in different châteaus in the regions surrounding Lyon.

The older children had been so helpful in taking care of the younger ones during the most sensitive moments of the escape. Lili suggested that they be the first to shower. A little water would help revive them. Then they could go to a nearby room for breakfast. The friars had prepared a simple meal of toast, cheese, and milk.

As Lili oversaw the older children, Élisabeth focused on the younger ones. They were starting to wake up. Many of them, bewildered and scared, called for their mothers and recommenced their crying. Élisabeth knew that as soon as their basic needs for rest, food, and cleanliness were met, they would be calmer.

Several volunteers helped Élisabeth get the younger children bathed. It had been several days since they had been able to tend to the most basic hygiene. The workers gently scrubbed off all the grime accumulated at Vénissieux, then dressed the boys and girls in clean clothes and took the children to the improvised dining hall. After many days of extremely meager rations, the children clapped excitedly to see the white bread and fresh milk. They scarfed down all that they were offered.

The first families were scheduled to arrive at nine thirty in the morning. The workers knew the day would be as long and arduous as the previous few had been, though with different risk factors. Everything had to be done with haste and order and, above all, without raising the suspicions of the neighbors or any authorities.

Lili had prepared a program of activities for when the children awoke. They would pass the long wait better if they were pleasantly distracted, and this way the workers could perhaps keep the crying to a minimum. The convent walls were thick, but a child's wail had a way of traveling. Lili had hung long curtains along one side of the hall. Youth actors from the troupe Jeune France came to demonstrate local dances and lead the children in songs and games.

Meanwhile, Madeleine called together the older teenagers. Very few families had been able to accept an older adolescent, so most of the teens would go to a Jewish Scouts camp in Haute-Loire until they could be placed in a long-term home.

"Here are the scout uniforms to put on. This way people won't suspect you," she told them.

The adolescents eyed the uniforms warily. They looked like military wear, and these children had been running from such uniformed people for years. But they finally accepted the clothing, and the girls went behind one curtain and the boys another to change.

One of the girls who had helped the volunteers the most held the uniform at an awkward angle and did not move toward the curtains. Lili went up to her.

"You all right, Lotte?"

"Yes, but I don't want to go to the scouts' camp. My father told me to try to get back together with my brothers and sisters. They're here in Lyon. I know the address."

"Are you sure that's what you prefer? It's dangerous to be out on the streets. I know that the gendarmes are looking all over for us."

Lotte Levy gave the social worker a confident smile. "I want to see my family. I'd rather be captured again than go any farther away from them. I have a feeling that if I leave Lyon, I'll never see them again."

Lili hugged the young woman. Despite her surety, Lotte cried softly onto Lili's shoulder.

"Do you have any money?" Lili asked.

The girl wiped her tears and nose and shook her head.

Lili handed her what she would need for the trolley and said, "One of our workers will go with you to the stop and see you on your way to Villeurbanne."

"They don't have to do that."

"It's safer that way. You'll look less suspicious if there's an adult with you."

Lotte said goodbye to the social workers and looked one last time at the children. They were still in danger, but at least they were not on the trains, headed for death like their parents.

Lotte left with one of the volunteers. They went down the stairs of the hill where the convent sat and reached the plaza where the trolley passed. The worker kissed Lotte on the forehead and waved her off. Lotte watched the streets of Lyon from the trolley window. They were starting to bustle with people. Twice she felt herself nodding off but forced herself to stay alert.

In Villeurbanne, she looked all around but was unsure in which direction the house lay. She felt lost and wanted to cry. Then she heard something she never would have expected.

"Lotte!"

It was a familiar voice: her older brother! He swooped her up in a hug and wept with her. With his hand in hers, he led her back to the home of the family that was housing the Levy siblings.

"Do you know what's become of Mom and Dad?" he asked cautiously.

Lotte looked at him steadily. He had grown in the weeks they had been separated. He was so thin, and his white skin contrasted starkly with his black hair and dark brown eyes.

She wanted him to know the truth, though it would have been easier to lie.

"They . . . they were sent to Germany." Her voice was barely audible.

"Will they come back?"

Lotte was quiet as she gathered her thoughts. Then she shrugged and said, "I don't know, but we're not going to give up hope. We've been in danger other times, and we've somehow survived up to now. The important thing is that we're back together again."

The siblings made their way up the avenue, then turned down a narrow side street. The blue sky was peeking out between the old, soot-covered buildings. That place was no paradise, but it would allow them to hold out a bit longer. Freedom might lie just around the corner, or perhaps it was out of reach forever. Both children had learned by then that the only way to bear up under the uncertainty and fear was to simply live one moment at a time, aware that it might be the last.

Chapter 43

EPISCOPAL PALACE

Lyon
AUGUST 29, 1942

CARDINAL GERLIER HAD BEEN awake for hours when the members of the rescue commission arrived to give him their report, though his rest the night before had been so fitful that it could hardly have been called sleep. He had spent the hours praying for the children and their caretakers, begging God to bring the dangerous undertaking to a successful end.

Father Glasberg led the group, taking the stairs to the main floor at a run. When he saw the archbishop and cardinal of Lyon, he bowed and kissed his ring. Gerlier was not hung up on protocol, but he allowed the ceremony. He had spent years advocating for the working class in Lyon. Many colleagues considered him too liberal for church work.

"Tell me what happened. I'm burning to know," the prelate said as he sat and invited his visitors to do the same.

"The majority of the children who were being held at Vénissieux are now safe," Glasberg said.

Gerlier did not hide his relief and joy. "Oh, God be praised!"

"They're in the convent waiting on families to come pick them up. But this part of the operation is as delicate as the previous. It might take us over twenty-four hours to get all the children placed. We don't know what the prefect's next move will be, or the intendant's, or the prime minister's, though we know they don't want to upset the Nazis."

"Father Glasberg, it's unthinkable that these good French servants have put a political matter above the well-being of innocent children. This war is bringing out the worst in too many people, though clearly not everyone." He nodded to the men before him. "The Holy Father has asked us to make every effort to save innocent life, though without risking the freedom of the church. The Nazis and the Fascists have us directly in their sights."

Jean-Marie, Glasberg, and Georges listened attentively to Gerlier's words. He saw the exhaustion etched on their faces and called for his assistant.

"Some coffee for these men, please."

"Thank you, Your Grace," Georges said with a sigh. He could barely remain upright.

Glasberg returned to the subject at hand. "We might need a convent to hide the older children in. We don't have families for all of them yet."

Gerlier spread his hands wide. "The Diocese of Lyon is at the complete disposal of these children."

The assistant returned with a tray loaded with coffee and pastries. Until that moment, the commission workers had not allowed themselves to feel how hungry and tired they were. Even so, it was still too early to rest or let down their guard.

"There's something else I'd like to ask of you . . ." Gilbert Lesage began.

Everyone turned toward the Protestant. He had been one of the first to mobilize volunteers in Lyon around the Vénissieux crisis. Cardinal Gerlier, known for his ecumenical spirit and for his support of Amitié Chrétienne, leaned forward.

"Do proceed, my friend."

"You've mentioned writing a pastoral letter to the churches in this diocese. If you were to do that now, in defense of the Jewish children, I believe that would make a real difference. The Vichy authorities don't want a disgruntled population, so if this whole situation came to light, their hands would be tied in going after the children."

The cardinal stroked his chin before answering.

"You realize what you're asking me to do?"

"The archbishop of Toulouse has already spoken out against the persecution of the Jews," Father Glasberg offered.

"I would hate to lose my privileged relationship with our president, which has allowed me to free no small number of people from prison and worse."

"Your Excellency, your work to help France's true patriots is invaluable. But if we don't do something, the Nazis will look for the children. And they always seem to find what they're looking for," Gilbert said.

The cardinal sipped his coffee. He was a man just like any other man. He knew what had happened to the bishops who openly opposed the Nazis in Germany and Poland. His respected visitors were kindly requesting that he commit political suicide and risk being replaced by a prelate in the pockets of the current political leaders.

"You're asking me to take a leap of faith. Sending a pastoral letter throughout the parishes will be taken by the government and by the Nazis as an act of war. I'll be raising the church up against the Vichy regime."

"We can't sit here with our arms crossed while the Nazis murder thousands of innocent people. What you would do isn't an act of war—it's an act of justice," Father Glasberg offered. The cardinal coming out with a public statement was crucial in his eyes.

Gerlier stood and walked to the lectern where an open Bible rested. His eyes passed over the words for a few moments before he turned back to his guests.

"I'll write a letter focused on the children. That way they can't accuse me of meddling with internal government affairs. They are the ones infringing upon our laws by deporting the innocent."

Father Glasberg, Gilbert, and Georges also got to their feet, relieved. A letter from Gerlier could halt the government's attempts to find the children, though the Nazi reaction would still be fearsome.

"Thank you, Your Eminence," they said.

Once he was alone again, the cardinal returned to his rooms and recommenced his prayers. Sweat was pouring down his neck. He was a human being with all the same fears and desires as other mortals. He knew his life would be on the line.

Back on the street, the men split up. Father Glasberg and Georges returned to the convent in the black Citroën while Gilbert returned to his office. From there he could monitor the movements of the authorities and the Nazis. They began the long wait to see if all the families would stay true to their word and come to take the children to safety.

Chapter 44

LOVE

Lyon
AUGUST 29, 1942

SYLVAIN LÉVY WAS THE first parent to come collect the child he had been assigned. Many of the volunteers helping in the rescue operation were French Jews. They understood better than anyone the discrimination that their foreign brothers and sisters were facing. The man, with his smiling face and rosy cheeks, was joined by his oldest daughter, who had brought a doll. They understood what a difficult position the refugee children were in and hoped that a simple toy could help ease the family's future adopted daughter.

Lili welcomed the Lévys into the convent. Sylvain was well known among Jewish aid organizations. He had been bringing food and other basic supplies to foreign refugees for quite some time.

"Mr. Lévy, thank you for being so prompt," Lili said.

"Of course. I can only imagine what this poor girl has gone through, and I didn't want to drag out her anguish any longer.

The sooner she finds a home to rest in and get back something of normalcy, the better for her."

→>-<←

Élisabeth found Eva Stein and took her hand. The child followed her with her head down. Dark rings circled her eyes that were red from crying. She wanted to ask Élisabeth for news of her father—had he been on that bus the day before?—but she did not have the courage to open her mouth.

Sylvain's daughter knelt and handed Eva the doll with a smile. Eva hesitated and looked to Élisabeth.

"It's all right—it's for you."

Eva took the doll from the older girl's hands and gently held it to her chest. Sylvain's daughter also handed her a lollipop, which finally elicited a smile.

"We want you to come home with us," the daughter said. "We've got loads of toys, and you can play with all my brothers and sisters. You'll have a really good time."

Eva's mouth puckered as if she would cry. The older girl stroked her cheek and gave her a hug. Eva let herself be held, and she wept softly. The others swallowed back their own tears.

"Thank you for everything," Lili told the Lévys.

"No, thank you and all of you workers. You've saved all these children," Sylvain said, his voice cracking as he waved toward the mass of children playing and imitating the dances of the youth actors helping them endure the long wait.

Joseph Weill double-checked his list and confirmed that all was in order. He was supervising the handoff of the children to the families. The plan was to keep sibling groups together and to prioritize placing the children in homes with families rather than religious institutions whenever possible. Furthermore, the adults responsible for the children were to respect the Jewish customs and beliefs of their charges.

Lili and Élisabeth said goodbye with a twinge of grief. Up to then they had viewed the moment of family placements as an enormous relief, a sign that the plan to rescue the children was working. But what they felt was a sense of loss. The children would be much better off with their new families; even so, the social workers were sad to see them go.

→>-<←

Horst Finder, one of the oldest adolescents, left the convent with the intention of locating his mother, who had been in the hospital when he was detained and taken to Vénissieux. Lili had helped falsify his age so the gendarmes did not send him to the bus with the other adults, but now he needed to find his family. Lili gave him directions for how to reach his mother's current hiding place, but the young man was so sleepy and disoriented that he could not remember what he was supposed to do after turning a few corners.

He walked aimlessly for a while until he saw a group of German soldiers. They eyed him and started walking toward him. Keenly aware of the danger he was in, Horst crossed the street. A priest buying a newspaper from a stand looked up and saw what was going on. As if speaking to the newspaper salesman, the priest said, "Don't say anything, but follow me, just not too close."

Horst walked after the priest under the Nazis' gaze. His heart was pounding in his chest and several times he thought his legs would give out. He forced himself not to look at the soldiers and to keep the priest in sight.

The clergyman stopped in front of a van and whispered, "When you hear the motor, hop in quick."

The priest disappeared into the van and a moment later the engine roared to life. Horst opened the door, slipped in, and sank down low as he closed the door after him.

"I'm Father Orbillot. I'm going to take you to Sainte-Foy-lés-Lyon, where there's a community of Marist Brothers who will look after you."

"But I've got to find my mother. This is the address." Horst held out the piece of paper Lili had given him.

"I can't take you there; it's too dangerous. Stay with the brothers for a few days, and then they'll help you get to her."

Horst began to cry. He knew the man had saved his life, but he was afraid it meant he would never see his mother again.

→>-<←

As the stranger helped Horst escape, Joseph Weill made sure the adoptive families left with the right children. When he saw that Georges had returned from visiting the cardinal, he suggested they sit together over a cup of coffee.

"I have something to ask you," Joseph said. "We need an OSE coordinator who will deliver the children to the families that can't come for them. It's a risky job."

The young man smiled. He had been with the Resistance for some time and had already decided that he would do whatever was needed, even if it cost his life.

"I'd love to do it."

➤➤◄◄

While the two men talked, Lili distributed among the children pieces of cake made with great love and affection by the mothers of the scouts. It was their way of helping out.

When she saw that Joseph had gone back to reviewing his lists, Lili went up to Georges. "Hey, how are you doing?"

"Oh, like the rest of us—foggy-headed with a frenetic sense of vertigo. I think this is the closest I've felt to a hangover my entire life."

Lili laughed. It was not their lot to be carefree, relaxed young people who poured themselves into studying, falling in love, and whiling away their days unconcerned. Now, every movement they made and every step they took was marked by the desire to see things change.

"It's already so hot in here, and it's only noon," she said with a sigh.

"It's because we're all in this one room. Children are like little ovens cranked up to high."

Lili leaned over to Georges and kissed his cheek. He looked at her in surprise.

"I don't know what tomorrow will bring," she said by way of explanation, "but I want to tell you that I love you. The moment I first saw you, my legs went weak. When all of this is over, I'd like to go out with you."

Smiling, Georges touched the spot on his cheek where her lips had brushed against him.

"Holy smokes! Nothing like this has ever happened to me!" He grabbed her hand, cocked an eyebrow, and led her to a discreet corner where he could kiss her properly. As the couple snuggled into each other, more than half the children continued waiting for their adoptive parents. Time kept passing, and the danger increased. A Nazi official was after them, willing to do anything and everything to get those children and their caretakers shipped off to Germany.

Chapter 45

HOURS OF ANGUISH

Lyon
AUGUST 29, 1942

THE HEAT INTENSIFIED AS the day went on. The children were sweaty and irritable because of the lice and bedbugs they played helpless host to. The damp straw stuck to their young bodies. As the majority of the adoptive families took their children away, the feeling of abandonment grew in those left behind. The adults sensed that any children left at the convent by evening would fall prey to complete desolation.

Jean-Marie asked Maribel to get the Fixler girls ready while he escorted Denise Paluch to number 10 rue Lanterne where they were to meet a pastor's wife named Mrs. Roland. From there, Mrs. Roland would take Denise to their home in Montée de la Boucle. The girl and the young man left the convent cautiously. The asphyxiating heat at least had the effect of clearing the streets. They walked for some time before reaching rue Lanterne. Just as they were turning, they spied a gendarme marching toward them.

Jean-Marie tensed up. He noticed a new pain in his neck but tried to chat casually with Denise as if he were a young father.

"Where are you headed in this heat?" the gendarme asked, not unkindly.

"We live just down the road, Officer. It's not the kind of day for a long stroll."

The gendarme looked up as if to confirm that the sun was to blame and then studied the girl.

"What's your name, sweetie?"

"Alice," Jean-Marie was quick to answer.

"Alice? What a nice name."

The policeman dug around in his pocket for something, and Jean-Marie thought that his luck had run out.

"Here, Alice," the officer said, pulling out a lollipop.

"What do you say, honey?" Jean-Marie asked, nodding his permission for her to take it.

"Thank you, sir."

The gendarme walked away smiling. They let out a sigh and continued down rue Lanterne. They knocked at a door on the third floor, which was opened immediately by a smiling woman with light eyes.

"You must be Denise Paluch," she said quietly when they were inside.

The child smiled back at the woman.

"Well, Denise, we're going to take a little trip, and I'm sure you'll love our house and get along famously with my children."

She took Denise's hand and nodded to Jean-Marie.

Jean-Marie wrestled with the emotion on his face and said, "Thank you for all that you and your family are doing. May God pay you back richly." He waved goodbye to Denise.

Leading Denise to the stairs they had just come up, Mrs. Roland called back, "Thank you to you and your coworkers for giving these children a chance at life."

→►◄◄

The Iehle family came for the Fixler sisters. Mr. Iehle ran the Lumière factories and on the side was a very active member of the Resistance. The couple lived in the nearby neighborhood of Feyzin but had come in their own car. The factories still had gasoline, and, unlike the majority of the population, Mr. Iehle could make use of his car with no difficulty. The Nazis were sequestering more and more of the country's natural resources, which meant that the restrictions and scarcity of war fell ever heavier on the population, though for their own convenience the Nazis tried to keep the people as pacified as possible.

The sad looks on the girls' faces made Mrs. Iehle momentarily hold back the hug she had intended to give them. But she shook off her hesitation and embraced them all at once before leading them out of the convent and quickly into the car.

Waiting nearby in the wings, Mela Bäcker fiddled incessantly with the earrings her mother had given her. Lili had told her that her adoptive family was coming next.

"Look, Mela, this is Mr. Henri Schilli. He's a friend of Sylvain Goldschmidt, the father in the new home where you'll be staying."

"The rabbi was so sorry he couldn't come personally, but we're overrun in the synagogue right now. We're doing everything we can to hide as many of our brothers and sisters as possible. Besides the children, as you know too well, a few other categories have been exempted from deportation, but we fear that the authorities will use any excuse to detain them again. So we're getting them into hiding in different places."

"Don't worry; we understand completely. We know that Mela will be in good hands."

Mr. Schilli looked around at the thirty-plus children still waiting to be picked up.

"Do the rest of these kids have a place to go?" he asked.

"Most of them, yes. People have been very generous."

Lili noticed how his Adam's apple trembled. "It's hard to believe that anyone would want to harm these innocent children. Their crime? Being born into a Jewish family? What kind of world are we living in?"

Lili looked at the children as well. They were tired and sweaty, and some trembled with fever. She had no words for the man's questions. Like him, she could not fathom the hatred of the Nazis and many of her compatriots toward others simply due to different religious practices. The human heart, so full of fear, was a mystery to her—capable of committing the vilest crimes against truth and humanity while claiming to do good.

→>-<←

Hélène Lévy escorted Mina Grobel to an area of Lyon that brought back many memories for the girl. It was Félix Jeantet's street in the Saint-Cloud neighborhood. Mina's father had worked as a diamond merchant with Mr. Jeantet. Mr. Grobel's family had been in the jewelry business for generations, and for him, it was the only way to make a living in a foreign country.

Hélène took Mina to the exact building where her father's shop had been. Above the shop lived the Schiari family. They knocked at the door and waited.

"Good afternoon. I've brought Mina Grobel to you," Hélène said when the door opened. The woman who looked out had a harsh face.

"I thought she was younger," was all the woman said.

"Don't worry. Mina is very well behaved and will be of great help to you in whatever you need."

"How old is she?"

Mina answered the question directly. "I'm twelve."

"Oh, well, all right. Come on in."

Mrs. Schiari stepped aside and Mina started up the stairs. She turned to wave goodbye to Hélène. Her eyes held such pain and fear that Hélène was tempted to take Mina back with her, but she knew that this was the best they could find for a girl of Mina's age.

→>-<←

Hella Jeserski picked up her suitcase with a resigned sigh. She was hesitant to leave the convent, though she knew that the rest of the children eyed her with envy. They all wanted to leave and forget the nightmare they had just endured. One of the social workers helped Hella with her suitcase. She would be traveling to Ruoms, the city south of Lyon where she had lived before the raid and would stay with Mrs. Bernard. The kindly widow would take good care of Hella until the OSE could get her safely out of the country.

→>-<←

Diana Wolfowicz, eight years old, was flustered by the heat and her itchy blond hair. Then she was told that Jeanne Rosenstiel was there to pick her up. Mrs. Rosenstiel was a middle-aged woman who for years had tried unsuccessfully to have children. The woman gathered Diana into a tight embrace the moment she saw her, sweat and lice and all. Here was the child she had never been able to have. They marched off hand in hand, leaving the rest of the children forlorn.

The afternoon was stretching on. Those who remained were losing hope of ever being taken home by new parents. Then they heard the barking of a dog. It was a playful bark, not the bark of a hunter.

Lucien Nouet entered the great hall with his huge German shepherd. All the children ran to see the creature.

"What's her name?" Élisabeth asked, scratching the dog's back.

"Mirza. The children can pet her; she's harmless."

Lucien owned a well-known café and had been supporting the work of the OSE and Amitié Chrétienne for some time.

Playing with the dog momentarily banished the accumulated fatigue, the desolation of being left behind, and the constant fear that the police would show up. The children ran and laughed as they were made to do.

Élisabeth separated one child from the boisterous group and brought him over to Lucien. "This handsome little man is Sylvain Rosenblatt," she said.

Lucien picked up Sylvain and put him on Mirza's back. "Look, Mirza, this is your new rider and friend, Sylvain."

Hilarity entered Sylvain and he laughed and laughed as he clung to the lurching dog. The other children watched with envy. When Lucien left with Mirza and Sylvain, melancholy once again settled in. One who would be leaving soon, Oscar Furst, began to cry inconsolably. Not even his brother, Manfred, could get him to calm down. Maribel thought for a moment and then brought a bowl filled with milk. All day there had been an elusive cat pacing at the window of the hall. He sniffed the offering and slipped inside the room to drink. The children approached him gingerly, and the cat allowed himself to be patted and stroked. This distraction calmed Oscar as nothing else had been able to.

Marguerite Kohn entered the hall and looked for the two boys she was to take home. Maribel pointed to Oscar and Manfred.

"Would you mind waiting just a minute? The boy has finally calmed down thanks to this cat."

Marguerite nodded and slowly made her way to Oscar. He paid her no attention as she began to stroke his head. His eyes were for the cat only. Then Marguerite spoke.

"Do you know that in my house there are two cats? Would you like to come meet them?"

At that, Oscar looked up. "Really?" he asked.

"Oh yes. And there are five children there too. All of them like to play. You won't ever be bored; I can promise you that."

Oscar and Manfred left willingly with Marguerite. Before the rest of the children's spirits could fall again, Lili served a snack with the help of the scouts. While the children ate, Maribel confirmed that the Weisel family had agreed to take Samuel Weichselbaum and his twin younger sisters.

"They should be here soon," Maribel told Samuel.

The Weisels, friends of the children's parents, showed up promptly, but the twins did not want to leave with them. They were fixated on the cat and kept passing him back and forth. After much creative cajoling and distractions, the Weisels finally managed to lure the girls away from the animal.

The group was shrinking, but there were still several children waiting to be picked up. One of the last to leave was young Émile Meisler. Sarah, one of the Jewish Scouts, picked him up and settled him on her bike seat. She then pedaled to the home of Rabbi Brunschwig. The family had agreed to take the boy after the desperate request from his parents the night before, communicated by Father Glasberg.

Adoptive families came and went, and the hall started to empty. The volunteers felt torn between the joy and relief at seeing the young ones placed in families where their needs would be met—and a sense of loss. In those few intense hours the social workers and scouts had come to love the children who were all alone in the world and had lost what they valued most: their parents.

Chapter 46

CONVALESCING

Lyon
AUGUST 29, 1942

JUSTUS HAD TRIED TO escape the first day he was in the hospital, but his side hurt too much. After the operation, he had awoken with pain throughout his body and a very fuzzy head, confused about where he was. He was young and was recovering quickly, but he still felt weak. The good part about his current captivity was being fed well, thanks to the purees and stews that tasted like heaven to the undernourished boy. It felt like ages since he had eaten hot food or come close to feeling full.

Justus got up carefully and stared out the window of his room. He was on the fourth floor, so the window was not a viable escape route. Then he cautiously opened his door and checked the hallway. A gendarme was sleepily puffing on a cigarette. Just then a nurse turned a corner. The policeman straightened up and began talking with her. He was so caught up in the conversation that Justus easily could have escaped without notice.

By the time the nurse reached his room, Justus was lying back in bed.

"How are you today?" she asked.

"Well, it hurts a little."

"Quit whining, chum. Your operation happened thanks to the good graces of the French state."

Her reply took Justus aback. Apparently the nurse saw herself as the defender of the Republic's public health system.

"Tomorrow you'll be out of here. They can't send you back to camp because everyone's already been shipped off, but they'll catch you up to your group, and within a few days you'll be put to work. No more living large like the parasites you people are."

Justus sat up and met her eyes squarely.

"What do you mean by that?"

The woman frowned, displeased that he had the audacity to retort.

"All you foreigners have come to France to steal our jobs and run our culture into the ground. Now that you don't have those worthless politicians protecting you, your time has come. The country is crawling with Jews and Red Spanish Communists, but really you're all just one and the same: leeches."

Justus did not reply. He knew it was pointless to argue with someone like that. As soon as the nurse left the room, Justus crept to the door to see if she had stopped again to talk with the policeman. She had. He threw on his clothes as quickly as he could, slipped out the door, and sprinted toward the stairs.

The gendarme heard the footsteps and turned to glimpse Justus. He jumped to his feet and tore after the boy, hollering, "You damned fool!"

Justus took the stairs three at a time, feeling the pull of the stitches but knowing that pausing was not an option. On the bottom floor he frantically looked for the exit and ran toward it. He was starting to tire, and the pain in his side was now piercing, but he did not stop.

On the streets of Lyon he ran in the direction he guessed was south. He had been in Lyon before but did not know the streets. He crossed the river and glanced back, dismayed to see the gendarme still following him. Justus feared being stopped by a pedestrian but kept pushing himself on. Twenty grueling minutes later, he found himself in front of a church. He went in, ran to what seemed to be an office, and knocked at the door. A middle-aged man with dark hair and a graying beard opened and studied him with surprise for a moment before ushering him in.

"They're after me," was all Justus managed to say between gasps.

"You'll be safe here," the pastor said, leading Justus to one of the back rooms as they heard a loud banging at the door.

The knocking continued. When the pastor opened, the gendarme demanded, "Why didn't you open right away?"

The reverend wiped the policeman's spittle off his face and calmly answered, "I was praying."

"A young man came into the church. Have you seen him?"

"I see many people all day long."

"I'm talking about right now, just a minute ago."

The pastor shrugged his shoulders.

"Oh, you damned Masons. You pastors will be the next to fall."

"I'm no Mason, sir. Now, if you'll excuse me," he said, moving to close the door, but the policeman stuck out his foot.

"I'm coming in."

"No, you aren't. This is the house of God and it's protected by the laws of France. Come back with a search warrant. There are still laws in this country, much to the chagrin of many of you."

The gendarme's face puckered in anger, and he wagged his finger in the pastor's face. "I'll be back with the warrant, don't you doubt it. You know what the punishment is for housing a fugitive. And since you're so keen on the law, I'll make sure the weight of it falls on your head."

The reverend closed the door and leaned his back against it. He let out a long breath and then went to look for the boy.

"We've got to go; it isn't safe here."

The pastor drove to the Amitié Chrétienne offices to see Father Glasberg. Justus would recover for a few more days in the home of Mrs. Lelièvre.

When he was strong enough, Mrs. Lelièvre helped Justus get out of Lyon. She accompanied him by train to Valence, where Justus hoped against hope to find the boys he had met at the Vénissieux camp.

Chapter 47

ONE HUNDRED HEBREW CHILDREN

Lyon
AUGUST 29, 1942

T HE MEMBERS OF THE rescue committee were at their wit's end. Some of the families who had agreed to house children rescued from Vénissieux had backed out. By ten o'clock at night, there were still too many children left in the convent. If things had gone according to plan, by that time all the children would be safe in their respective new homes, or at least en route to them. Father Glasberg called Gilbert, Georges, and the rest of their team to see what else they could do to get the remaining children out of danger before the day ended.

"What can we do with the children no one has come for?" Élisabeth's voice held the anguish that was also visible in her tense, exhausted face.

None of the adults had rested the entire day, and the team that had been in the convent around the clock was worn thin both physically and emotionally.

Gilbert was frustrated with the families who had gone back on their commitment, but he could hardly blame them. If the authorities discovered someone collaborating with the Resistance, they and often their entire family would be jailed. He ran his fingers through his hair and said, "The only thing I can think of is to write a leaflet and distribute it among our networks. There are enough members of OSE and Amitié Chrétienne to take in the remaining children."

"A leaflet? And what happens if it falls into the hands of the police or the Nazis?" Lili asked pointedly.

Everyone murmured in agreement, but Father Glasberg leaned forward and said, "I think it's worth a shot. We're out of time, and we should get it printed up right away. Georges, you write something up and take it to your printer friend. The OSE and Amitié Chrétienne will distribute it immediately. The children who haven't been picked up yet will have to stay here at the convent overnight. If any of them are still here by noon tomorrow, then we'll take them to a safe institution."

"But will it be safe to stay here at the convent till tomorrow?" Maribel asked.

"What other option do we have? We'd be taking a much greater risk if we carted a group of kids around the streets of Lyon at this hour of the night," the priest replied.

"Is there enough food?" Gilbert asked the social workers.

Élisabeth answered, "Enough for dinner and breakfast."

"Well, let's get to it." Father Glasberg rose to his feet and they all dispersed to their various tasks.

Georges jotted down the urgent message and took it to a trusted printer. Half an hour later, they were already passing out the leaflet among friends, acquaintances, and members of the organizations represented by the commission. Within an hour, the news had spread all around.

One of the OSE members left his leaflet on the kitchen table of his apartment. A gust of wind from the open window carried it out, twirling in the air until it landed on the street three floors below.

A policeman making his nightly rounds saw the fluttering paper and knelt to pick it up. What he read stunned him. He immediately headed for the commissary and showed the leaflet to his superior. Not long afterward, the paper was on the desk of Lucien Marchais, the intendant. Marchais boiled with rage when he realized the entire city knew that the Jewish children from Vénissieux were in hiding. The Resistance had gone too far in undermining the government's authority, and he would not let this pass. He picked up the phone and alerted the camp director, Cussonac, and the prefect, Angeli. They had to find those children as soon as possible and get them to the Germans. If they failed, the Nazis would have one more reason to do away with the free zone's independence and turn the entire nation into Nazi slaves. France's honor was at stake.

Chapter 48

BACKUP

Lyon

AUGUST 30, 1942

T HE LEAFLET WAS IN Klaus Barbie's hands by midnight. He was still in his office dealing with a few urgent matters. Since his trip to the camp before dawn, he had barely had a moment to think about the children who had escaped. But as he studied the leaflet, he was convinced that the French authorities were too inept to fix the situation on their own.

He read the paper for the hundredth time and then crumpled it up and threw it in the trash. He did not have many soldiers in the city. Officially, the SS and the Gestapo were not authorized to interfere in the free zone of France, though extrajudicially was another matter.

The captain called for his secretary, who ran in right away.

"Radio for all of our units within fifteen miles. I need all available SS members for a special operation."

"An official operation, sir?" the secretary asked.

Klaus frowned. "I'm the one who decides what's official and what isn't. Is that clear?"

The woman nodded and ran out of the office. Klaus put on his bomber jacket and grabbed his hat. A glance out the window showed him that the city was calm, as if the war and all its misery were something far off and unreal. But it was very real and still going on. The Germans had not yet finished their masterwork of bringing Europe into submission and turning the world into Germany's backyard. Planet Earth would become a showcase for the superiority of the Aryan lords. Klaus walked out after securing his pistol to his holster. His blood was boiling now. The sensation of the hunt inebriated him far more than alcohol ever did. That was what he loved about his job. It made him a higher being, godlike in deciding the life and death of mere mortals.

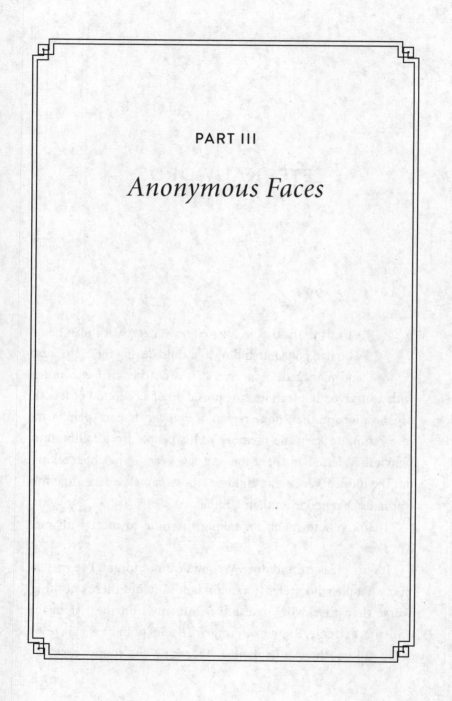

PART III

Anonymous Faces

Chapter 49

ETERNAL WORDS

Lyon
MARCH 6, 1999

VALÉRIE HAD AN APPOINTMENT with Jean Lévy, who had gone into hiding as a child during the Holocaust and managed to survive. It was not her first encounter with a survivor, but Jean was the president of a coalition of Jewish organizations in the Rhône region of France. He had spent years researching to keep the memory of his people from falling into oblivion. Valérie had spent the past few years of her life seeking out the hidden Vénissieux children, those nameless faces that the war had separated from their families.

"Thank you so much for taking the time to meet with me, Mr. Lévy."

"It's my pleasure and duty. We Jews cannot forget. I've met so many people who prefer to remain ignorant, but there's nothing worse than that. Now that anti-Semitism is on the rise again and the extreme Right is acting freely in public, we have to teach our youth what happened. There's no end to my work. It's overwhelming because, no matter how much we do, it's hardly a drop in the ocean."

"But drop by drop we'll fill up that ocean," Valérie said.

The man smiled. He was beyond the age for idealism and had never been particularly gullible. Yet age had helped him see the broader context of things and appreciate the contents of the human heart.

"For many years I didn't speak openly about what I'd been through. The Nazis robbed us of even the normalization of who and what we were as survivors. Of course I'm much more than just a Jew: I'm a Frenchman; I'm from Lyon; I'm a father, husband, professional, and all of that. But the essence of my core will always be Jewish."

Valérie felt a stab of pain in her heart. She had no idea what it was like to have her identity stolen and to feel like an eternal stranger in her own land.

"But you did always know that you were a Jew?"

"Yes, of course, but with my community destroyed, what did it mean to be Jewish? Our people have survived all these centuries because we've established strong communities wherever fate or providence have taken us. The Nazis destroyed the daily rhythms of going to synagogue; they stopped us from gathering with our Jewish brothers and sisters, from eating together, and from learning from our elders. More than half of France's Jews were murdered. Many others left for Israel, and the population now is just a fraction of what it used to be. You know rue Juiverie in Old Lyon? That street in the original city shows that Jews were in Lyon as early as the Roman period. Louis the Pious bestowed his goodwill on my people and allowed them to practice their faith in peace, but persecution ramped up in the thirteenth century. My people managed to get back into the region a few decades later, until 1394. That's when they were expelled almost indefinitely.

"For hundreds of years there were no Jews in this city, at least not officially. Our freedom was reinstated thanks to the French Revolution, and we could come out of the shadows. Napoleon defended us for the most part, and we lived in relative peace until the Nazis came. Jews were held in high esteem during the nineteenth century: most of my people were in business, and the government paid the salary of the community's rabbi. The Grande Synagogue de Lyon was built along Quai Tilsitt during the Second Empire. After the Great War, many Jews from Morocco arrived looking for a better future for their families."

Valérie nodded, familiar with the history but grateful for the personal touches Jean added.

"It's a long, sad, and beautiful history. During World War II, Lyon was the headquarters of the Jewish Resistance in France. But you know what happened with the raids of Klaus Barbie, that German butcher. Until liberation in September 1944, it was the darkest period of history for all the Jews in the region and throughout France."

Valérie was recording their conversation. She wanted to know all she could about life for Jews in their country.

"Our community has grown a lot in the past few years. The Jewish population in Lyon is one of the biggest in France. At the same time, Jews have left for Israel or the United States, especially after the bombing at the Jewish community center in Buenos Aires in 1994. Then right here in Lyon in '95 there was the car bomb outside the Jewish school . . ." Jean shook his head.

Valérie had followed the news about those attacks against the Jewish community. It seemed impossible that things like that were still happening on the cusp of the twenty-first century.

"There's no better time for people to start remembering what happened in the past," she said.

"It's always the right time to remember the past. Thank you for trying to find those children. I at least was able to keep my identity, but they lost theirs forever."

Chapter 50

THE VIOLIN

Lyon
AUGUST 30, 1942

THE NIGHT WAS LONG and even hotter than the previous one. The temperatures did not reflect the fact that summer was winding down. Most of the thirty-some-odd children yet to be placed with a family finally fell asleep, but Rachel Berkowicz had tossed and turned restlessly. She managed to relax into a dream only a few minutes before the social workers served breakfast.

The day before, during the long wait at the convent, she had played her violin several times to entertain the other children. The case was now doubling as her pillow as the outside light filtered through the windows of the hall.

"Good morning, Rachel. How are you today?" Lili asked.

"Tired, hungry, and hot," she said frankly.

"Yes, I'm afraid we all are. But no trial lasts forever, as my dad used to tell me."

The girl sat up a bit. Lili sat beside her and handed her a croissant and a glass of milk.

"Do you miss your mom and dad?" Lili asked.

"Mainly my dad and my stepmom. I haven't seen my real mom in a long time."

"It's all so hard, isn't it?"

"As long as I can remember, we've always been going from place to place. I never really know where I'm from."

The maturity of Rachel's analysis seemed incongruent with her slight, disheveled, eight-year-old body. Lili smiled at her and said, "Well, you can be from wherever you want to be."

"That's not what the Nazis think. They say we're a plague on the world."

"The Nazis are full of nonsense, Rachel. Don't listen to what they say. I think a family is coming to pick you up today."

To Rachel, the wait in the convent was confirmation that she was now completely alone and unloved. She wondered if it would have been better to stay with Fani. Her answer was hardly audible. "Why has it taken so long for them to come get me?"

Having no direct answer, Lili said, "Your adoptive family is from Saint-Sauveur-de-Montagut, the Merlands."

"What are their names?"

"I looked at the list but I can't remember very well. I think the wife is named Paulette."

"Paulette Merland . . . that's a good name; I like it." Rachel nodded to herself with a milky smile. The food and Lili's words had improved her mood.

As Rachel and Lili talked, Madeleine and René Fraure arrived at the convent along with their friend Paulette Merland. Dr. Joseph

Weill had been the one to contact them about adopting children from Vénissieux.

The three adults teared up immediately upon entering the hall and seeing a group of familiar faces. A handful of the Vénissieux children had lived in Saint-Sauveur-de-Montagut for some time before the recent raid. Just a few days prior they could be seen happily running and playing in the streets. Now they were unhealthily thin and haggard, with circles beneath their eyes and sadness darkening their faces.

Madeleine Fraure wiped her tears and said, "Hello, children, we've come for all of you."

The children stared at her mutely. They had seen these adults around town but had never spoken with them.

Lili said, "This is Anna and Jules Szrajbe, Hélène Raychmann, and Jean Baumel."

Rachel was hiding behind Lili, holding her violin case.

"And this is our violinist, Rachel Berkowicz."

Paulette knelt beside Rachel and put her hand on the child's shoulders.

"I remember you, little one. I've heard you playing violin many times."

Rachel did not know what to say.

"Your dad is a barber, isn't he?" Paulette went on.

"Yes, but now he's . . ." Rachel's face crumpled and she could not finish the sentence. Paulette hugged her, and Rachel let herself cry.

"But now you're safe," she cooed.

"Will I stay with you or with them?" Rachel asked between sniffles, pointing to the Fraures.

Madeleine Fraure piped in, her eyes twinkling, "Not with us, honey, but with Mrs. Merland. That way you'll be living with the best and nicest family in town. They'll take good care of you until you can be with your parents again."

The three adults held as many small hands as they could while exiting the convent. The children were relieved and happy. They were so tired of fear, desperation, and suffering. Walking away felt like a chance to live normally again.

→>-<←

As the group headed to Saint-Sauveur-de-Montagut left, Father Glasberg entered the convent in haste. It was almost noon, and there were still too many children without family placements. He called Joseph Weill and others to a meeting in a side room.

"Things have gotten dire. Time is against us, and I've been informed that, besides the gendarmes, the SS is on our trail, sent by a captain named Klaus Barbie, the same one who was at the camp overseeing the deportations. Plus, the adult Jews deported from Vénissieux are held up north of Lyon at Chalon-sur-Saône, which is where the handoff to the Nazis occurs. Apparently the police up there informed René Bousquet that there are fewer refugees than promised and there aren't enough children. The prefect, Angeli, has ordered an immediate search for the children, and he's ruthless."

"So they're holding up the shipment to Germany until they find the children," Joseph concluded.

"Exactly. Because of this, our top priority is to empty this hall. The prefect knows that Gilbert Lesage and I are behind all of this. He's sent his men after me to bring me in for questioning."

"So you two need to go into hiding immediately," Élisabeth said, worried.

Glasberg nodded. "I'm not worried for my own safety, but I don't know what I'd be capable of revealing during torture."

Lili frowned before speaking.

"The gendarmes would go that far?"

"For them, we've now become terrorists, enemies of the state who are endangering national security," the priest explained.

"But that's ridiculous—a bunch of lies!" Lili protested.

"Well, it's the truth according to them, and that's what matters. I'll keep out of the way so the gendarmes don't arrest me until the children are out of danger. Then they can do whatever they want with me. But that's why the lists with all the addresses of the families have to be destroyed as soon as our operation concludes. Yes, Joseph?"

Joseph nodded gravely.

"Okay, so let's get to it. There's a lot left to be done."

Father Glasberg left the meeting room and studied the faces of the remaining children in the hall. With every fiber of his being, he hoped those innocent souls would get out of there alive. Their parents were stuck crammed together in foul, unsanitary train cars en route to either immediate death or slavery until they starved. But their sons and daughters deserved the chance to survive.

The priest went out beneath the pounding sun. The few passersby hurried from one shady spot to the next on their errands. Common sense told him to hide and stay safe, but he had never paid much attention to the voice of self-protection. His mission was not yet over, and he was willing, if necessary, to pay with his life in order to save those children.

Chapter 51

GERTRUDE

Outskirts of Lyon
AUGUST 30, 1942

W HEN THE BUSES FROM Vénissieux had stopped at the train station on August 29, Gertrude Krauss had hidden under her seat. She stayed there undetected as the gendarmes shuttled the rest of the refugees off and into the train cars. There she remained curled up until the buses returned to their garage on the outskirts of Lyon. After a long time of stillness and quiet, Gertrude crept toward the empty driver's seat and tried to open the door. It would not budge. She managed to get a window open enough to force herself through. She fell hard against the ground and twisted her left wrist. But she hopped up immediately, her senses on heightened alert. She found herself in a hangar where the buses of a local business were kept.

She groped toward an exit and slipped out to a deserted street. It was still dark out, though the sun was just starting to peek over the horizon. She walked for hours with no particular direction and in constant fear of being caught by the police. She wanted to get as far away from the buses as possible, in case her absence had been detected by the gendarmes overseeing the deportation.

She did not know where to go. She was hungry and hot, and her head was aching with all of the stress. She started at each little noise. Eventually she remembered a woman from Amitié Chrétienne who had talked with her once. Mrs. Langlade was a kind house-wife who had a small vegetable and fruit stand at the downtown market. Gertrude headed that way. She had to ask for directions several times and then wait for the market to open. Once she was inside, she searched for the woman's stand.

When Gertrude emerged from behind a nearby stand, Mrs. Langlade recognized her right away. She immediately threw her shawl over Gertrude's head and shoulders and led her away from the market.

"What's happened?" she asked, walking quickly.

Gertrude dissolved into tears. She had escaped, but she was the only one from her family not on the train to Germany. After sketching the details of her improbable flight, Gertrude concluded, "But I have nowhere to go."

"Don't worry, my dear. Come with me."

After walking half an hour, they reached the doors of a convent. Mrs. Langlade knocked, and a nun soon greeted them with, "May the Lord bless you. How can I be of service?"

"We need to talk to the mother superior," Mrs. Langlade said.

"Sister Margot is in a meeting at the moment."

Mrs. Langlade nodded and leaned closer. "I'm with Amitié Chrétienne. This girl needs sanctuary. Will you allow us in?"

The young nun opened the door and led them to the cloisters, down a long hall, and to the waiting room outside the mother superior's office. A few minutes later, a small, pudgy woman emerged with a wide smile.

"Merciful Lord! Please, come in."

Inside the office, Mrs. Langlade explained the situation.

The mother superior turned to Gertrude. "We'll shelter you here in the convent, where you can pass as a novice. Do you know anything about Catholicism?"

Gertrude shook her head.

"Never fear, we'll teach you so you won't stick out. From now on you'll be the novice Ana. Don't tell anyone where you're from or why you're here—not a soul. I trust my sisters, but there are others who come in and out of the convent. One never knows who's a spy for the government or the Nazis."

Gertrude nodded and teared up again. She could barely get out her question: "Why are you going to all this trouble for me?"

"Sometimes people think they're doing good when all they're doing is padding their selfish lives. The banalizing of goodness is what's destroying the world. Doing what's right is always harder than doing what's wrong. It's far easier to hate than it is to love, and causing damage is simpler than healing. But we're here to do what's right and good. Helping you is, without question, the right thing to do."

As she hugged Mrs. Langlade goodbye, Gertrude said, "I'll never forget what you've done for me." Gertrude knew that Mrs. Langlade's actions would not go down in history; they would never be remembered by anyone else or commemorated in a book. But for Gertrude, Mrs. Langlade had made the difference between dying and living. It was the greatest miracle on earth that someone would risk her life for a stranger. Gertrude vowed to try to do the same. She did not want the banalizing of goodness to successfully replace the power of a generous heart.

Chapter 52

GILBERT

Lyon

AUGUST 30, 1942

ANGELI POUNDED THE TABLE with his fist. The prefect wanted Gilbert Lesage to tell him right that minute what they had done with the children, but Gilbert was not easily swayed. He had joined the Quakers some time before and had spent many years helping people in difficult situations, especially refugees. A longtime lover of ideas, he had studied philosophy in Paris until he realized that the pretty words were pointless unless they turned into concrete action. His life took a major turn in 1929 when he met the Quaker Ella Barlow. That is when he became a Quaker and dedicated his life to promoting peace. He had lived in Berlin in 1932 and 1933 as Hitler came to power and the world fell apart before his eyes. The Nazis expelled him from the country when they became aware of Gilbert's activities. Back in France, Gilbert was planning to go to England, but he was asked to head up the aid to refugees in Paris. The rise of Nazism had led to a flood of Jews escaping from Germany to France. Among other jobs, he had also helped Spaniards fleeing their country since the start of their civil war. When war broke out in Europe, Gilbert had been obliged to join the army. After the armistice between France and Germany was signed, he went to Vichy to offer his services to the newly formed government. There, an old friend, Mr. Laborie, recommended Gilbert for a post with the Ministry to Family and Youth. He eventually wound up in Lyon as the inspector general of refugee services for the Ministry of the Interior.

Angeli knew that he was not dealing with any do-gooder Quaker. "You know that I can send you straight to jail or hand you over to the Gestapo for interrogation. We ourselves can't interrogate you the way I'd like, not until I find enough proof, but the Germans aren't inhibited by such formalities."

"All I can say is that the children are in a safe place, which I will not reveal. Do as you see fit, Prefect."

Angeli knew that Gilbert was well connected, including with the cardinal of Lyon.

"Damn it, get out of here at once!" he growled.

Gilbert took his hat, made a mocking bow, and sauntered out of the room. As soon as he was out of earshot, the prefect called the intendant.

"I couldn't get anything out of Lesage. We've got to get Vichy to call the cardinal and pressure him to turn the children in."

"I'll call the prime minister right now," Lucien Marchais answered.

→>⋅<⋅

An hour later, the president of the Republic, Marshal Pétain, called his friend Cardinal Gerlier. When his assistant alerted him to who was on the phone, Gerlier cleared his throat. He knew what the call would be about.

"My dear marshal, at your service."

"It's a pleasure to hear your voice, Your Eminence. A little problem has been brought to my attention. A group in Lyon has taken custody of a large number of children that the German government has claims on. I appreciate your zeal for the young, but the Germans have assured us that no harm will come to the children."

The cardinal was quiet for a moment. He picked up his glasses from his desk and put them on. Before him was the letter he was drafting to distribute among the parishes of his diocese.

"My good marshal, I admire your efforts to steer France back to the path of Christianity. I know that you're pressured from all sides. For you to call me about this matter indicates the depth of your concern. First, I want to beg you to protect these children. I do not trust the word of the Germans. They are capable of doing anything and everything to get their way. These children are French. Even more importantly, they are innocent."

"I guarantee you that they will come to no harm."

"Mr. President, it is not within your power to offer such a guarantee. Once they are beyond French borders, we can do nothing for them. My esteemed marshal, a Christian society cannot be built upon a foundation of tyranny, hatred, and disdain for life. Our Lord Jesus Christ himself was a Jew. Would you have deported him to Germany, Marshal? The church will do everything within her power to protect these children."

It was the marshal's turn to be silent.

"Is that your final answer, Cardinal?"

"The final answer is in God's hands, sir, but if you are referring to whether or not I will reveal the whereabouts of the children, I will not do so even under torture."

Marshal Pétain slammed the receiver down in fury. He looked up at his prime minister and said, "Laval, bring the full power of the state down on the accomplices of this treason."

Laval saluted and left the room. Then the former war hero let loose a string of curses against the curates and prelates of his country. There was nothing of the savior of France left in Pétain. He was little more than a lackey in the Nazis' hands, grasping at the smoking embers of a world that had fallen to pieces long ago. The marshal purported to represent all that was worth rescuing in France; in reality he was the symbol of the collaborationist regime eager to sell its soul to the devil to keep the French flag flying over history, however stained by blood, tears, and death it was.

Chapter 53

FINAL HOURS

Lyon
AUGUST 30, 1942

JOSEPH WEILL ASKED FATHER Glasberg about the cardinal. They all knew that if he relented, the entire team would end up in jail and the children on a train to Germany.

"Up to now he's given no sign of backing down," the priest replied, "but it's a matter of time before they track us to the convent, and there are still about twenty kids without homes."

Joseph shrugged. "We're doing all we can, but several families have gotten cold feet."

"I just can't believe that within the whole city of Lyon and the surrounding areas, we can't find a few more families in solidarity with our mission."

Gilbert, who had made sure no one followed him from the commissary, was pensive. Finally he spoke. "I think we should make another visit to the cardinal. The pressure is intense, and betrayal wouldn't be surprising . . ." He trailed off.

The other two studied their Protestant colleague carefully.

"You doubt the word of a member of the church hierarchy?" Joseph asked.

"It's the prefect and the intendant I don't trust. They've got orders to find and deport the children, and they have ways of achieving their goals."

The three men arrived at the episcopal palace half an hour later, surprised to see the intendant's black Citroën parked at the entryway. Fearing they were too late, they dashed up the stairs past the secretary and let him know their intentions as they ran.

The cardinal was standing and pointing to a glowering Marchais. "I've already told you I will not reveal the whereabouts of those children. They are now charges under my care. Is that understood?"

"You're committing high treason, a crime punishable by death." The intendant got to his feet and turned his head when he heard the three men at the door. "This is not the end of the matter, Gerlier. I've asked nicely. You've forced me to resort to more direct methods." He stormed out of the cardinal's office and down the stairs. The cardinal, Glasberg, Joseph, and Gilbert knew where he was headed.

Marchais told his chauffeur to drive straight to the Gestapo's headquarters, not far from the episcopal palace. There, he got out of the vehicle and asked to see Captain Barbie.

A few minutes later he handed the SS officer one paper that listed the names of the children who had disappeared from Vénissieux and another with the names of those known to have been involved in their escape and hiding.

"This is everything?" Barbie asked.

The French official nodded.

"Including the addresses of the collaborators and their families?"

Those words sent a chill up Marchais's spine. He was aware that he was dealing with the devil himself.

"Yes, everything we know is written there, but I hope you won't go too far."

At that, the German burst out laughing. "Then why have you come to me? You think I'm going to tickle the information out of them? You've come to me to take these terrorists down a notch. How are terrorists and enemies of the state treated? With all the force of law, of course, but more importantly, with all the force of our moral superiority. It's very hard for people like them to understand that these children are a cancer to France as they were to Germany—a cancer with rosy cheeks and innocent faces, perhaps, but it turns into a malignant tumor that destroys the entire social organism."

The intendant was silent, his head slightly ducked. An alliance with evil always brought disastrous consequences, but it was Marchais's last resort before his superiors released the hounds on him.

→>-<←

Meanwhile, at the episcopal palace, the three men continued talking with the cardinal.

"They know the identity of Father Glasberg, and they suspect Gilbert. You two should go into hiding immediately."

"But we can't go now, not while there are still children waiting at the convent," Gilbert said, displeased at the thought of hiding like a coward.

"We'll get the children to sanctuary somewhere. We're hours away from August 31. It's too risky to keep waiting on families," the cardinal answered.

They knew the prelate spoke with the voice of reason, but Father Glasberg and Gilbert would rather die than risk the children falling into Nazi hands.

Father Glasberg crossed his arms. "I'll go into hiding tomorrow, but as long as the children are at the Carmelite convent, I've got to be there overseeing the operation. It's safest for them to be placed in families outside the city. Our team of social workers is still working and leaving no stone unturned to get the children out of here."

Chapter 54

LAST CHANCES

Lyon

AUGUST 31, 1942

THE CHILDREN SPENT ONE more hot night in the convent. After two of the longest days of their lives, no one wanted to be in the Carmelite convent anymore. The novelty of all the games, singing, and dancing had long since worn off. The hay on the floor of the hall was disgusting and rank with urine, fleas, and lice. Food was running short, and the four remaining children were a real concern for the caretakers that morning. On top of the trauma of being separated from their parents, they were now languishing in a state of abandonment. It seemed that no one wanted them. When Father Glasberg entered the hall, everyone there looked to him. Lili, Madeleine, Charles, and Georges went up to him, hoping to hear a solution for the last few children.

The children were also looking at him with plaintive, anguished eyes. Jean Stern, Marcel and Miriam Frenkel, and Rachel Kaminker were the last of the unfortunate children waiting to be taken away.

Father Glasberg shook his head and broke the news to his colleagues. "We haven't come up with any good options."

Discouraged, they dispersed to make a few last calls.

When they came back together, Lili announced, "My mother's coming for Jean, but she can't handle any more than one."

"That's fine because I've finagled it so that Mrs. Berheim is coming to pick up the Frenkels. She should be here soon," Charles said.

And another family had agreed to get Rachel Kaminker out of the city and to the Peyrins château.

→>-<←

An hour later the large hall was completely empty. Finally, nearly two-and-a-half days after arriving at the convent, the last of the children had been smuggled to safety.

With the mission complete, Father Glasberg accepted his lot of going into hiding for a while. The remaining workers got busy destroying all the evidence.

"It's good, but I'm sad they're gone," Madeleine mused to Lili.

"I feel the same," Lili said, hugging the psychologist. They had met only a few days prior, but the bond that formed between them was unbreakable. "It's only been a couple of days, but they feel like my cousins or little brothers and sisters."

Madeleine started to cry. "I'm sorry, it's so unprofessional of me," she said with a cracked voice.

Lili rubbed her back and said, "It's all right. It's all going to work out." She spoke in hope against reality; the war had already gone on for three years and seemed like it would never end.

The Nazis had lost precious few battles and were likely to be the masters of France for a long time.

Madeleine nodded and then moved off to continue cleaning.

Lili joined a few of the scouts gathering up the things the children had left. Georges came up to her then and held out his hand. She took it and stepped away.

"It's all over," Georges said.

"Well, I wouldn't go that far," she replied.

"Still, I want to take you out to dinner tonight. Let's have a good wine and pretend none of this ever happened, that it was just a nightmare that very conveniently introduced us to each other."

Her serious eyes stared into Georges's.

"I don't want to forget what's happened. They've been the best and worst days of my life. But yes, I accept your invitation to dinner. However, I've got to shower first and get a fresh, pretty dress on."

"You're beautiful no matter what you're wearing," he assured her.

Lili smiled and smacked at his shoulder. "Oh, you men know all the right ways to lie."

Life would go on despite all the suffering. But a dark shadow loomed. Evil would not rest nor make a truce with the noble souls who resisted it.

Chapter 55

BLOWS

Lyon
AUGUST 31, 1942

WHEN GILBERT LESAGE HAD left the cardinal's office, he had returned to his own office and continued to deflect any direct questions about the whereabouts of the children. He stayed there all night, occasionally nodding off, but mainly working out the countless details of how to support the families who had taken in the children. Early that morning he headed back to his apartment to gather a few things before making himself disappear. Some pastors had advised him to seek refuge in a French village close to the Swiss border. In case danger followed him there, he could escape to Switzerland. Others had recommended a monastery in the south until things calmed down, though rumors indicated that the days of the free zone were numbered. The Germans were about to launch a new campaign against Russia. If they took the colossal country, nothing would stand in their way. The hopes raised by the United States entering the war were floundering. The Yankees were more caught up with fighting in the Pacific than in freeing Europeans from Nazi tyranny.

Gilbert opened the door to his apartment and Charly, his little terrier, lunged at him.

"Forgive me for abandoning you, my little friend. But you can come with me now."

Gilbert puttered about packing his suitcase. As a Quaker, he lived a simple, ascetic life and would take only the essentials. He owned few material things. When he left this world, all that would remain would be the memories of him cherished in the hearts of those he had helped.

He packed two pairs of pants, three shirts with worn collars, a few changes of socks and underwear, a couple of ties, a watch that had belonged to his father, a few old photos, and five books, along with his ancient Bible.

He shut the suitcase and looked around the apartment that had been his home for a few months. He had no special memories here. It was simply the place where he went to sleep at night after the endless workday.

He put some food in a backpack along with a knife, a thermos of coffee, and a map of France.

He picked up Charly and went to the door. Then he heard the noise. Half a dozen boots were marching up the stairs, the noise reverberating throughout the building. Gilbert was petrified, unsure of what to do. He thought about climbing up to the roof and trying to jump to the building next door, but he was no longer a lithe youth. He would either break his leg or get shot.

So he set down his suitcase, opened the door, and stroked Charly as he waited.

Two gendarmes and four SS soldiers stopped at the door.

"Are you Gilbert Lesage?" a rotund gendarme asked, breathing heavily from jogging up the stairs.

"Yes, sir."

"You're under arrest."

"What am I accused of?"

"Sedition, falsification of documents, obstruction of justice, and treason," the policeman rattled off flatly.

Gilbert raised his eyebrows. "And do you have a warrant for my arrest?"

The gendarme had no answer, but one of the SS soldiers grabbed Gilbert by the arm and said, "That won't be necessary. Terrorists have no rights in France, you damned Jew!"

"I'm not a Jew, however much I would like to be. But I am French."

"Then it's even worse; you're a traitor to your race and to your faith."

Gilbert smiled at the irony.

"You think that's funny?" the soldier spat out. He then punched Gilbert in the stomach. Gilbert doubled over and his glasses fell off. The gendarme knelt to pick them up, but one of the Nazis crushed the lenses under his boot.

"Never fear, he won't need those where we're going," the German said with whimsical cynicism.

Two of the SS officers picked Gilbert up between them, and that was how he descended the stairs, his feet dangling awkwardly in the air. Charly's barking echoed down the stairwell.

"But what about my dog?" Gilbert asked. The Germans laughed to see the animal chasing after them, growling loudly but too timid to bite them. When the soldiers shoved Gilbert into the back of the van they had arrived in, Charly got in front and barked louder than ever. A soldier aimed at him with his pistol, but the sergeant stopped him.

"You're going to waste a bullet on a dog?"

Then the burly sergeant grabbed Charly by the scruff of his neck. Charly whined in terror. The German looked into the dog's small brown eyes, like two shiny buttons against a woolly white coat. "So you're a Jewish dog, aren't you?" And with that ridiculous question, the sergeant threw the animal hard against the wall of Gilbert's apartment building. After one strangled cry upon impact, Charly fell lifeless to the ground.

That was when Gilbert began to cry.

The van, bearing none of the customary markings of a police car, sped away. Gilbert knew his detention was extrajudicial, but that was the prerogative of the Nazis who, as lords of the land, did as they pleased.

➤◄

Klaus Barbie went down to the basement of the Gestapo head-quarters. He found the dark, chilly rooms quite pleasant. They were the landscape of the hell the Nazis fashioned to their own liking.

Gilbert was tied to a chair. His face was already swelling with bruises. One lip was split and his nose bled in a slow trickle. He had held out as long as he could, hoping to give his colleagues as much time as possible.

"Well now, I believe the time has come for you to tell us where the children are being held. My men were just getting you ready for me. You'll find my methods much less indirect. It means nothing to me that you have the cardinal, the pope, or Marshal Pétain behind you."

"I think you might want to check in on your humanity," the Quaker answered.

"How's that?"

Gilbert stared at the SS officer. He looked like a very ordinary guy in shirtsleeves, without his sinister black uniform.

"When you treat us like beasts, it shows you're even more beastly than we are."

"I see you're sorry for the loss of your dog. Well, me too. Animals can't be blamed for disagreements between men."

The paradox struck Gilbert: the two-legged animal looming over him was sadder about the death of his dog, Charly, than he was about the hundred-some-odd Jewish children he was so desperately trying to find.

"It's sad that people like you are in charge of the world, though this state of things is certainly nothing original. It's always been the low-life riffraff that directs history."

Klaus responded with a blow that spun Gilbert's head hard.

"I'm a reasonable person like yourself, but I lack patience. Why do you risk your life for those Jewish rats? I'll never understand it."

"Of course you can't understand it. You've relinquished your soul. What good does it do to gain the world yet forfeit your soul? What has Hitler promised you? A horse farm, a new car with your own driver, a hefty monthly payment the rest of your life? And that's a worthwhile exchange for your eternity?"

"The only eternity is what exists right here and right now. Tell me where the children are!"

Gilbert closed his eyes and imagined himself far away from that room, at home with his parents when the world was small and almost perfect, where his father's shadow could protect him from all evil.

Klaus let loose his fury with blow after blow. After pulverizing Gilbert's face and chest, the Nazi held his victim's face up.

"Not so cocky now, are you?"

Gilbert wheezed out, "You're a pathetic schoolyard bully, violent to cover up your cowardice."

The next hit to Gilbert's chin left him unconscious for a few minutes. When he came to, one of his hands was tied to a desk in front of him. The implements told him what was coming next. He would lose his fingernails and then his fingers one by one.

Barbie sighed. "Well, this is your last chance."

"Hold on," Gilbert panted. "I'll tell you what you want to know."

The German set the pliers down. They had reached his favorite part: the submission of the human spirit. Years ago he had learned that all men had a price, that they could hold out only so long. There was a threshold for each body, beyond which it was willing to do anything to survive.

"The children are at 10 Montée des Carmélites. It's the Carmelite convent."

"I would hate for you to be deceiving us. Then I would be obliged to remove your eyeballs after your toes and fingers."

"I'm not lying. Go and see for yourself."

Klaus Barbie washed his hands in a porcelain sink, dried them, and then put his bomber jacket back on.

"Well, quite a pleasure to make your acquaintance, Mr. Lesage. Unfortunately for me, the prefect and the intendant have inquired into your whereabouts. If not, you could have joined some of your colleagues at a camp in Poland where your kind receive the treatment they deserve."

The SS official left the basement, and two soldiers untied Gilbert. They allowed him to wash his face and put on his jacket. He hollered as the water touched his wounds. Then he made his slow, painful way back down the hallway. To his surprise, the gendarmes who had arrested him that morning were still there. One of them flinched at the sight of Gilbert and helped him back to his cell.

"I'm so sorry about this," the gendarme whispered into his ear. "We're all on your side."

Those words lifted his spirit. He felt like the prophet Elijah after facing Jezebel and the prophets of Baal: exhausted, emptied, and alone. Yet there were thousands, perhaps hundreds of thousands, of French who had not bent the knee before Hitler and his regime of terror. They were waiting for the moment to rise up against the tyranny that murdered the innocent, forced their children to work as slaves in Germany, and stole the food they worked so hard to grow in the pure, fertile fields of France.

Gilbert sat down on the cot in his cell as best as he could with every part of his body throbbing with pain. One thought consumed him: Had he held out long enough for the last child to be moved to safety? His own life was of no consequence to him. He had already fulfilled his duty, the mission for which he had been created: helping foreigners regain part of their dignity. He was prepared to pass through the door to eternity and gaze upon that perfect world in which there would be no more injustice or pain, the new garden of Eden for all human beings.

Chapter 56

ASSAULT

Lyon
AUGUST 31, 1942

BY TWO O'CLOCK IN the afternoon, several police units were gathered at the door to the Carmelite convent. A few passersby stopped to watch but most lowered their heads and kept walking. It was better to keep a low profile and avoid any run-ins with the police. The prefect was standing with the officers, ready and willing to attack the building if the friars refused to open, but that proved unnecessary. The door hinges creaked open and two men wearing habits stood aside to let the authorities pass.

The police asked no questions but began searching the entire grounds. They soon arrived in the large hall where the children had spent their grueling days of waiting.

Only one person was in the large room: Madeleine Dreyfus, the psychologist. She had returned to make sure no documents had accidentally been left behind. Her brows arched when she saw the police.

"Where are the children?" the prefect Angeli demanded.

She smiled and said flatly, "Ask Cardinal Gerlier."

Angeli spat out, "They're not here. The information from the SS is false."

"We should search the offices of Amitié Chrétienne on rue de Constantine," Marchais said. Then he told the policemen to arrest Madeleine.

As Madeleine was taken to the commissary in one police car, others raced toward the headquarters of Amitié Chrétienne with their sirens blaring. There was little traffic, and the cars that were out willingly yielded to the police vans.

Inside the Amitié Chrétienne offices, the police found Father Chaillet. He had helped with the rescue operation indirectly, primarily by appealing to the cardinal for support.

The police arrested Chaillet as well. That was all that the prefect and the intendant had to show for their efforts. The solidarity of a group of volunteers with different religious beliefs and political ideas had managed to stump the authorities and hide the children right under their noses. It was up to the government's lackeys to try to find the children before all traces disappeared.

Chapter 57

MIRACULOUS EXIT

Lyon
AUGUST 31, 1942

GILBERT LESAGE WAS LYING on a cot in a cell in the Gestapo basement. Every one of his bones ached, his body was covered in bruises, and he could still sense the unpleasant taste of blood on his lips. He had been given nothing to eat, but at least his captors had promised that he would soon be taken to a French police commissary. He counted on the mediation of Cardinal Gerlier to get him freed from there.

Just before midnight on the day of his capture and torture, he finally drifted off to sleep, despite the hunger and cold. It did not last long. Approaching footsteps woke him, and someone loomed in the doorway of his cell. When the door opened, the light from the hallway momentarily blinded him.

"Gilbert Lesage, you'll come with us now."

The voice spoke with a German accent. Gilbert trembled with renewed fear. He had never thought of himself as a hero. He was simply one of the mortals who could not tolerate injustice even though working against it brought many sleepless nights.

Gilbert put his shoes back on. They were the only thing he was wearing that was not bloodied. Then he offered his wrists to be handcuffed.

Walking down the long hallway and up the stairs required more effort than any other walk Gilbert had taken in his life. There was a Nazi on each side of him. When they finally emerged on the main floor of the building, Klaus Barbie was waiting for them.

"Mr. Lesage, you have some powerful friends, but they can't complain when a prisoner is shot when trying to escape. It's just part of a prison guard's duty, no?"

"I have no intention of fleeing."

"It's not necessary. A bullet in the back is sufficient justification for your death. An unfortunate diplomatic event, to be sure, but one that will be forgotten within weeks."

Gilbert was shaking again. The guards led him outside and tossed him into a van. Splayed out in the back, he thought back over his life. Though there had been times of loneliness and sadness, on the whole he had enjoyed a life of meaning and purpose. He was aware that such was more than most people could say.

The vehicle stopped a mile or two from the Gestapo headquarters. Gilbert heard boots on the asphalt and then the opening of the door.

"Out!" a loud voice barked at him.

Gilbert made the effort to get out, but with his hands tied and his body in severe pain, he was not having success.

"Damned traitor!" the guard yelled, grabbing Gilbert's right arm and yanking him out of the van with such force that Gilbert landed hard on the street. He was forcefully made to stand. Gilbert rocked unsteadily on his feet before the men. There was no moon, and the dark, predawn streets were unlit. The only light came from some houses a few blocks away.

"Run!" the same soldier commanded.

Gilbert stood stock still, knowing full well what it meant to run.

The German shoved his cocked pistol into Gilbert's face. "Run!" he repeated.

So Gilbert turned and started hobbling as fast as he could. It became a slow, stumbling run, as rapid a movement as the searing pain in his legs allowed.

The soldier took aim and waited for Gilbert to move far enough away. When Gilbert was about one hundred yards away, he fired. But there was no blast, only a click. The Nazi looked at his gun, cocked it again, and pulled the trigger. Yet once again it misfired.

"Son of a bitch!" he screamed and grabbed the other soldier's gun.

By this time Gilbert was some two hundred yards away. The protective darkness began to envelop him. The German fired, but that second gun also misfired. He repeated the cocking and misfiring routine until the prisoner had disappeared into the shadows. Gilbert stayed well hidden when the Nazis ran up on foot, searching with their flashlights, and again when they drove the van up and down the streets with the headlights flashing in every direction.

When it had been quiet for a very long time, Gilbert emerged and started walking. It took him until dawn to reach the episcopal palace. It was the one place he could hope for safety.

One of the housekeepers found Gilbert slumped against the gate and recognized him right away. With the help of another servant, they carried the limp man to a room beside the kitchen. They laid him gently on an unused bed and ran to alert the cardinal.

Gerlier had woken up an hour before to begin morning prayer. When he heard the sound of hurrying footsteps, he leaned over the second-floor banister to see what was going on.

"Antoine, what's all this noise?"

"We found Mr. Gilbert Lesage wounded at the gate. We've taken him to a room beside the kitchen."

"Call a doctor immediately. I'll dress and come down to see Mr. Lesage."

Gerlier had an unpleasant feeling in his chest and had to pause for a few deep breaths as he put on his pants. That week had been the most difficult of his life and career to date. When his pastoral letter was made public, he knew that he would be in the sights of his enemies and of the Nazis, but what other option did he have? He had sworn to serve Christ, even if it cost his life. Yet he was loath to further compromise the already weak Vichy republic.

When Gerlier had gathered himself together, he walked down the stairs slowly, making sure to hold on carefully to the banister. He went into the room where Gilbert was. The man's bruised, discolored face and swollen eyes made him nearly unrecognizable.

"Holy Father in heaven . . ." Gerlier sucked in his breath. "Who did this to you, my friend?"

Gilbert lifted his head. With swollen eyes and no glasses, he struggled to make out who was before him.

"Ah, Your Excellency. Thank you."

"Rest assured, you'll be safe and tended to here. It's the very least we can do for a brother. But tell me, what happened to you?"

Lesage gave a brief account of his torture and how divine providence had allowed him to escape.

"Can you give me the name of the Nazi official? I'll present a formal complaint to the German government in Berlin."

"Klaus Barbie, though I fear his government already knows what he's doing. But the children—how are they?"

The cardinal sat on the edge of the bed.

"Don't worry. As far as we know, they are all well. With God's grace, the mission has been a success. But we cannot afford to lower our guard. The gendarmes are still looking for them, as, apparently, are the Nazis."

The prelate's words calmed Gilbert. He had feared that his betrayal put the children in danger.

"Rest now until the doctor arrives, my friend," Gerlier said.

Gilbert closed his eyes. He immediately fell into the deep, restorative sleep only possible when a body knows it is in a clean bed in a safe place.

The cardinal returned to his office and called Father Glasberg, requesting that he come to the episcopal palace immediately. Gilbert was not the only one who needed to be in a safe place. The cardinal was worried about his priest. The Nazis were determined to capture the children from Vénissieux and were willing to do anything it took to get them.

Chapter 58

VALENCE

Valence
AUGUST 31, 1942

THE PLANS OF HUMANKIND rarely work out. Men believe themselves to be the lords of the universe but are nothing more than irrelevant, fleeting particles. Those were Justus's musings when he arrived in Valence. His friends were not there. He thought about making another attempt to cross the Pyrenees alone but feared the repercussions of being captured again.

In case Justus changed his mind about the Pyrenees, Mrs. Lelièvre had given him the address of someone in the La Baume-Cornillane neighborhood. A Protestant woman named Mrs. Sayn was willing to house Justus should he desire to stay in Valence.

The young Jew had lived on his own for a long time, and the thought of adapting to a new homelife did not appeal to him, though uprootedness equated to a deep, aching sadness. He was a despised foreigner on the run who did not fit in anywhere. What happened to him was of no concern to anyone. Justus had thus concluded that his existence in the world was superfluous.

He avoided main roads as he made his way to Mrs. Sayn's house, walking along the train tracks and amusing himself by testing his balance. In the distance a train was approaching. Naturally, he made to step aside, but paused. The approach of the mighty machine sucked him in with magnetic fascination. This could be the escape route. It could all be over, right then. Nothing made sense anymore. He thought about his parents. Surely they were dead by then, just like his aunts, uncles, and cousins. So he was alone.

The train came on quickly, slicing through the air in an intense burst. Justus was at the level of the engine's light, and it momentarily blinded him. He covered his head with his hands. His mother's face flashed before his closed eyes and her whisper coincided with a fleeting thought above the train roar: *"Live, live for us, for your ancestors. Don't let them destroy you. We all live through you. Don't forget us."*

Tears then blurred Justus's vision as the white smoke of the approaching locomotive covered the dark horizon. He stepped back and let the iron beast pass. It raced by, whipping Justus's face with angry air, a punishment for not allowing it to carry him with it.

Justus dragged his sore body up off the ground and dusted himself off. He walked slowly through the night hours until he reached Mrs. Sayn's house. It had started raining. The hot summer air turned into a tempestuous, chilly wind. A middle-aged woman answered his knock. Her gray-streaked hair was pulled back in a bun. She had a sincere smile and vivacious eyes.

"I'm Justus Rosenberg . . ." he began.

"I know, honey. Come in. It's not a pleasant night to be out."

As soon as Justus crossed the threshold, a very old, almost forgotten sensation rolled over him: home. While a pot of soup heated, Mrs. Sayn made up the bed for Justus. They chatted pleasantly enough during dinner.

"So how are you right now?"

Justus did not know how to answer. Her concern seemed genuine.

"Well, I feel really alone." Speaking those words out loud unleashed a tide of pent-up tears.

The woman moved from her chair so that she could hug him. "Well, you're not alone anymore, and you'll never have to be again."

The wind continued to howl in the darkness outside. But a candle had been lit inside that house that no storm could snuff out: the hope of two strangers brought together in a companionship that rose up against the death and pain of loneliness. It was hope against hope.

Chapter 59

DINNER

Lyon
SEPTEMBER 1, 1942

DINNER THE NIGHT BEFORE had been magical for Lili. Heretofore she had not had luck with love. She had never been one to pine after this or that man, and natural shyness had kept her from revealing her feelings to the two boys she had had a crush on. But things with Georges had been different. From the very first, she had sensed that he was the man for her, and for forever. That gave her the courage to act on her feelings. She had not wanted love to slip away again.

They had dined at a small restaurant in the old city. There were fewer and fewer restaurants open. The dwindling variety of foods available and general lack of supplies had forced most tea shops, cafés, and restaurants to close. One of the few still holding out was the Parisien, a hole-in-the-wall with five tables. It was on a narrow street just beyond the city's original Jewish neighborhood. The fat, friendly-faced, and very chatty Louis Pompadur kept the place running. Georges had reserved one of the candlelit tables, though only two other tables were occupied when he and Lili arrived.

Back in the room she rented the next morning, Lili replayed the entire evening in her mind.

"Welcome to my humble home," the restaurant owner had said with gallantry and led them to their table.

"The Germans have kept the best wines for themselves, but I've managed to get my hands on a Bordeaux that I'm sure you'll love." He showed them the bottle and waited for their nod of approval before uncorking it. The two young lovers studied the limited, handwritten menu and made their requests. A short while later the table was full of steaming plates.

"I hope it's all to your liking!" Mr. Pompadur said before retiring.

Lili and Georges began eating without a word, restrained by a shy modesty. Finally, Lili broke the silence.

"I've been advised to disappear from Lyon for a time, but that seems ridiculous. What can they really do to us?"

"Well, things are a bit stirred up at the moment, and it seems like a good idea to me. We think that Gilbert and the psychologist have both been arrested."

Lili dropped her fork. "They've arrested Madeleine?" She looked around frantically. What would happen to her friend? And if Madeleine could be arrested, perhaps it was better for Lili to go into hiding.

"Yes. So I really would recommend going somewhere; maybe lie low at your mother's house for a few days."

"What are you going to do, Georges?"

He shrugged. "There's so much to do here in Lyon and in the rest of the department. There are more children being held in other detention camps."

"But it's so risky."

"Yes, but someone's got to do it."

They continued eating. Lili's left hand rested on the table, and Georges took it in his own.

"We're living through some really difficult times, but I wanted to ask something of you," he said. Lili stared into his eyes, the shadows cast by the candlelight flickering over his lovely face. "I want you to wait for me. When the war is over, I want to marry you."

Lili's heart skipped a beat and she caught her breath.

"That would be . . ."

Georges looked at her, waiting for the answer that would determine the rest of his life.

". . . wonderful." She smiled.

Georges knelt in front of her beside the table and held out a ring. "It was my grandmother Rose's and has been in the family for generations."

Lili offered her hand and felt electricity run through her as Georges slipped the engagement ring onto her finger. "Yes, yes, oh, heavens, yes!" she cried.

Georges then stood and kissed his fiancée's honey lips. The other couples in the small restaurant turned. They stared half in celebration and half in confusion at how love had found a way forward in those dark times. Lili and Georges were ready and willing to challenge fate and entrust their souls to each other forever.

Chapter 60

MADELEINE

Lyon
SEPTEMBER 2, 1942

THE YOUNG PSYCHOLOGIST HAD spent two days in a cell but, to her surprise, had not been tortured or even questioned. She wondered if the authorities had simply forgotten about her. Having only been served scant meals of weak broth with minuscule, tough shreds of chicken, Madeleine felt very weak. She focused her energy on keeping her mind intact. She did not want to succumb to the panic or insanity threatened by incarceration.

Her cell was small, a mere two by three yards. There was no outside light, and one faint bulb in the ceiling was lit for eight hours a day. Thanks to that, she knew more or less when day and nighttime were, though she was beginning to lose track of time. She spent part of her awake hours recalling with as much precision as possible any and every book she had ever read. She also thought about what life would be like when she was free again. But it was getting harder and harder to concentrate.

The light flicked off, and Madeleine knew that another day had finished. To her surprise, a soldier opened the door to her cell. He handcuffed her wrists and motioned with his head for her to follow.

"Where are you taking me?" Madeleine's voice was raspy from disuse.

The man said nothing. Perhaps he had not even understood her question. They arrived at a large, sparsely outfitted room. It boasted a tall table with some tools and a wooden chair, a metal cabinet with locked doors, and a dilapidated desk with a lamp.

Two men were waiting for them in shirtsleeves. The tall, burly one had arms that bulged with muscles and the face of a simpleton. The other was shorter and slighter, but his look made Madeleine's stomach churn.

That man said in a singsong voice, "Please, have a seat, madame."

"Why am I here? What have I been accused of?" Madeleine said without moving.

"Well, for the moment you're not accused of anything, but the charges floating around you are quite serious. You and your colleagues have illegally kidnapped a group of children in the care of the Vichy government who were to travel to Germany, not to mention the falsification of documents and the obstruction of justice. We could even add terrorism, since we're aware of your participation with the Resistance."

Madeleine frowned. "That's ridiculous. I work for a legally registered association. I'm a pacifist, and I've never used a weapon."

"Mmm, there are many ways to cause damage to the state. Weapons aren't always involved."

"I want a lawyer."

"Allow me to introduce myself. SS Captain Klaus Barbie at your service."

"I'm French, and I'm in my country. According to the laws of France, you can't interrogate me."

"You'd be surprised by what all we can do in your country." He placed his gloved hands on Madeleine's shoulders. "Now, you're going to be a good girl and tell me the names of everyone involved in this little matter. If you tell me everything, you might get out of here unscathed. If not . . ." His eyes indicated the table with the tools.

Fear was nearly choking Madeleine. "What are you going to do to me?"

"Nothing good, I can assure you of that."

Madeleine studied her options for a few seconds. The man standing too close to her was not to be taken lightly.

He continued, "Don't feel guilty—just tell me the names. Your friends would do the same in your shoes."

"I-I don't know anything," she stammered.

Klaus moved even closer and, with one swift jerk, ripped off all the buttons of her blouse. Her white bra now stood out against her dark olive skin.

"Don't make me hurt you."

She looked at him imploringly.

He shook his head and said, "You're the only one who can stop what's about to happen."

Madeleine tried to think about something else, to detach, but when Klaus removed her first fingernail, she knew she could not hold out.

After stating all the names of her colleagues and giving as much information about their whereabouts as she knew or could guess, Madeleine took a very deep breath, hoping her suffering was over.

"Now, so that you can see I don't hold any ill feelings toward you for your earlier hesitation, you and I are going to have ourselves a good time," he said, yanking down her skirt.

Madeleine wept. She knew that she would never be the same. But even at that moment she held on to her earlier musings of life after imprisonment, if she could only survive this and overcome the guilt.

Chapter 61

THE LETTER

Lyon

SEPTEMBER 6, 1942

WHAT IF THE OTHER dioceses asked the cardinal for permission to read his letter throughout the parishes of France? Pierre Gerlier hesitated as this thought occurred to him. He was unsure what the repercussions would be if the missive in his hands were made available to the rest of the church. Rome had sought a policy of appeasement to curb the growing persecution against Catholics, but they would not be able to stay silent forever. Gerlier knew he was not the first to rebel against the collaborationist policies of his government. Monsignor Saliège, the archbishop of Toulouse, had spoken out just days before. The mass deportation of Jews that fateful summer had moved many hearts, but Saliège was one of the most important and influential men of the church in France. He chose not to hold his tongue.

Cardinal Gerlier wondered how to go about loving his enemies, those despicable men who did such damage in the world. But he knew that if he did not love them, he would sow hatred instead, and there would never be peace, only vast devastation.

Gerlier's own people had been taken, the sheep from his flock in Lyon, and this infuriated him. The letter penned by his brother Saliège was clear and to the point. Saliège's words stirred even Gerlier's conscience.

For the hundredth time, Gerlier read back over the letter written by his archbishop friend.

My dearest brothers,

There is a Christian morality, a human morality, which imposes duties and recognizes rights. These duties and these rights are an inherent part of human nature. They come from God. We can violate them, but no mortal has the power to suspend them.

A sad spectacle has unfolded in our times: children, women, men, fathers, and mothers are treated as lowly farm animals; family members are separated from one another and shipped off to unknown destinations.

Why does the right of sanctuary in our churches no longer exist?

Why are we defeated?

Lord, have mercy on us.

Our Lady, pray for France.

In our diocese, scenes of terror took place in the camps of Noah and Récébédou. Jews are men, Jews are women. It is not true that anything and everything can be done to them, can be done against these men, against these women, against the fathers and mothers of these families. They are part of the human race. They are our brothers like so many others. A Christian must never forget this.

France, my beloved fatherland France, in the consciousness of all your children flows the tradition of respect for the human person. Chivalrous and generous France, I have no doubt, you are not the one responsible for these horrors.

Once again the words of the short missive left Gerlier breathless. He could not improve upon the rhetoric, the style, or the heart behind them. He was convinced that the one they served, the Jew from Nazareth, would be proud of their letters. That Jew had come to the world to save what had been lost, not to spread more hatred and evil among humanity. Gerlier looked at his own letter and prayed again for God to protect all the Jews and Catholics in France. Then it was time. He stood, donned his holy robes, and headed for the cathedral of Lyon to officiate. His lot had been cast.

Chapter 62

A SUCCESS

Saint-Sauveur-de-Montagut
AUGUST 28, 2001

I T WAS A VERY special day for Valérie. Seated in front of her at an old café that had borne witness to the joys and sorrows of its clients for decades were two of the girls who had survived the Vénissieux camp: Lotte Levy and Rachel Kaminker. The two women studied Valérie with the kind eyes of people who have suffered much and forgiven deeply in order to continue on with their lives. She smiled at them.

"I've learned as much about you two as your paperwork and a few photographs can tell. At times it's been hard to believe that you're real, as if all the information about the camp were just history, a history I've been digging up from the dust of the past. But here you are—flesh and blood."

"Yes, dearie, and some of us are a little more fleshy than others," Lotte, the more rotund of the two, said with a giggle.

"Oh, it's so delightful to meet you!" Valérie gushed.

"The pleasure is ours, truly. We've been told that you're re-searching everything that happened the last week of August 1942. At that time we should've all been jittery about going back to school, smelling our new schoolbooks, complaining about our uncomfortable new shoes and satchels that were wearing thin. But instead we were packed into buses that took us to hell and stole what we loved most dearly in life." The muscles in Rachel's face strained with the effort to control her emotions.

"Sometimes things just happen. Existence itself is suffering and pain, as well as love and life. Who would we be now if we hadn't gone through all that? We'll never know. Obviously we'd be very different, but there are important lessons to be learned from the ups and downs of life—things that can't be learned in history books," Lotte added with her sweet voice.

Rachel tsked and said, "But we haven't come here to get our new friend all sad. Valérie, you'll know probably better than we do what happened. We were young, terrified, and so confused that, to be frank, I can hardly remember any of it. It's probably for the best, though what is forever emblazoned into my mind—the memory that torments me most—is the way my mother looked the last time I saw her. It was a look of complete desperation and fear. She had always overprotected me, and I think the poor woman didn't think I could survive without her." Though she had gotten control of her face, her eyes belied the pain behind her words.

The three women chatted for some time, telling one another everything they knew or could remember.

Eventually, Valérie asked, "Did you always know who you really were, your real names?"

Lotte nodded. "I did. I could remember everything from my life before the camp because I was fifteen when they took me to Vénissieux. And it was only me, not my parents. We were eventually reunited. But I think that afterward, if the family I ended up staying with had tried to convince me that I was someone else, they could've done so. It's always been so painful to go back and remember."

Lotte looked to Rachel, wondering how she would respond. Rachel thought for a few moments before answering. "No, I didn't know who I was and still don't know. I don't know much about my family of origin except that they were all killed in concentration camps. We're a generation of lost names and lost lives. Our identities disappeared that stormy, scary night. There under the rain and lightning, we became other people."

Valérie turned off the recorder and took the hands of the two women. "Your lives will not be lost forever to the impetuous winds of history. You and the other children rescued that night are more than the blue documents on which your parents rescinded their rights in order to save you."

Lotte and Rachel smiled through their broken hearts. They were now mothers and grandmothers. Deep inside they were also still scared, lost children who escaped from hell one August night as the skies let loose their fury against the accursed earth—the earth where parents were capable of turning away from their children to save them from the tyrannical yoke of Nazi slavery.

"It's strange how bonds of love can form between strangers, but I feel like I've known you for years," Valérie said.

"Love is much more than a feeling or an emotion. It's fundamentally a choice, and you have decided to love us—at least, the lost girls of Vénissieux that we were."

Valérie nodded. Rachel was right. She loved her research and loved the names written on dingy old documents. She did not yet know and love the flesh and blood version of those names sitting in front of her.

"Still," Rachel went on, "we want to thank you for digging up our history. For so, so long we never dared to talk about what happened, not even with our own children. Forgetting seemed better. But that's not right. If we lose the memories, we'll be left with nothing—just orphans of the truth."

Lotte smiled. To lighten the mood, she suggested, "So are you picking up the tab?"

Valérie laughed. "Of course! It's my pleasure. Had you two stayed in touch?"

Rachel and Lotte looked at each other and smiled.

"Well," Rachel said, "for a time some of us were able to, but you know how life goes. We went on about the business of living. Fate joins us together with certain people for certain times. Sometimes we think it'll be forever, but often it's just a brief moment, and then we're separated again like strangers. That's why we treasure in our hearts all the people who've shared their lives with us. We might lose them and realize too late that there was so much more we could have shared with them."

Valérie stored up Rachel's words. Then she asked for the check. As the three women said goodbye, Valérie was more committed than ever to finding the rest of the formerly lost, scared children of Vénissieux and giving them back their identities so they never had to hide again.

Chapter 63

THE FAITHFUL

Lyon
SEPTEMBER 6, 1942

THE CARDINAL ARRIVED AT the church and took his place on the throne. That morning the nave was full to bursting. Nazi occupation had a direct impact on the people: the reigning uncertainty had become a great ally to the faith, or at least to gullibility.

When the deacon took the address from the cardinal's outstretched hand, Gerlier held his breath. He was deeply concerned about how the people would react. At the end of the day, the people were the only ones with the power to end the tyrannies of men.

The deacon cleared his throat before reading, seemingly aware that this was a pivotal moment in his life and career. History was about to be made.

"'The deportation measures currently being carried out against the Jews lead to scenes throughout our region that are so painful that we have the imperative and painful duty to voice the protest of our conscience. We are witnessing the cruel breakup of families from whom none are spared, neither due to age, weakness, nor illness. The heart aches at the thought of the treatment suffered by thousands of human beings and aches still more so thinking of the treatment they are yet to face.

"'We do not forget that the French authorities have a problem to solve, and we can appreciate the difficulties the government faces.

"'But who could reproach the church for, in this dark hour and in the face of that what is imposed on us, clearly and loudly affirming the inalienable rights of the human person, the sacred nature of family ties, the inviolable right to sanctuary, and the imperious demands of charity made by Christ to be the distinctive mark of his disciples? It is the honor of Christian civilization, and should be the honor of France, to never abandon such principles.

"'It is not on violence and hatred that we can build the new order. We will only build it, and peace along with it, on the respect for justice, on the beneficial union of minds and hearts, to which the great voice of the marshal calls us, and through which the centuries-old prestige of our homeland will flourish once again.

"'May Our Lady of Fourvière help us hasten its return!'"

A long, uncomfortable silence followed the reading. Eventually a well-dressed man toward the front stood up and started clapping. A frumpy-looking woman a few rows away joined him, and within seconds the entire congregation was on its feet giving an ovation to their pastor, Cardinal Gerlier.

He stood, too, and approached the pulpit. As he spoke, the crowd of the faithful quieted and took their seats again.

"The wise Solomon says that there is a time to speak and a time to remain silent, a time for war and a time for peace, a time to scatter and a time to gather. There is a time for everything. Today it is time to shout to the four winds from all the parishes of France that what makes us great is our love for truth and justice. The church has often erred by attempting to impose its creed on others; it has erred when it has attacked the Jewish people, who are God's chosen people through whom the Messiah and Savior of our souls came. It is time for men and women, children and adults, poor and rich—all of God's children—to refuse to collaborate with evil. It is time to ask those who rule over us not to make us choose between our conscience and their unjust laws, between good and evil, because we will choose to follow our conscience and will choose the good."

The people got to their feet once again. It had been a very long time since they heard such valiant words, words that put love before hatred, honor before the cowardice into which the French government had sunk. Tears on many faces bore witness to how deeply the cardinal's message moved them. It was a message to reconnect France with its soul. The cardinal continued.

"We ask the government of Marshal Pétain to return to the path of the right and the good. If not, it will be judged by history and by the supreme tribunal, which will serve justice to each man and woman for the good and evil they have done or allowed in this world. The court of God brooks no appeals, and we will all give defense in it. We cannot look away, nor do we wish to. The children of France are our children. Their innocent faces will not see the camps of Germany; they will not succumb to the ignominious curse of hatred that besieges Europe. Leave the children in peace! Jesus told the children to come to him because the kingdom of heaven belongs to them, and no one can be saved without first becoming like a child. The authorities want to rob us of France's greatest treasure, a treasure to which nothing in the Louvre, the halls of Versailles, or any of our towns compares: it is the treasure of our freedom and brotherhood. Yet since these are intangible, they can never be taken from us, though our very lives be destroyed. We are not afraid of the authorities. We fear only what can take eternal life from us, but the authorities can do nothing against the reign of peace, love, and truth."

The cardinal was drenched with sweat when he stepped away from the pulpit. He staggered to his throne, and a priest helped him settle into the seat. Then he looked up and saw the enlivened congregation. It had been quite some time since the French had felt proud of being French. The cardinal had returned some of their dignity to them. With that, he intuited something had changed. He wondered if it might be the beginning of the end. It may yet require time and blood, but the Germans and their accomplices had at least suffered a sizable moral defeat.

Chapter 64

FEAR

Lyon
SEPTEMBER 7, 1942

PIERRE LAVAL PICKED UP the telephone with dread. The president had told him he must place an immediate call to the military commander of German-occupied France, Carl-Heinrich Rudolf Wilhelm von Stülpnagel. Laval was to communicate that the French government would no longer cooperate in the deportation of more Jews, whether foreigners or French nationals. The prime minister knew that this could very well mean the end of the shaky independence of the free zone, but the old marshal had left no room for questions. Public opinion had spoken. After the cardinal of Lyon's pastoral letter, protests had broken out across the country. Pétain saw his government as dependent on the French, not the power of the Germans.

"Commander, this is the prime minister speaking."

There was no answer beyond the sound of heavy breathing.

"The president has communicated to me that we must suspend the deportation of foreigners and French citizens of

Jewish background. We are obliged to cease all actions of this nature until further orders."

The German gave no reply. With an army career of nearly forty years, von Stülpnagel's entire life centered around the defense of his country. He was from a Prussian family of the old guard that prized honor, loyalty, and duty. His cousin Otto von Stülpnagel had previously held the post in France but had been forced to resign when he refused to carry out Hitler's strict orders against the growing French Resistance. Carl, who had reluctantly accepted the deportation of Jews, was therefore quite aware that opposing Hitler equated to personal and political suicide. For some time he had flirted with covert opposition to the Führer within the German army, but as long as Hitler continued to win battles, von Stülpnagel knew that no one could overthrow him. The SS and the Gestapo were pressing von Stülpnagel for full compliance with racial laws and repression of German enemies. To him it was clear that Himmler was vying for the power that the army still held in Germany.

Finally, he spoke. "Are you aware of what you are asking me to do? The Führer has given very clear orders. He wants all European Jews in Germany by the end of this year."

"I'm very sorry to say that we are unable to meet his demands."

"The Führer does not accept no. You'll have to face the consequences. You are German allies and must respect the agreements between our nations."

"Yes, sir, and you're aware that I support German victory—without it, we all lose, and the Bolsheviks will rule the world—but the French people do not want to deport the Jews."

"Since when do the people make the decisions? Real leaders tell the people what they must believe and do. Repress the protests and get your house in order, or we'll have to do it for you."

Laval was silent. He knew that at that moment the Nazis did not have enough men to take over the entire French territory and that the Eastern front was consuming most of their energies. Besides, they needed France in order to continue the war effort, and a couple thousand Jews were not going to break the strong ties between Vichy and Berlin.

Carl-Heinrich Rudolf Whilhelm von Stülpnagel continued, "I will communicate your government's decision to my own. There will surely be repercussions of some sort. It won't be long before our troops will spread throughout the entire country. Clearly the Vichy authorities are incapable of maintaining order and keeping their word."

Laval took the threats seriously, though he presumed that Hitler would eventually calm down and appreciate all the other ways in which the Vichy government showed its loyalty to the Third Reich. Laval's folly was proved a few months later.

Chapter 65

THE LEAFLET

Lyon
SEPTEMBER 7, 1942

KLAUS BARBIE WAS FURIOUS. A leaflet declaring open opposition to the Germans was circulating throughout Lyon. Cardinal Gerlier and his minions had challenged the occupiers, and Klaus would see that they paid dearly.

He cursed as he read the small paper again.

> YOU WON'T GET THE CHILDREN
> Following German orders, Prefect Angeli demanded that 160 Jewish children aged two to sixteen be handed over to him.
> These children were entrusted to Cardinal Gerlier by their parents, who Vichy had already handed over to Hitler.
> The cardinal declared to the prefect:
> "You won't get the children."
> This conflict is open and public.

The Church of France stands against the ignoble racist Tartar.

French people of all persuasions, of all beliefs, listen to the call of your conscience; don't let the innocent be handed over to the executioners.

The Resistance Movements

The captain had sent his men to round up all Resistance members who had collaborated in the Vénissieux operation, but they were nowhere to be found. It would not be easy to bring a people as proud as the French into submission. Yet Klaus was set on doing so.

He wrote to the Gestapo offices in Berlin requesting more men, materials, and resources. Klaus still had time to curb the Resistance, but if he did not act soon, the nuisance would spread throughout the Reich's territories. Anyone and everyone would think they could stand up to the Germans without suffering the consequences. The Aryans were much more than simple mortals; they were the race chosen to rule the world. He would let no one dare to stop them.

Klaus ordered that anyone implicated in the Vénissieux operation be brought to his secret jail. It was a pity that Gilbert Lesage had escaped and that Alexandre Glasberg could not be found, but at least he knew where Father Chaillet was. If he patiently followed the string, he would end up capturing them all and dismantling the Resistance in Lyon. This would no doubt lead to a promotion, and perhaps Klaus could return home to his family, where he would be received as a true hero, the guarantor of the purity of the Aryan race.

Chapter 66

REENCOUNTER

Brotteaux Neighborhood
SEPTEMBER 18, 1942

L ILI HAD GATHERED HER belongings and, with new identification papers, moved to a neighborhood on the other side of the city. Hoping to escape the attention of the authorities, she had dyed her hair and changed jobs. The only one who knew where she lived now was her mother. That was why the knock at her door one afternoon startled her so badly. But her heart raced in a completely different way when she looked through the peephole and saw Georges Garel standing there.

The day after their magical dinner she had gone to his house, but he was in hiding by then. Lili feared that it had been too good to be true and that what seemed like a real chance at love had fallen through. Georges had fled to save his life and had been hiding out at the home of a friend. As soon as he could get false identification papers, the first thing he did was go out and find his love. He had not forgotten for one second their promise to marry, though the circumstances were highly unfavorable to their plans.

Lili threw open the door and wrapped her arms around Georges's neck, peppering him with kisses. "Oh, I've missed you so much!" she managed to say.

Georges looked all around and answered, "We'd better take this inside."

They kissed all the way down the hall and were only half dressed by the time they tumbled onto Lili's bed. The desperation of the last few weeks fueled their lovemaking. After an endless hour of bliss, they leaned back against the pillows and shared a cigarette. In the magic of the moment, it seemed like nothing on earth could separate them again.

"How did you find my new apartment?" Lili asked.

"Your mom. I figured you would have told her about me."

Lili smiled. "Has anyone ever told you how pretentious and arrogant you are?"

"For what—presuming you had told your mom that you went and got yourself engaged? I just figured that would have come up, you know. If I'm so pretentious, why do you like me?"

"For your looks," she joked, kissing him again.

Lili got up and returned a few minutes later with coffee.

"Do you know where the others are?" Georges asked.

"No, and it's better that way. They're hunting for all of us."

"I get the feeling that something changed, like the Nazis' good luck has run out. Now it's our turn."

Lili was amused. "Do you always get so optimistic after sex?"

"Ha, no, it's just that the streets are flooded with tracts against the Nazis, and there are big V's for victory painted on lots of walls. It's like people have lost their fear and respect for the occupiers."

Lili rested her head against Georges's chest. "Do you think we'll ever go back to normal life again? I used to never want a normal life. It's like I needed a war to make me realize that what really matters is exactly what we already have but don't care about. Like walking together and holding hands, having a picnic in the country, drinking fine wine with cheese, watching the leaves fall from the trees, and maybe having an adorable baby with your eyes."

"Someday we'll get all of that back, and you'll become Mrs. Garel. We'll have . . . twenty children!"

"Hmm, for the sake of getting places by car, three or four should suffice."

They spent the rest of the afternoon dreaming and making love. Despite it all, life did march on, and they had to learn how to move forward. They could not put everything on hold until the Nazis were defeated. Who knew when death would knock on their door? What mattered right then was to guzzle the cup of their existence to the dregs, leaving nothing for later. In those times, the future did not exist. Only the present was real.

Chapter 67

MARGOT, MAURICE, GABRIELLE

Mâcon
OCTOBER 11, 1942

TWO GENDARMES KNOCKED AT the door of the Koppel family. After being rescued from Vénissieux, Margot Koppel had been reunited with her grandparents and was now living with them since her parents had been sent to Germany on the trains. Margot was helping her grandmother fix breakfast when they heard the knock. The three Koppels were petrified when they saw who was on the other side of the door. The coffee began to boil and its fragrance filled the air. The toast was still warm when the policemen bound each Koppel's hands and led the family outside. A group of neighbors had gathered to block the gendarmes' way, but the policemen pushed through to the black van.

"Why are you doing this? What crime have we committed?" the grandfather asked, still in shirtsleeves.

"We're just following orders," the corporal answered tersely.

Margot was crying. At eleven, she could not understand why people hated her so much that they would chase her down across the country. She missed her parents, fully aware that they had likely already left behind the sad life they had the misfortune of calling their own. Though the echoes of the war seemed far off, little by little everyone began to feel its effects.

"God will not forgive you for this," the grandmother said as the gendarmes forced her head down and shoved her into the van behind her husband and granddaughter. The neighbors were yelling in protest. They threw rocks and whatever they could find at the van as it drove away.

→>—<←

As Margot and her grandparents were being shipped to Auschwitz, Gabrielle and Maurice Teitelbaum were biking the last stretch of road to the Swiss border. At fifteen and thirteen years of age, they looked the part of lost children searching for their parents. Yet their parents had disappeared into the dark night at Vénissieux, and the Teitelbaum siblings, rescued that same night, held little hope of ever seeing them again. When they glimpsed the demarcation line of the border, they stopped to catch their breath and marvel at the sight. They had not stayed long with the family who picked them up from the Carmelite convent. The father had turned out to have a nasty, violent temper that he reserved for the Jewish children. So they had fled. They knew that their younger siblings were safe in the children's home in Izieu. After the war, Gabrielle and Maurice would come back for them and start over at being a family.

As they resumed pedaling, they saw a car approaching with several gendarmes inside. The children increased their speed as much as they could. There were only about five hundred yards between them and freedom.

The car sped up and cut them off, sending the children flying from their bicycles. Maurice hopped up and started running, but Gabrielle was pinned underneath her bike.

"Maurice, help!" she cried.

Maurice, just a few yards from the border, turned back. The gendarmes were out of the car now and headed toward his sister with their pistols raised.

"Wait!" he screamed. He dashed toward Gabrielle and got her free, and they set off again.

But a mere lunge from a gendarme allowed him to catch Maurice by the leg. The boy fell hard against the grass. His sister kicked and bit at the gendarme, but two other policemen ran up and knocked her down. The wet grass pressed into their faces. Maurice lifted his head up enough to glance at the precious few yards that separated them from freedom. His eyes filled with furious, helpless tears. Once again the last image of his mother flashed before him: her blank, ruined stare as the bus drove her away from Vénissieux.

The policemen shut the children in the back of the car. As the vehicle drove back into France and toward the police station, Gabrielle and Maurice gripped each other's hands. At least they were together. They prayed that would remain the case.

Chapter 68

FINAL STOPS

La Baume-Cornillane
NOVEMBER 20, 1942

M RS. SAYN'S HOUSE WAS a haven of peace. But Justus could not just sit idly by and let the war continue. As soon as he had the chance, he made contact with a few friends he had known from his days working for Varian Fry, and he tried to get involved with the Resistance. At first he thought that someone as young and inexperienced as he was could never do much; he did not know how to use guns, explosives, or even the clandestine radios. But he was accepted into the Gallia network. The Resistance did not have many weapons, but it tried to sabotage certain infrastructures and take out soldiers and officials foolish enough to be found alone in the country's cities.

Late one afternoon, after he'd completed a simple mission of mixing up road signs to confuse the Germans, Mrs. Sayn was waiting for him with dinner.

"Why are you so late today?" she asked.

"I apologize. I was with some friends and we got carried away."

Mrs. Sayn saw right through him. "I want you to know that if the gendarmes or the Nazis capture you, we'll both pay the consequences."

Justus sat and stirred his soup. "I don't want to put you in danger, but I can't sit around doing nothing. Tomorrow morning I'll start looking for somewhere else to stay."

"You don't have to do that, Justus; all I'm asking is that you be very careful."

The young man nodded. Mrs. Sayn sat beside him, and they began to eat in silence.

Taking a sip of wine, Mrs. Sayn asked, "What would you like to do and be once all of this is over?"

"Well, it may be hard to believe, but I love French literature. I'd like to continue studying and then teach at the university level."

"Do you know that my room is stuffed to bursting with books? I'll bring some out tomorrow."

Justus smiled at his protector. She was not necessarily like a mother, but she was the closest thing to a mother he had had in several years.

"Thank you so much for helping me."

"I'm not courageous enough to pick up a weapon, but I want to serve France with the few gifts that the good Lord has given me. I lost my son in the war before this one, as well as my husband. So all that's left for me is to help others in need."

Easy silence reigned as they finished the hearty soup and simple wine. Words were superfluous. They had learned to be company for each other, keeping loneliness at bay and joined in solidarity for at least one stretch of their journeys.

Chapter 69

THE PRIEST

L'Honor-de-Cos
NOVEMBER 25, 1942

F ATHER GLASBERG KNEW THAT all the children except three had survived and were safely in hiding. Their well-being was all that mattered to him. He could not explain why, but he felt himself to be French despite being from the Ukraine; just as he had always felt like a Catholic, despite his Jewish background. He was constantly the opposite of what the rest of the world said he should be. He imagined that the Vénissieux children felt something similar.

For his safety, the cardinal had sent Glasberg to serve as a parish priest in a church far from Lyon. The small chapel in the village of Léribosc in Occitania could have seemed like an embarrassing, exiled demotion. To Glasberg, however, it was paradise on earth. He had lived in many cities and had traveled throughout many countries, but in that private corner of the world, he discovered the peace that nature brings.

Glasberg took long morning walks. Roe deer, eagles, foxes, and all sort of wild animals were daily sightings. In the afternoons, he visited his parishioners, most of whom were of advanced age. He sat and drank coffee or played cards with them. As pastor of this kind of flock, Glasberg was content to let life unfold as it wished. The world continued its course, and he no longer felt responsible for saving it. He knew that such rest was a gift from God, a kind of parenthesis in his life, and he was willing and eager to enjoy it.

That day he studied the pattern of snow forming over some nearby mountains. The destruction wrought by discontented men crazed with ambition and greed had no place there. The mountains seemed to say, "Let the world keep spinning no matter who rules it—we'll still be here."

Father Glasberg thought about the children and the three interminable days they had spent together, bonded through worry and sleeplessness. He suspected that his life would have been worth it had he managed to save only one of them, but there were over one hundred! He wondered where they were and what they were doing right then. Each of those individual lives had the potential to become a multiplying force of happiness and love. He was aware that the good he had done for those children was good done for the whole of humanity.

He sat on the rock bench in front of his humble abode and gazed at the fields, now barren for the winter. He imagined the leafless trees and fruitless stretches of land resurging with life in the spring. That was the way of things. No matter how unbearable the obstinate cold of winter, life would rise from the ashes. Behind each death lay a new beginning, just as a seed must die to produce its abundance.

Chapter 70

ANOTHER PARADISE

Le Chambon-sur-Lignon
MARCH 2, 1943

MADELEINE DREYFUS HAD MANAGED to escape the clutches of Klaus Barbie. A French woman who cleaned the Gestapo building had gotten ahold of the key to Madeleine's cell and helped her escape. Madeleine, bewildered and internally destroyed, was cognizant enough to make her way to Élisabeth Hirsch's house. Élisabeth took her friend to a convent where she could hide in safety. Meanwhile, Élisabeth processed false identification papers for Madeleine and arranged for her to be escorted to a remote area in the Alps region of France, the village of Le Chambon-sur-Lignon.

That place was a paradise of healing for Madeleine. The Protestant pastor André Trocmé and his wife, Magda, welcomed her as their own daughter.

Nearly the entire community was dedicated to helping Jewish children suffering the effects of the war. Madeleine's emotional and physical wounds healed as she began to work as a bridge between Lyon and Le Chambon-sur-Lignon.

"How are you, dearie?" Magda asked one day as Madeleine was sorting out the paperwork for some of the children they had recently received for shelter.

"I was thinking about Lyon and everything that happened last August. Sometimes I wish I'd never gotten involved. It came with a very high price tag."

Magda took a seat beside her.

"That's true. You paid for it."

"But then I think about the suffering of those parents. I had to ask them to give up their children! And they knew they'd never see them again."

Magda closed her eyes and shook her head. "I can't even imagine what they were going through. If someone took my children, I've no idea what I'd be liable to do."

"Sacrifice is a difficult road, but it takes us to places beyond selfishness. Every night I remember the faces of those children and wonder about their lives now. If we hadn't done something, they would've been killed."

Magda put her hand on Madeleine's shoulder. "We can't save the whole world, but each one of us, in little ways each and every day, ends up making a big difference. Back in the day, my family had a hard go of it when they had to leave everything behind in Russia. But when I look back on it, if it hadn't been for the suffering they faced, I would never have ended up here, never have met André, perhaps never have dedicated my life to helping others. As aristocrats, my family had it all, but maybe not the most important thing: love. We can't take anything from this world with us, but the love we've sowed will endure."

Madeleine smiled at her friend. She had also sowed love. The harvest had produced something greater than what she had been forced to sacrifice. Klaus Barbie had stolen her innocence and damaged her body, but she knew that her soul was intact. He, on the other hand, was a vile and selfish being incapable of love. One day he would have to pay for what he had done, whether in this world or the next. Madeleine did not hate him and had managed to forgive him. She knew that forgiveness sets the victim free from the prison of hatred and bitterness in order to love again.

"This, too, shall pass," Magda said, as if reading Madeleine's mind.

"Sometimes I think it would be better if it doesn't pass. I've never felt so happy and full of life."

The two women sat together in silence, musing over how much they had received from giving themselves to their neighbors. It had been entirely unexpected. If they had known earlier, they would have done even more for others. They had learned that happiness was found in the face of a child or anyone who needed their help.

Chapter 71

ÉLISABETH

Barcelona
MAY 9, 1944

É LISABETH HIRSCH LEFT HER post as director of the OSE once the children from Vénissieux made it to safety. The idea had been for Madeleine Dreyfus to take over, but shortly thereafter the psychologist had had to flee to Le Chambon-sur-Lignon. Élisabeth had been helping Jewish children in exile since the 1930s, but she knew that continuing to operate in France would very likely lead to her capture and death.

Élisabeth reached Catalonia and crossed into Spain without difficulties. On the other side of the border, members of the Jewish Resistance met her. Thanks to the aid of a group of Spanish diplomats, they were helping shuttle Jews from various countries east of Spain to Palestine and the United States.

Élisabeth's first few days in Barcelona were marvelous. For the first time in many years she felt safe, without having to look behind her every five minutes. She rented a small apartment on the famous street Las Ramblas. She spent part of her time helping the Jewish Resistance network and the other part visiting the sites of the city and enjoying the Spanish spring.

It was hard for her to believe that, despite the dictatorship and the lack of basic material necessities, the Spaniards continued enjoying life. People spent so much time out in the streets, walking, having a drink on the countless and ubiquitous terraces, and chatting exuberantly.

On one of her excursions around town, she saw an old and unpleasant acquaintance. It was one of the Nazis she had come across during her time in Paris. That could only mean one thing: Germany was losing the war.

Élisabeth tended to avoid the news. She was tired of battles. Reports of the fighting appeared in a scant few paragraphs of the heavily censored Francoist newspapers, but she knew that even those terse lines covered up hundreds of thousands of human dramas.

The network for smuggling European Jews out tended to begin in Barcelona or Valencia, then stretch to Madrid on its way to Lisbon or by boat to the Americas from Cádiz and other parts of Europe.

Élisabeth had saved hundreds of children in and from different concentration and detention camps in France. She had also led many expeditions of supposed Boy Scouts to get them into Switzerland. Yet the children of Vénissieux held a special place in her heart, and it was to them that her memories returned over and over again. Never before had she been part of such a tightly knit team, and never before had she been part of an operation that rescued over one hundred children in just one night—one dramatic night followed by several heart-stopping days.

As the months passed and life went on, she wondered what had become of the children. Were they happy? Had misfortune found them after all? Would their pasts forever hold them back, or would they move on with new and different identities? No child was prepared to leave their parents under such dramatic circumstances. Yet Élisabeth had learned that human beings have more resilience than what seems possible at first glance.

After a year in Spain, Élisabeth missed France, the country that had welcomed her. Born in Romania, she had arrived in France as a child. Her brilliant brother Sigismond had helped found the Éclaireurs Israèlites de France, the Jewish scouting movement. But both Sigismond and his beloved wife had been sent to Auschwitz. Élisabeth presumed they had met the fate of nearly everyone else sent there and that she would never see them again.

She knew that their young son and her nephew, Jean-Raphaël, was still alive and even at his age was active in the Resistance. The damned war had taken almost everything sweet from Élisabeth's life, but it had also allowed her to see just how far she was willing to go to bring about change.

Élisabeth went out onto her terrace. In the distance, almost at the horizon, a speck of ocean cheered her. The immense blue always made her feel so small and unimportant, aware that Earth was just a tiny planet amid a vast universe—so she could not fathom the meaning of human life and, more poignantly, the evil that humans seemed set on doing to one another.

Élisabeth reread the letter lying on her desk. It was from Maribel Semprún, now safely in Switzerland after escaping first the war in her own country of Spain and then the war in France.

Élisabeth sat in the chair she had dragged out to the terrace and listened to the murmur of foot traffic and the horns of passing cars. At that moment she finally identified what it was that she loved so much about Spain: discovering that blessed normalcy could one day be part of her life and her country's life again. Then she could once again be Élisabeth Hirsch, just an average woman hoping to be happy in life.

Chapter 72

SAVED

Tourelles Barracks, Paris
AUGUST 17, 1944

AFTER YEARS OF HELPING people avoid detention and concentration camps, Gilbert Lesage had finally landed in one himself. He studied himself in the mirror as he shaved: his sunken face, now creased with wrinkles, had aged more than he would have expected during those nearly five long years of war. He buttoned up his shirt and went out to the yard. The internment camp, which had been set up within former army barracks, housed all sorts of people, especially members of the Resistance. Gilbert limped slightly on his right leg, a gift from Klaus Barbie during his brief stay in the Gestapo jail in Lyon. Gilbert had since heard many stories about Barbie's nefarious deeds throughout Lyon. He only hoped the man would one day be made to pay for his crimes.

"Good morning, Pierre. Did you get ahold of a newspaper? I'm ready for this war to be over."

"The Allies are at the gates of Paris. It can't be much longer till we're liberated."

"Well, they're taking their precious time," Gilbert said, half joking. Since the landing in Normandy, the Allies were not advancing through France fast enough for his liking. "It must be the heat," he said, fanning his chest with his hat.

"Gilbert Lesage," a voice called from the other side of the yard.

Gilbert approached the guard cautiously.

"Yes, what is it?"

"You're wanted in the infirmary."

Gilbert figured it must a summons from his old friend Michel, an Alsatian doctor who tried to keep the camp's prisoners in decent health despite the lack of medicines at his disposal.

At the infirmary, Michel closed the door to his office once Gilbert was inside.

"The last transport is preparing to leave," the doctor said, getting straight to the point.

"What? They can't. The Allies are just miles away," Gilbert retorted.

"That's exactly why. We're free manual labor, and they're still hoping to win this war. Hitler still claims that his radio-guided missiles will bring the British to their knees."

"No one believes that anymore."

"Maybe not, but the Germans have no choice but to try to hold out. The Russians are eating them alive. Pretty soon they'll be in German territory and will get their revenge."

Gilbert shrugged. He would never understand the self-feeding, never-ending cycle of hatred that refused each passing generation the chance to start from scratch. "So why did you want to talk about it with me?"

"Come here."

Michel scooted the cot where he examined patients. It was covering up a panel in the wall that Michel took off to show Gilbert the hole behind it.

"It fits only two people."

Gilbert frowned. "Then what about all the others?"

"It fits only two people," the doctor repeated.

"Why me? There are young men out there, kids with the rest of their lives ahead of them. And fathers—no one is waiting on me to get out of here."

"Look, you've saved the lives of thousands of people—who knows, maybe even tens of thousands. You're the best human being I've ever met."

"Well, I'd like to save one more while I'm at it," Gilbert retorted.

"Today you're going to have to let me save you."

Gilbert was surprised to find himself tearing up. He had not expected to ever be saved, and he did not even think his life was worth the trouble.

"Come on," Michel insisted. "Get in before the Germans come around."

"Thank you," was all Gilbert could say as he fought to restrain his tears.

"There's no time for sentimentality; in you go."

The two men knelt and crawled into the small cave, pulled the bed back against the wall, and fixed the panel in place. Then they held their breath and waited.

The Nazis deported a sizable number of men from the Tourelles Barracks that day. Gilbert and Michel could have been among those final unfortunate Frenchmen. Their former fellow inmates were sent to German extermination camps and weapons factories where they perished from the working conditions or the physical and psychological abuse from their captors.

A few hours later, when Gilbert and Michel crawled out of their hiding spot, they found the camp nearly abandoned. A handful of older men remained, along with a few prisoners who had managed to hide during the final roundup. Only they saw the Allies enter and officially free the camp.

Gilbert joined the others at the main gate. Soldiers wearing French uniforms forced it open.

"Thank you," Gilbert said to one of them.

"We're from the Leclerc Division," the soldier answered in heavily accented French. He was a Spaniard.

At that, Gilbert burst out laughing. He would never have guessed that a group of Spaniards would be among the first units to liberate Paris. History was full of ironies, but that one beat them all.

Small tanks bearing the names of Spanish cities drove by the old barracks. Those soldiers, who had been fighting since the start of the Spanish Civil War in 1936, were now headed to Germany to pay Adolf Hitler back for all the bombs he had dropped on innocent people throughout Spain.

Gilbert joined the inmates cheering the soldiers beneath the intense August sun. He remembered back to August two years prior, in other barracks in another French internment camp. In Lyon he and his colleagues had stood up for the cause of justice and saved 108 children from the talons of the Nazis. How he hoped that Europe would never have to face something like that again—hoped that their fight for freedom and human dignity had been worth it all.

Chapter 73

LAST WISHES

Saint-Sauveur-de-Montagut

AUGUST 20, 1944

RACHEL HAD BEEN WITH the Merlands in Saint-Sauveur-de-Montagut for nearly two years. Time seemed to have made the wounds of the summer of 1942 disappear, though the girl still missed her mother, her stepmother, and, most of all, her father. Her new adoptive family and other members of the Resistance had taken good care of her. Yet there was a lonely ache in her soul that never left her. Rachel often dreamed of being back in the old Roman theater in Alba-la-Romaine. Those millennial rocks seemed to understand her more than anyone around her. As often as she could, Rachel would go to a quiet park in Saint-Sauveur-de-Montagut where she could imagine being back in the theater. She would take out her violin and prop it between her chin and shoulder, teasing from its strings the saddest notes in the world. Rachel would play for at least an hour, letting the music carry her far away until her fingers hurt and her heart calmed down. Then she would sit in silence, watching the play of the sun and shadows in the trees all around.

That day was different. Rachel was finishing her improvised concert when someone came up behind her and stopped to listen. Rachel was unaware of the presence; all of her senses were concentrated on the music, her true liberator. When the wind carried the final note out of the park, she heard a familiar voice.

"Rachel."

At first she stood paralyzed. Had she imagined it?

"Rachel."

The second time her name soared through the air, the girl turned and gazed at the woman standing in front of her. She dared not move for fear that the figure would vanish like a ghost.

"Mama?" she asked. When the figure nodded, Rachel yelled her mother's name aloud again through tears, placed her violin down, and threw herself into the woman's arms.

They said nothing for some time. Interlocked arms and faces pressed together, their skin nearly burning. That was enough. Then Chaja knelt to be on Rachel's level. Both of their eyes were flooded with tears.

"Oh, my daughter, you're here, you're alive, you're all right. It's a miracle. My goodness, how you've grown. But why are you so thin?"

"I'm fine, Mom," the child answered, happily letting her mother correct the mismatched buttons of her blouse and wipe a few stains from her face.

Chaja stood back and stared into Rachel's eyes, which were Zelman's. Chaja knew Zelman would never return. Her little girl no longer had a father. Chaja started crying all over again. Her ex-husband had been a good man. He was hardworking and honorable. He had not deserved to die like a despicable criminal.

The two of them walked hand in hand to the Merlands' home. As soon as Mrs. Merland saw Chaja, she knew what was going to happen. She had known this day might come and was glad for Rachel's sake, but Paulette would have loved for Rachel to stay with them forever.

"Thank you," were the first words that Chaja said to the woman who had helped save her daughter's life.

Paulette dried her hands, still soapy from washing dishes, on her apron and said, "Any woman would have done the same."

Chaja climbed the stairs to the front door and held out her hands. Paulette took them and could not help but notice how dry and rough they were. Chaja's hands had seen much harder work than what raising one daughter required.

"Thank you," Chaja repeated.

Something between the two women broke open. In different ways, they were both mother to the same sweet, affectionate girl they loved so dearly. Rachel hugged them both at once. In that embrace, time slowed down and ceased its lurching. From then on for Rachel, minutes flowed into hours with the harmonious, rhythmic cadence life was meant to have: time in motion seasoned by love and peace.

EPILOGUE

Lyon
AUGUST 26, 2012

VALÉRIE PORTHERET STUDIED THE faces of the authorities and the survivors who had turned out for the commemoration ceremony. In that unassuming street of an old industrial area, thousands of people had lived through hell on earth seventy years prior.

She waited for the ceremony to come to a close before approaching an older woman. At seventy-eight, Rachel Berkowicz looked very good for her age.

"Forgive me for bothering you; I'm Valérie Portheret. For twenty years I've been researching what happened that night at Vénissieux and in the days that followed."

Rachel smiled. "I don't think I'll be much help. I've forgotten nearly everything. I think my old brain wanted to shield me from all that pain and suffering. I was only eight when it all happened."

"I'm so sorry about all of it," Valérie said, moved to tears at having Rachel before her.

"You needn't be sorry, my dear. The rescue operation saved our lives. One of the few things I do recall is Lili Garel holding my hand and walking me to the mess hall."

Another wrinkled, gray-haired woman came up to them.

"Look, Lili, this young woman is studying about what we went through in 1942."

At ninety-one years of age, Lili still retained her mental clarity, her memories, and even her spry gait.

"Oh, Georges would have loved to meet you. He was always talking about it. He said it was a youthful adventure. That's how we experienced it anyway. I think that if we'd been older, we would never have dared to attempt what we pulled off."

Valérie could not shake the surreal shock of seeing those two women together after so many years. Since 2003, Valérie had dedicated herself to locating one Vénissieux survivor after another. She still had a number to go, but Lili and Rachel were two of her favorites.

"What happened to your old violin?" Valérie asked.

The wrinkles on Rachel's face stretched as she smiled. "I went back to Belgium with my mother in 1945, and the violin came with me. Life was hard, very hard. She worked as a domestic servant, and we shared one tiny room. Sometimes in the summers we would visit my adoptive parents, the Merlands. I kept playing violin and in 1949 I immigrated to Israel. Eventually I married Wolff Rajzman and helped to start the marvelous Tel Aviv orchestra. I've been very happy. I've had a long, full life. I think I've taken advantage of the second chance Lili and the others gave me. I kept my father's old violin. One day it will go to my granddaughter and remind her of how I was reborn one hot August night during the worst storm of my life—not just the thunderstorm but the storm of hatred that shook Europe and the whole world. I hope nothing that terrible ever comes around again."

Lili gave Rachel a hug, and tears coursed down both of their faces. Then they placed a handful of red carnations at the commemorative plaque. After saying goodbye to Valérie, they made their way slowly to the cars.

Valérie dropped her camera into her backpack. She was no longer the young woman who, with such passion, had started the race of her research project about the children of Vénissieux. But safely in her heart she stored the long list of names and lost lives that had once again found their way home.

REFERENCES

Martin Buber, *Tales of the Hasidim* (1933; repr. New York: Schocken Books, 1991), 250.

Pierre-Marie Gerlier, "Communiqué de son eminence le Cardinal Gerlier Archeveque de Lyon," September 6, 1942, original translation.

Benoît Hopquin, "The Painful Rescue of Jewish Children from the Vénissieux Camp," *Le Monde*, August 27, 2020, https://www.lemonde.fr/m-le-mag/article/2020/08/27/le-douloureux-sauvetage-des-enfants-juifs-du-camp-de-venissieux_6050084_4500055.html.

Valérie Portheret, *Vous n'aurez pas les enfants* (France, 2020).

"Un kilomètre à pied" (English translation found in chapter 32) is a popular French children's song similar to a nursery rhyme. Unknown origin.

CLARIFICATIONS FROM HISTORY

THE STORY OF VALÉRIE Portheret is real: I first learned about her and her work from the French newspaper *Le Monde*. Her story has moved French society. It also brought to light the country's opposition to remembering the treatment of Jews during World War II and the obstacles in the academy to historical research into that period, especially during the 1990s.

In 1992 Valérie Portheret wanted to become a judge. She had studied law but had not yet written her final research project. She decided to focus on Klaus Barbie, the infamous "Butcher of Lyon," but her research led her down a different path. At first, her professors did not want her to study those subjects. At the time, the Jean Moulin Lyon 3 University was a bastion of anti-Semitism that denied the existence of the Holocaust. Yet Valérie was determined to continue and did so with the support of professor Jean-Dominique Durand, who risked everything to back Valérie.

Valérie learned of l'Enfant Caché, known in English-speaking regions as the Hidden Child Foundation, which led her to the Peyrins château. There, the son-in-law of the former château director showed Valérie the logbook of the children sheltered at the château. It was no small task to sort out the names of

French children from the Jewish children whose names had been changed.

In a meeting of LICRA, the International League Against Racism and Anti-Semitism, Valérie ran into one of her neighbors, René Nodot. He had been active in the French Resistance and had written a pamphlet about the children sheltered at the Peyrins château.

These are all facts, though the order of events has been changed and the conversations have been imaginatively recreated. It all began in Lyon in August 1942, when orders came to deport the region's Jews. Klaus Barbie, chief of the local Gestapo, and his henchmen chased the Jews down to the farthest corners.

Although it is true that Klaus Barbie was in the region at the time of the Vénissieux roundup, he was not authorized to take action in Lyon until the fall of that year, which kept him from personal involvement in the search for the children rescued from Vénissieux. There are many other documented cases of his hunts for children, including those hidden at the children's home in Izieu. He was also accused of numerous cases of torture and rape. After living penalty-free in South America for several decades, in 1983 he was returned to France, and four years later, he was sentenced to life in prison. He was convicted of the deportation of some 7,500 Jews to concentration camps and of involvement in the arrest and torture of thousands of other people, many of whom were members of the Resistance. Barbie died four years later of leukemia.

→>-<+

It is true that Valérie dedicated herself to identifying the names of the 108 children and locating them personally. Thus began a journey that lasted more than twenty-five years, a journey to return to those children their original identities and to listen to their stories. By 1994 she had identified the names of 93 of the 108 children from a list found in the archives of the Alliance Israélite Universelle, a French organization. In 2003 she uncovered eighty-two of the waivers from the Vénissieux camp in which parents signed away their parental rights and entrusted their children to the members of Amitié Chrétienne. Among the children on the list of those rescued from Vénissieux was a girl named Eva Stein. Eva was one of the last children Valérie found, and not until 2018. Altogether, Valérie has identified the names of all 108, has reconstructed the stories of 90 of the children, and has personally met with as many as of the children and the rescue workers as possible.

→>−<←

The case of the priest Alexandre Glasberg is also real. Glasberg had visited Germany in the 1930s and seen the plight of the Jews. Cardinal Gerlier put Glasberg in charge of care of the refugees arriving from Europe, and he set up several welcome centers for families who made it out of Vichy-run camps. When the Germans wanted to take the Jews of Lyon, Glasberg did everything in his power to free as many people as possible from Vénissieux. He concocted a plan with Germaine Chesneau to help keep 108 children from being deported, even though the children would have to lose their born identities forever. The plan was possible due to an ambiguous order from the Vichy government that children abandoned by their parents were not to be deported. Thus, the families of Vénissieux had to give up their parental rights in order to save their children, not knowing if they would ever see the children again.

→>-<←

As Valérie went about locating the Vénissieux children over a twenty-five-year period, she reconstructed the timeline of what had occurred at the end of August 1942. In the process, she learned the stories of many other people, like Ruth and her family, who tried to escape the raid in Lyon. They were Czech Jews who had lived in France since 1938, and Ruth's parents were photographers. One neighbor hid them, but another neighbor, who hated Jews, denounced them. Thus they ended up in Vénissieux.

The story of Rachel Berkowicz's life is also based on facts. She and her family escaped from Belgium when the Nazis arrived, and they settled near Lyon. Her father had previously fled Poland.

After more than two decades of researching, searching, and documenting all that she learned, Valérie presented her doctoral thesis.

Characters including Gilbert Lesage, Pierre Gerlier, Élisabeth Hirsch, Charles Lederman, Georges Garel, and Lili Tager are real, as are many others. The real persons of Madeleine Barot and Madeleine Dreyfus were telescoped into one character herein. And a few details from history are conflated into one day for the sake of storytelling.

May this novel serve in praise of the great humanitarian effort of these fine people.

TIMELINE

1939

September 1: Germany invades Poland, initiating World War II in Europe.

September 3: Great Britain, France, Australia, and New Zealand declare war on Germany.

September 17: The Soviet Union invades Poland.

September 27: Warsaw surrenders.

November 30: The Soviet Union invades Finland.

1940

March 12: Finland signs a peace treaty with the Soviet Union.

April 9: Germany begins the occupation of Denmark and invades Norway.

May 10: Germany invades Belgium, the Netherlands, and Luxembourg.

May 10: Neville Chamberlain resigns and is replaced by Winston Churchill.

May 15: The Netherlands surrenders to Germany.

May 26: The British Expeditionary Force evacuates from Dunkirk.

May 28: Belgium surrenders to Germany.

June 10: Italy declares war on Great Britain and France.

June 14: The Wehrmacht enters Paris.

June 16: Marshal Philippe Pétain is named leader of the Vichy government.

June 18: The Soviet Union invades the Baltic states.

June 22: France signs an armistice with Germany.

June 30: German occupation of the Channel Islands begins.

July 10: The Battle of Britain begins.

October 28: Italy invades Greece.

November 22: The Ninth Italian Army is defeated by the Greeks.

1941

February 12: The Afrika Korps begin their offensive in North Africa.

April 4: Germany captures Benghazi.

April 6: Germany invades Yugoslavia and Greece.

April 13: The Soviets and Japanese sign a neutrality agreement.

April 17: The Yugoslav army surrenders to Germany.

April 27: Germany captures Athens.

May 20: The airborne invasion of Crete begins.

June 1: British forces on Crete are defeated by the Germans.

June 8: Allied forces invade Syria.

June 22: Operation Barbarossa begins—Germany invades the Soviet Union.

June 28: The German Army captures the Belarus city of Minsk.

July 15: Germany captures Smolensk.

August 16: Germany captures Novgorod.

September 8: The siege of Leningrad begins.

September 19: Germany captures Kiev.

November 3: Germany captures Kursk.

December 5: The Germans halt their offensive against Moscow.

December 7: Japan attacks the United States' military base in Pearl Harbor.

December 7: Japan declares war on the United States.

1942

February 15: Singapore falls to the Japanese.

July 3: Sevastopol falls to German control.

August 26: Jews are rounded up in Lyon and the surrounding regions.

August 26–27: Prisoners arrive at the Vénissieux camp.

August 29: The children are smuggled out of the Vénissieux camp and hidden in Lyon.

August 29–31: The children are sent to families in the region.

September 6: Cardinal Gerlier shares a pastoral letter about protecting Jewish children.

October 23: The Second Battle of El Alamein begins.

November 8: Operation Torch begins.

1943

January 14: The Casablanca Conference begins.

January 23: Britain's Eighth Army captures Tripoli.

January 31: Germany surrenders Stalingrad.

February 8: The Soviet Union retakes Kursk.

February 14: The Soviet Union retakes Rostov.

May 13: Axis powers surrender in North Africa.

July 10: Operation Husky begins.

July 25: Benito Mussolini's Fascist government in Italy falls.

September 3: Italy signs an armistice with the Allies.

September 10: Germany occupies Rome.

September 23: Mussolini declares the establishment of a Fascist government in northern Italy.

September 25: The Soviet Union retakes Smolensk.

October 13: The official Italian government declares war on Germany.

November 6: The Soviet Union retakes Kiev.

1944

January 6: The Soviet Union advances through Polish territory.

January 22: The Allies land in Anzio.

January 27: The siege of Leningrad ends.

March 19: The Wehrmacht occupies Hungary.

April 10: The Soviet Union takes Odesa.

May 9: The Soviet Union takes Sevastopol.

June 4: The Allies liberate Rome.

June 6: The Allied landing on Normandy beaches begins.

June 28: The United States Army takes Cherbourg.

July 3: The Soviet Union retakes Minsk.

July 20: Operation Valkyrie fails.

July 24: The Allied offense against German defenses in Normandy begins.

July 28: The Soviet Union takes Brest-Litovsk.

August 4: The Allies liberate Florence.

August 15: The Allies land in southern France.

August 25: The Allies liberate Paris.

August 28: The Allies liberate Marseille and Toulon.

August 31: The Soviet Union takes Bucharest, the capital of Romania.

September 2: The Allies liberate Pisa.

September 3: The Allies liberate Brussels.

September 3: The Allies liberate Lyon.

September 4: The Allies liberate Antwerp.

September 5: The Soviet Union declares war on Bulgaria.

September 22: The Allies liberate Boulogne.

September 30: The Allies liberate Calais.

1945

April 30: Adolf Hitler dies by suicide.

May 7: Nazi Germany surrenders unconditionally to the Allies. World War II ends in Europe.

DISCUSSION QUESTIONS

1. What is the purpose of hope in this story? How do people like the social workers maintain hope when all seems lost, when no day seems better than the one before?

2. Consider how various characters see the world—both in their differences and in their similarities. Do you relate to one character more than the other? If so, how and why?

3. What does this story tell you about the power of love? About the power of sacrifice?

4. Of the many losses portrayed, what do you consider the greatest loss in this story?

5. Which character do you admire the most?

6. How much did you know about this period of history before you read this novel? What did you learn, and what did the story teach you about the nature of wars in particular?

7. Do you think there are instances of everyday heroism that have been lost to time and circumstances? How does that affect how you view history and your own story?

8. How does the truth of this story change the way you read and experience it?

From the Publisher

GREAT BOOKS

ARE EVEN BETTER WHEN THEY'RE SHARED!

Help other readers find this one:

- Post a review at your favorite online bookseller

- Post a picture on a social media account and share why you enjoyed it

- Send a note to a friend who would also love it—or better yet, give them a copy

Thanks for reading!

ABOUT THE AUTHOR

Photo by Elisabeth Monje

MARIO ESCOBAR, a *USA TODAY* and international best-selling author, has a master's degree in modern history and has written numerous books and articles that delve into the depths of church history, the struggle of sectarian groups, and the discovery and colonization of the Americas. Escobar, who makes his home in Madrid, Spain, is passionate about history and its mysteries.

Visit him online at marioescobar.es

X: @EscobarGolderos

Instagram: @marioescobar.oficial

Facebook: @MarioEscobar

ABOUT THE TRANSLATOR

Photo by Sally Chambers

GRETCHEN ABERNATHY worked full-time in the Spanish Christian publishing world for several years until her first child was born. Since then, she has worked as a freelance editor and translator. Her focus includes translating and editing for the *Journal of Latin American Theology* and supporting the production of materials related to the Nueva Versión Internacional and New International Reader's Version of the Bible. Chilean poetry, the occasional thriller novel, and a book on Latin American protest music spice up her work routines. She and her husband make their home in Nashville, Tennessee, with their two sons.